A Creative's Anthology

My creativity flows from the world around me / I'd become a writer for the ages in my liminal space. *How did I get here...?* He practiced holding his breath. **He counted from one thousand backwards.** By then it was quite dark and to ... mist had begun to ooze up from the damp earth. She thought of the splat of raindrops on the do ... ther ... -encased home and the clatter of runoff cascading from the gutters through the root filters ... own into cisterns. **The world suddenly went dark.** The birdsong wakes her in spring and in summer.

COURAGEOUS + CREATIVE - VOLUME 1

... the full sun, be ... trudged their way from one trai ... t ... *living* just ... en sun-re ... from ... th ... in t ... the sh ... y object ... hin ... eye. I stood in the ... ing roo ... paine ... ning those few quiet moments. To take her m ... ndr ... walk, taking great big steps ... lin ... nd. The way the moonlight streams between buildings and illuminates a small section ... the still po ... Morning sunlight filters through closed blinds ... It happens quickly, the swi ... from night t ... nd ... nty ... un ... ood ... e ... e ... h the hea ... *Dearest* L ... *It* ... I ... *find you* I ... I ... o ... who ... und ... hat ... y ht ... in ... ed I ... nind. De ... going-sp ... e dive team's ... the quiet ... the ... te w ... almost impe ... r ... ight settles on ... e high desert. Rolling clouds re ... ver ... fo ... ing m ... s, ... efly the moon cuts through and illuminates the distant valleys in brilliant light.

The water sat their dru ... of them, attempting t ... co ... t ... d an "oops!" as a splash of her cock ... ss. He was a blank, growing up in a succession of good intentioned foster homes, always th ... e table, afraid to eat until ... e "real" members of the family had filled their plates. **My arms crack down against the unforgiving, unyielding surface of the ocean as I swim towards safety.** Deep in the cloudless canvas of s ... black-a ... warbl ... low in aimless circles. Phan took a sip of rye. He wasn't inclined toward hard spirits but he ... would quiet his thoughts, blunt his worries. My creative foundation is built on the ... ts, stat ... e ... emori ... s of those bigger than me who found me lacking. They tried to fathom th ... ent o ... yster ... that was their grandfather, his hidden complexities, and the p ... that b ... e ... at c ... something you see every day." I don't know her, but I follow the old wom ... king ... on once defined by mountains dotted with green and purple life, now lay bleak and bro ... greeted Sara as she entered the kitchen with two bags of groceries. I watched as I ... ad ... used hands, avoiding eye contact with me. I narrowed my eyes. It is 7:20 a.m ... human being descending the stairs, his leaden feet fiercely colliding with each ...

You always sneak in like it isn't your house. Positive sighting / ... and alone / Eager hands creak / Sleek Circles / shark in home waters. / The loud sound of displaced water hitting ... against the rocky shore ... appears to be like that of a forever-thirsty man gulping water down his parched throa ... No order for the m ... o life for the god, just dead earth-an even field for all. Her hand's movements, broad a ... tense, at no p ... er ... shaken by the growl of the storm, or by the thick droplets of rain that crackled in hast ... os ov ... of of the theater. She steers clear of the burnt offerings, a small pile of charred fish bones and ... She starts her shift extra-early, ignoring your "Do Not Disturb" sign ... On the path to the forge ... r husband's fea ... She turned off the bed-side lamp in her Utah motel room.

The sound of it jolts me awake. **The loathsome break in the night suffocates t ... rs ... my min ... e's some old** feller that's standin' in front of it ... said he owns the tree and ain't nobody gonna cut it down ... i ... vin the old school. I've been scrambling to keep up with the new skool. Adapt or die, right? It's a hot, o ... ja ... te summer day, the type where the air is so wet your clothes never dry and all the old folks fan themselves with a newspaper, shake their heads, and say "Oh, it's a scorcher." **I stretch to the sun, angling my broad leaves toward it, drinking in the late afternoon rays.** I am awake. I am alert. I am aware. Please don't leave me here. These shoes don't fit.

Edited by
Leisa Greene, Kurtis Hassinger, and Dustin Nelson

Courageous Creative
Copyright © 2022 by Indie It Press, LLC

Vol., 1.

Editors: Leisa Greene, Kurtis Hassinger, and Dustin Nelson
Cover art: Fred Charles
Cover design: Andy Schmidt
Cover *Courageous Creative* title design: Sierra Shaw
Interior book design: Leisa Greene

PRINT ISBN 979-8-9856477-0-9
EBOOK ISBN 979-8-9856477-1-6

Indie It Press
Missoula, MT
IndieItPress.com

Printed in USA by IngramSpark
IngramSpark.com

Dedication

This book is dedicated to artists that take risks who find themselves influenced by the world around them in the forgotten in-between spaces of the creative.

Keep Your Face To The Sun by Sasha Snow

Contents

Where Does It Come From (They Ask So Casually)

Clara Olivo

My creativity flows from the world around me
The things I see when I close my eyes…

The hugs and hits that came from being
the youngest of four in a home of tortured souls
Survivors of our own undeserved hell

The sounds of screams for attention
over the deafening beat of the 8 am cumbias
that fueled my tired mami's soul as she cleans
the mess from the night before because
cleanliness is next to godliness
and here we practice ~~leave no trace~~

The inescapable sounds of celebration and pain
that only colonized people can bring
when singing of survival and glee
Before we learned the words
and names of *displacement*
and *diaspora*

The bitter-sweet taste of freedom
como el mango verde de mi juventud
The forbidden fruit of knowledge picked too early
Melting forgotten memories onto my tongue
tastebuds rejoicing at the delicious surrender

as the jugito de limón drips down my lips
Glistening my chin leaving a story
that only my skin can tell

The growing pains of wanting to fit in
E x p a n d I n g/retracting
back into the bite-size shape
of my younger body but

There is no space for youth here!
They've stayed behind!

Locked in the room of their memories
where movement stays hidden and
discovery of self lays cold and deep
in the slumber of depression
Where songs by boy bands and Slipknot
built the loudest walls that kept them silent and safe

Waking up to the glory of reflection
Rising to the opportunity to feel and reclaim
The sacred tears cascading down my face
Glistening truth in every drop

My words rising with the tide
Blessing me with hopes for a future
I have yet to see

A hope that moves me to speak my truth
May you hear it loud
May you know it well
Because in this truth is a history
you were never meant to hear

Liberation | Imprisonment

Part One

Mountains in Sky

By Alisa Hartley

ONE

Writing in the Liminal Space

Annie James Thomas

Someone posted a 10 by 16-foot garden shed for sale on my local community selling site this morning. It was a gray post and beam structure, finished on the outside, unfinished on the inside, with a very small front landing; and it was ready for delivery.

Although I won't buy it, I wanted it. Images of a writer's garden paradise populated my brain. While shoegaze vinyl spun on a turntable, I'd sip coffee in the early hours of each glorious morning from the deep recesses of my backyard. There's a lake to the rear of the property, and the main house to the front. In the middle, in this in-between of creativity, I'd tweeze thoughts from my brain like strands of daybreak fog, capturing them for all infinity with the clackety-clack of my electric typewriter.

I'd become a writer for the ages in my liminal space.

If your liminal space[1] isn't a garden party, is it the gently brewed rumble of a coffee shop? The quiet single hour in your person-free home? The leg-brushing clamor of a rush-hour train, when the thoughts of another passenger hitch a ride onto yours and feed your outgoing monologue?

The idea of the liminal space is one that writers inherently know well. The concept of liminality stems from the Latin, "limen," meaning "threshold," or a point of entry or exit.[1] Placed in the context of time, a liminal space is the in-between, or transition. For many, it's waiting on the transformation. When fraught with pen to paper, writers have experienced liminality otherwise as theoretical, physical, or metaphysical.

Theoretically, I am a perfectionist in my mind who struggles with external paper translation. I envision a Picasso painting and then convince myself that I've produced childlike scribbles. Physically, I wrestle with clunky dialogue, editorial revisions, accidental changes in tense, or unintended head-hopping. Metaphysically, I own love-hate relationships with the craft as I carefully construct scenes while driving or showering or insomniating. Yet, I block my own flow at the keyboard; instead of typing, I welcome distractions of unfolded clothing, unpacked dishwashers, and unscripted life.

I'm writing this piece on New Year's Day. It's a liminal day; a day that represents an entirely fresh year to write my heart out. Creative intentions have been declared in the form of texts sent to my writing partner. The year has begun strong. My novel-in-progress remains untouched, because it is the only large piece that I can mess up at the moment. In its current state, it is half-drafted, but in half-drafted perfection. I will cross that threshold when I'm ready.

I won't buy the garden shed. As a writer of decades, I know that I've existed in many spaces, and a physical building, however dreamy, is not the solution in my search for writing perfection. Rather, it is the search itself, the ability to exist in the neither here-nor-there, the liminal space, that keeps the goal forever just out of reach. It is there that I exist, and there that I push. To be forever burdened by the need to strive and stride, and to step through that space, is to remain writerly fearless.

---

1. What is liminal space? https://inaliminalspace.org/about-us/what-is-a-liminal-space/. Last accessed 1 Jan 2021. Last updated 2016.

TWO

Free Fall

Darren Faughn

In a moment he was a bird stretching his wings after a long hibernation, the sun energizing every skin cell exposed on his body. He began to fall, gaining speed and momentum, like a boulder rolling down a hill. The next moment he felt his head crack; hairline fractures spread over his skull like wildfire. Then, everything grew dark.

How did I get here…?

The room was still. Heavy heels stamped down the hallway. A figure approached the door; their details were vague through the translucent glass. The knob turned and the door swung open. A woman stared at him; her expression jumbled. She wore a juniper-colored dress and a berry brooch pinned to her breast. She carried a stack of papers and folders in her arms.

"Who are you?" She flinched.

Pipes hummed in the wall.

"I think I was having a meeting," He replied.

"How did you get in here?"

"This is *my* office," feeling sure of himself.

The floorboards creaked as her posture stiffened.

"And *your* name is Emily?" She glanced at the nameplate.

He turned the nameplate around. It read *Emily Shafer, General Accounts Manager*. His brow furrowed. He grew silent.

"I think you should wait here," She said. "I'll be right back."

Why am I here?

 Before he could ask, the woman exited the room. She shut the door and the lock clicked. Her hurried footsteps echoed down the hall. The sea of office chatter broke and he could hear the woman say, "Holly, call the cops!"

He got up and began to pace around the room. His breathing accelerated. His memory of the last 24 hours suddenly sharpened. It happened again. The first time he woke up in someone's kitchen, halfway through a bowl of raisin bran with a shotgun cocked in his face. Behind the barrel was a grizzled old man with a white and stubble mustache.

 "Who are you?" The man asked. "Why shouldn't I kill you?"

He had thought for a moment. "Because I think I'm sick."

The old man lowered his gun and sighed, "Well, how's the bran?"

"Pretty good I guess."

"That's good. Finish up while I call the cops." He served three months in county jail for breaking and entering.

He sat back in the chair again. He ruffled his brown, greasy hair into a mess and caught his reflection on the woman's nameplate. He loathed his disheveled look: the bags under his eyes, unkempt beard growing on his cheeks, and brown stains on his teeth. He was tired.

He couldn't go back to jail. If he were charged again, he would get up to five years. He popped up out of the chair and jiggled the door knob, but the latch didn't release. His chest tightened, his breathing contracted to short-and-shallow pulses. The room spun around him like blades on a fan.

Behind the desk he opened a pair of french doors to a balcony overlooking the street below. He remembered a breathing exercise his therapist taught him in jail. *Five things you see.* "Red car. Blue car. Woman talking on the phone. Man eating a hotdog. Loose newspaper tumbling down the street." *Four things you smell.* "Hot dog. Gasoline. Ink. Frying oil." *Three things you can touch.* He latched onto the weathered rail, clinching the ivy leaves growing between his fingers. He felt grains of rust collect in the grooves. His heartbeat began to slow and then suddenly it came to him. "I have to jump."

THREE

How Long Has It Been?

Ellis Morten

L uke wasn't sure if any of this was real.

Where was he? On his back, on the couch. Charlie stood over him. He was talking, but there was no sound. Luke stared into his face, into the dark, into something wet and...

He wondered when he'd fallen asleep, and immediately started to panic because he *shouldn't be asleep*. His eyes flickered around the room. What could wake him?

There was something sharp and heavy on the coffee table. Before he could question it or stop to consider, a hand attached to his body reached for it. The hand jerked forward as soon as his fingers had purchase. He swung. The sharp, heavy thing lodged into something soft and yielding.

"Luke?"

He woke up. Charlie was kneeling in front of him. The end of the TV remote pressed into his eye. His hand gripped Luke's, gently encouraging the hard plastic away from his face. "What are you doing?"

Luke opened his fist. "Sorry. I'm sorry."

"It's okay." Charlie put the remote aside. "You weren't in your bed, I was just... Have you been out here all night?"

There was a dark and vaguely person-shaped shadow right behind Charlie. Luke reached for his phone. A beam of light sliced into the dark, chasing the shadow out. It was four in the morning.

"I'm sorry," he mumbled.

"I think you should go lay down."

Luke stared past Charlie's shoulder. The screen went black. The shadow didn't return.

Charlie worked most of the day, and he went to bed early. "I'm sad we can't spend more time together," he'd said to Luke on his first night, "but I'm glad you're here."

Luke hadn't slept since arriving. He didn't have the heart to admit it, or the spine. Nothing Charlie could do about it, and it was Luke's own fault for agreeing to come up here in the first place.

The week so far had been unseasonably cold. Luke's breath gathered in a cloud of vapor in front of his face. His hands curled around a mug that was belching steam. Charlie sat beside him, one leg tucked under his body, both shoulders tucked under Luke's arms. They sported skullcaps and shared a blanket. Charlie's leg rocked the chair lightly; the gentle swings nearly lulled Luke into slumber.

"So you like Vermont?"

"Ugh. It's so gorgeous up here." Charlie sipped his tea. "These woods are amazing," he said, gesturing to the expanse of trees that stretched out in all directions around the property. "And I love that I don't hear any cars at night. Maybe like, one or two. Really different from New York."

"I'm not used to the quiet."

"It's strange, but I learned to love it really fast." Luke felt an elbow nudge at his ribcage. "You ever think about leaving the city?"

Some sort of bug kept pounding into the light above them. An erratic *thump thumpthump thump thump*, like it was bashing its head in. *Say no say no say no.* A breeze cut through Luke's protective layers, and he shivered. "I never considered it."

Charlie took this in. "Well, I'd love it if you were closer, obviously," he said after a quiet moment. "I miss you a lot. Like, all the time. And I think a change of scenery will be really good for you. It did wonders for me."

7

"Are you asking me to move in?"

Charlie smiled sheepishly. "I'm not *not* asking you." He stared for a moment longer, then returned to his tea. "It'd be nice to live with someone again. And I always thought we'd live together well. I mean, no pressure, of course. Let's see how this goes first."

In the mornings, once the sun started to peek into view, Luke would retreat into the guest room and pretend to still be sleeping. He practiced holding his breath. He counted from one thousand backwards. He kept as still as he possibly could.

The curtains would rustle. Or footsteps would creak under the floor. Or the sheets on the bed would slowly bunch up around him. Charlie, elsewhere, never noticed, and Luke destroyed all physical evidence before it could be found.

(Thinking about it too hard made his skin crawl.)

He tried to earn his keep by cleaning, doing laundry, assisting Charlie in the kitchen during mealtimes. It didn't take long for them to find the same ease of being. Two years folded in on themselves, and it was like they'd never been apart at all. In a matter of days Luke warmed to constant hugs, to interlaced fingers, to a palm placed tentatively against the small of his back.

The TV was hissing. Luke was sitting upright, curled up against the back of the couch, gaze glued to static. The room around the screen felt impossibly, completely still.

A face was less than an inch from his own, just barely in the corner of his vision. Eye wide, unblinking, a gaze filled with malice. And here he was, incapable of lifting even a finger. Incapable of even feeling fear. Still as stone and staring at vibrating dots.

"It'll hurt him more if I say anything," he murmured.

The TV stopped hissing. Luke held his breath as a finger pressed into his eye. Cold spiked into his skull, followed by a searing, explosive heat.

The only thing he could think was *I have to do this again and again and again and again.*

He was never going to sleep again.

While Charlie made breakfast, Luke held an ice pack to his face.

His excuse, when he'd been found on the floor ten minutes earlier, was sleep-walking. He fell over and smashed his face into the corner of the coffee table. It was as good a lie as any other.

"Has this ever happened before?" Charlie set a plate of eggs on the table.

(Depends, he almost answered.)

Luke shook his head, then groaned softly and stilled. He was nauseous with exhaustion and he had a black hole of a migraine. His eye throbbed, and the stare still burned into him from nearby. It felt like a warning, or a test.

"Okay…" Luke wasn't looking, but he imagined there was a little wrinkle in the center of Charlie's brow. It always appeared when he got worried and frustrated about it.

"I'm okay. Promise."

"Luke…" Charlie sighed. "Is it… you know, your version of okay, or mine?"

Luke laughed humorlessly. He ignored the knife in front of him and cut up his eggs with his fork so he could keep holding the ice pack. Metal scraped against porcelain. The cold had numbed the entire left side of his face. "Obviously, not yours."

(It was always going to be like this. Charlie, stable, and Luke, on the verge. Unspooling, in need of someone to hold him together. It was always going to be like this, no matter how many restarts he had.)

"I figured." Charlie was quiet for a few moments. Luke looked up to confirm: the wrinkle in his brow was there, and his mouth was screwed up with concern. "Is there anything I can do?"

Charlie's phone rattled as an alarm blared. The picture on the screen hadn't changed after all this time. Luke had flinched the first time he saw it: Charlie, his arms wrapped around his then-boyfriend, Fletcher. It had been one of their last pictures together before Fletcher died. There was a smile on Charlie's face that Luke hadn't seen in years.

Charlie turned the alarm off. "Just work stuff. I can be late."

Luke felt breath against his skin. He'd cut up the eggs into increasingly smaller pieces but still hadn't taken a bite. "I don't know how to fix this."

"That's okay," Charlie said in a voice that almost made Luke believe him. "I have a few ideas. We'll figure it out. And we'll keep an eye on the sleepwalking." He paused, then wrinkled his nose. The tiniest of smiles twitched along his mouth. "Sorry. No pun intended."

Charlie brought him liquid melatonin. Sleepy-time teas. A bottle of pills. He downloaded apps on Luke's phone, wrote down research on sticky notes, told Luke he was welcome to join him in the master bedroom, if that was what it took.

Luke brewed the tea but let it go cold. He threw out the pills one at a time. He dumped the melatonin. He played the apps just long enough to describe the sounds: rain on tin roofs, rolling thunder, crackling fireplaces. But every night after Charlie went to bed, Luke would sit in the living room and wait for the sun to rise.

(And while he sat, a face hovered too-close.)

During the day, he came-to in different places. He would start off hovering over a coffee, and then he'd wind up in the garden with no memory of walking outside. He caught himself scrubbing an invisible stain on his shirt, his arms aching with the effort. He realized he was standing in the bathroom, staring at his reflection.

One eye was still swollen nearly shut. The other started rolling and rolling. The entire room tilted and pitched sharply. In the next second, his head cracked into the wall and he was on his knees.

And then he was in the attic, digging through a box of memories. Old clothes, pictures that were faded and waxy. Charlie smiling that smile, arms around Fletcher's waist. Luke stared at the dead man. A shadow blocked out half of his features; his left eye was shrouded in darkness.

A hand reached from beneath him, then. The fingers brushed his face— twitching, feather light touches with cold, cold skin. The touch traveled down his brow, pulled at his lip, slid over his chin.

(He found the term on one of the sticky notes. With so little rest, he had started to microsleep. He was losing pockets of time, his brain shutting down while he stayed upright and blinking.)

And then he was in the kitchen, cups tumbling onto his shoulders. And then the front porch, a sweaty glass of water pressed to his forehead.

Charlie found him there, later, and sat beside him. Grocery bags were left at their feet. Luke discovered a hand against his cheek. It was warm this time. Calloused and real and alive, nothing like the frigid touch from before. A soft, gentle circle pressed against his spine as Luke shuddered out tiny, gasping sobs.

He didn't ask questions. Not that night or the next, when Luke gave in for a while and crawled into bed, held onto him, then crawled back out. Charlie already knew what was happening. He understood the rhythm of Luke better than anyone. He'd pulled him out of the pit over and over and over. That was the worst part, Luke thought miserably while he pushed his fingers into his eyes to keep himself awake. He would keep collapsing, and once he was built back up, he'd rip up the foundation and collapse again. And Charlie would pull him out every time. He was a trap and a time bomb, and he hated it, but not enough to let Charlie go. He was certain there was no one in the world more selfish than him.

The last time he had a full night's sleep, Luke had woken up, slipped into his shoes, unplugged all the appliances, and walked to the bridge.

On his way, it started to snow. Luke was hyperventilating; he hadn't managed a deep breath the whole way there, and he was growing lightheaded. The night was soft around the edges, but the streetlights threw the cold, white-dusted railing into sharp relief. His hands were wrapped around the metal, shaking. His skin looked almost gray. His sweater was soaked to his skin.

Despite the temperature, the river wasn't frozen. But it should be cold enough. If he didn't shatter on impact, he might freeze to death before he drowned.

Luke threw his leg over the side, shifted his weight slowly until he found purchase on the tiny ledge that precipitated the water. His tremors nearly made him fall, right then. He still gripped the rail, his arms now twisted behind him. His toes dipped into the open air.

Fletcher stood to his left, watching intently.

Luke choked. His cheeks were stiff with frozen tears. "This is what you want, right?" All he had to do was tilt forward. "It's gonna kill Charlie."

His grip slackened, and his stomach flipped, and then Luke screamed and tightened his hold desperately. Then he climbed back over, gulping in lungful after lungful of bitter, icy air.

———

That stunt had landed him in the hospital with a bad case of pneumonia and round the clock surveillance. Charlie returned to the city he swore he'd never come back to. Luke made a lot of promises that they both knew he couldn't be trusted to keep.

Like always, Charlie got it into his head to save him. "Come stay with me," he'd blurted, one day, his eyes bright.

"Charlie—"

"*Please*, Luke. I'm so tired of only seeing you in a hospital bed. Please."

———

So, he was here. But of course, so was Fletcher. And being here made him worse. Fed his anger, his bitterness, his righteous disdain.

Luke wondered if he should disappear for a few days, first, or if he should just get it over with.

The road was empty. Spring had finally arrived, though sluggishly, dragging its feet. Only one or two cars a night, Charlie had said. Luke sat on the gravel, waiting for the flash of headlights. He hadn't *decided*, not really. He never did. But he was here; might as well get it over with.

The first car rushed right past before he could work up the nerve to launch himself onto the road. The next one spotted him and rolled to a stop. A window came down and a stranger asked if he needed help. Luke just laughed, then pushed himself to his feet.

(What was he doing? Right in front of Charlie's *house*?)

He walked back through the woods. Low branches scraped the top of his head.

He stumbled over exposed roots and he thought about that night, stepped from the present into the memory and back out again.

Fletcher was everywhere, around every corner, and the air was filled with accusation. Not just here but in the house. Charlie's broken heart was scattered in every room, hung up in every doorway. Luke was a coward for trying to die before he told Charlie the truth.

He wanted to go back to the house, but he was lost. He didn't remember which way he'd just turned. And when he blinked, he was in a different part of the forest entirely. He came-to while leaning against a huge bark, the shadows retreating with an approaching dawn.

"Why don't you kill me?" he asked.

Silence answered.

"If I tell him it'll make everything worse. I'll ruin his life."

(He didn't know what Charlie was talking about: the quiet was so much louder than the white noise of the city.)

"You always wanted me out of the picture. Just do it. Bash my head in. Throw me in the river. You can gloat the whole time, I don't care."

Still nothing, but this time, pressure built around his eye.

Charlie was going to find him out here later that morning. He'll already be worried sick, fearing the worst, when he'd stumble upon the scene. Luke was so wretched. All he did was hurt the person who cared about him the most. Charlie bringing him here was the worst thing that could have happened.

Luke fell asleep on the ground, and dreamed about the day he watched Fletcher die. He dreamed about the way that time had held its breath. He dreamed about the way his hand moved before his mind really decided, like it wasn't really him doing it. He dreamed about the way Fletcher's limbs twitched after the impact. The way his good eye rolled and rolled and rolled, looking for a path that didn't end in death. He dreamed about the hand on his face, as if Fletcher would cling to life, somehow, if he could only grab some of Luke's flesh.

And then Luke woke up. He was in the master bedroom, the morning so bright it bleached away all the colors. Charlie was laying beside him, arm deadweight on Luke's chest. There was a bloody crater where his eye used to be. The other was wide, wide open, a thousand miles away.

He woke up falling, with just enough time to feel his body smash to bits against the churning river.

He woke up with his fingers inside his eyes. They mangled through his corneas, caving everything inward. Nerves lodged under his nails. Fluid leaked down to his knuckles.

He woke up on the walkway toward the house, just after dawn. Charlie cried from the porch and ran to him. He crushed Luke into a tight hug.

"Where did you go?" Charlie wept. "I thought you... Don't do that again. Please don't ever do that again."

Luke wasn't sure if any of this was real. If he was being honest, it felt like a violation to even be breathing. Every inhale was a stolen one, taken from someone who deserved it more. There were so many other people who shouldn't be dead and here he was, wasting away.

"The melatonin doesn't help? The pills?"

Luke opened his eyes. He was on the couch, his head propped up against throw pillows. Charlie sat on the floor beside him, clutching his hand, crying. Luke wanted to cry, too, but he was afraid of what might come out of him if he did.

"I haven't been taking any."

"Luke... why?"

(Because your dead boyfriend is trying to kill me in my sleep. Because I killed him, and I didn't mean to, but that hardly matters because he's still dead, and he's still angry, and I still did it. Because I'm a terrible person. Because I've been running and I'm so tired of running all the time. Because the guilt is eating me alive. Because I love you but in the most selfish, evil way.)

Luke didn't answer. Charlie cried some more. "If you need me to take you back to the hospital, I can do that. I'll do anything. I just don't want to lose you, too."

14

Luke could feel his heartbeat in his eyes. "Going back won't help me."

"You don't know that, Luke. They can help you better than I can. You have to sleep eventually."

Luke thought about the first time he saw them together. Young. In love. Everything was so perfect. For the first time Charlie had someone stable, reliable. Not someone who was about to unravel at the seams. Something inside of Luke had known from the first day that he was finished. The end was fast approaching. Fletcher was going to take him away.

The sun was so bright. It hurt to keep staring at the ceiling. Luke rolled onto his side and gave Charlie both of his hands. They both held on tight.

"How long has it been?"

"Since what?"

"Since we've known each other."

Charlie pressed his lips to Luke's knuckles. "I think it's close to ten years."

"And I've never gotten better, Charlie."

"Luke—"

"Maybe I'm just not meant to get better."

Charlie froze. He blinked a few times. "How could you say that?" he whispered, lifting his eyes to meet Luke's. His face was a ruin of tears and desperation. "Why would you ever say that to me?"

"Charlie." Luke sat up. He put Charlie's face in his hands, and felt him flinch under his icy fingertips. "You are such a good person. You deserve so much more than this. You need to find other good people."

Charlie placed his palms over his wrists. "You're a good person, Luke."

"*No.* You need to find better people than me. People who can maybe come close to you. Like Fletcher. Find another Fletcher. People who aren't going to fuck everything up, all the time."

"Shh, Luke, you—"

15

"If I lost you, Charlie, I would be… I can't deal with any of this without you. But you can. You'll be so much better off without me."

"But— Luke. I don't—" Charlie's face broke open with grief.
"Please live, Luke. That's all I want. Please stay alive. I don't want another Fletcher. I want you. I just want you."

Luke felt something inside of him crumble. Fletcher was digging into his back, shouting silently. *Get out get out get out.*

They were holding onto each other so tight. How could he tell Charlie no?

———

It would be this, over and over. Luke falling apart. Charlie piecing him back together. Luke would pull him further and further into the pit every time he fell. He would let it happen. He would pick himself, over and over. He would stop anyone who tried to get in the way of that.

———

That night, Charlie made him stay in the master bedroom. Luke held Charlie as close as he could. Charlie kissed Luke's eyes over and over until they both drifted into sleep.

FOUR

It's Better That Way

Catherine Peacock

T hey say *"If you see something...say something."* But that's not always a good idea. Sometimes, the very best you can do is to keep your mouth shut and just keep on keepin' on.

I was finishing up the last run of my shift. The schedules were all humped up because when Hurricane Sandy made landfall on October 29, 2012, it flooded out a major section of the Sagtikos Parkway. I'd been on the job 27 years—I had seniority—so this shouldn't have been my problem. Senior staff gets their pick of the routes. But first Ulloa called out sick, then so did Grantham. Perkin covered that route the night before, but then he also called out sick. Three drivers short plus 13 buses down because all that flooding included the North Amityville Terminal.

The reason nobody wanted the Sagtikos run is because starting at about 3:00 PM, for the whole west-bound leg of the trip, the sun's directly in your eyes. There are moments when you literally can't see jack-shit in front of you. You have to slow down to a crawl and pray you don't hit some idiot steppin' off the curb with headphones on the ears and eyes glued to a cell phone. But don't go too slow or management's pickin' at your ass for not keeping the schedule.

The sun in my eye wasn't the issue. That was bad enough, but with the Sagtikos flooded, the run was diverted through Pilgrim State. Anyone from Long Island will appreciate the problem immediately. For those not from around here, I'll explain. Pilgrim State Psychiatric Hospital is closed now, but in its heyday, it housed tens of thousands of New York's mentally ill. Later came the soldiers returning from overseas with what today they call *PTSD*. It was a good hospital. Most of the patients were regular, ordinary folks who just needed a little help. The staff was caring. They helped thousands return to society with programs like a community garden run by the residents, adult literacy classes and workshops that provided jobs training.

If they'd just stuck to the script, none of what followed would ever have happened. But sometime in the 1950's some asshat bean-counter had the genius idea of relocating Plum Island's Hospital for the Criminally Insane to the grounds of Pilgrim State. Almost overnight the character of the hospital changed. The change meant the patients were not just ill, but ill, sick and *dangerous*. The staff—all the doctors, nurses, orderlies, housekeeping—all of them, went from helping people through bouts of anxiety or depression to constantly watching their own backs.

Then, in late October of 1962, some of the inmates escaped and went on a killing spree. They overwhelmed the orderlies, then went from building to building, indiscriminately slaughtering staff and patients. Those poor victims never had a chance.

I didn't know all the details, of course. It made the news at the time, but there was only a bare-bones reporting of the events. Officials cited "patient confidentiality" and "names withheld pending notification of kin." They buried the incident like they buried the butchered and mangled bodies. The thing of it was; Pilgrim State employed hundreds of local people. There wasn't anybody on Long Island who didn't know *somebody* who worked there. Rumors of the horrors of that night got out, even if a true accounting never did.

So, what was a crappy run became worse because now it took me through the hospital grounds. That abandoned old place was creepy as Hell. Shut down sometime in the 70s, the hospital sat empty and derelict. There were all these old gothic-style red brick buildings, including a church with stained-glass windows–still intact even after sitting derelict for so many years. One window showed the sacrifice of Isaac and Abraham, with Abraham standing over his son, ready to slit his throat. It was on my third pass on this route that I worked out what was *wrong* about the scene. There was no depiction of an angel poised to stop the downward plunge of the knife.

Driving the bus through, the first thing I noticed was how the buildings on either side of the road crowded out the light. Going across the hospital grounds, I almost wished I had the glare of sun in my eyes. At least there would be some light. But as soon as I made that left turn onto Sowwyn Road it immediately went from daylight to dusk. Like somebody turned out the lights. I'd see shapes out of the corners of my eyes. I worked hard to convince myself that all I saw were squirrels flitting in and out of the underbrush that hugged the road. My first time on Sowwyn, there was a woman screaming in the tall weeds. I slammed on the brakes before it registered that it was only a fox.

The windows of the buildings were sealed with rusted iron bars. The glass was all broken, with jagged edges like teeth in a dark mouth. I drove my bus along cratered roads choked with weeds and littered with decades of abandoned bottles and trash plus branches brought down by the storm. I never saw anyone on the hospital grounds. I just drove through as quickly as I could. But I couldn't help but notice the windows on the upper floors. Their broken panes reflected what little light there was in an odd way. The motion of my bus making its way down the road reflected from those dirty window panes. The reflection moving from one window to the next made it seem like there was something inside the building, watching and following me as I made my lonely run.

The runs were so empty because the hurricane knocked out power lines all over. With no electric, schools and businesses were closed, so most times it was just me in an empty bus. I hated that. That bus would make such a huge racket, the noise bouncing and echoing off the walls in contrast to the silence of the hospital grounds. I thought of my grandmother, who would have said:

"Boy, you make 'nough racket to wake the dead."

I wished I hadn't thought of that.

I saw the old lady two days after Hurricane Sandy struck. She walked slow and stooped; dressed in layers of what looked like shapeless gray sweaters. Her head was wrapped in a rag. Despite the tattered clothing and her obvious homelessness, she reminded me of my long-dead grandmother. The one I had just been thinking about.

She turned onto Sowwyn Road just as I got there in my bus. The lady was dragging a 2-wheeled wire cart overflowing with what looked like junk. She was struggling with the weight of it. The cart's wheels kept getting stuck in the ruts on the road. Even though she was not at a bus stop, and had not looked up in my direction, I pulled up alongside her, brought the bus to a halt, and opened the door. The hiss of the door opening made the old woman pause her struggles with the cart and look up at me.

"Aunty! Do you need a ride? Get in" I surprised myself. *"Aunty"* wasn't a word I had ever used, not even when I was a kid visiting the folks back home in Jamaica. But the word just came out of my mouth as naturally as if I had used it all my life. "Lemme give you a ride, Aunty." I called out to her again. "It's comin' full dark soon."

For her part, the old woman said nothing. She simply stared into my face for a long moment. Then she seemed to gather herself, as if remembering something she had forgotten. She said, "You're a kind boy. I can see that. But I ain't got no money for a ride."

She put her head down and renewed her struggles with the shopping cart. I couldn't let it go.

Now, if I ever got caught giving free rides to people, I'd be on the unemployment line faster than sea water pours out of an open hand. I had no interest in losing my job or pension, but management was miles away; parked on their fat asses in comfortable chairs. And ain't no way I was going to drive my empty bus through this deserted place and leave an old lady to struggle through on her own. It's true that in the two days I'd been on this run I hadn't seen a single soul on the grounds. But who the Hell knew who might be lurking around? Anyone could pull her into any of those empty buildings and do… whatever. She was an old, raggedy shopping-bag lady but she was a human being and I wasn't going to leave her. "It's OK, Ma'am, I have to drive this bus empty or not. Don't worry about the fare."

But she shook her head again. "I can walk, baby. I don't have too far to go. And you have things to do, I'm sure."

"Aunty, I certainly *do* have things to do. Namely, drive this bus. Come on. I'll help you with your things."

She looked into my eyes for a long moment: studying me, taking my measure. Then she smiled for the first time. I could just make it out in the fading light. Despite the rags, she had a quiet dignity about her. "Bless you, Son. I see you got the spirit of righteousness in you. To tell the Truth and spite the Devil, I'd be glad of a ride. I thank you kindly."

I stepped off the bus (another rule broken, but, hey! In for a penny, in for a pound,) and walked across the pitted road to where the old woman waited with her rusted wire cart. "Lemme help you, Aunty." With that, I grabbed the cart's handle, lifted it up over the pavement and walked back toward my bus. But as I did so, I gasped. That cart was *heavy*. Unbelievably so. I'm a big man. I'm 6-foot-4. I work out and I've kept myself fit ever since my baseball playing days. But I was *sweating* by the time I got that cart across the pavement and up the steps of the bus. I positioned it out of the aisle by wedging it next to the window of the first seat. Then I turned to help the old woman up.

But when I looked out the window for her, she wasn't there. I turned around in alarm, only to discover her directly behind me. I hadn't heard her follow me onto the bus, nor would I have thought such an old woman could move that quickly or that quietly. I hid my surprise and moved aside so she could sit down. "There you go Madam! Best seat in the house. Make yourself at home and just let me know when you're ready to get off." Her only answer was another smile. I got back into my seat, and continued along Sowwyn Road. I was surprised at how dark it had become in the short amount of time I had the bus stopped. I drove a little further along, maybe 100 feet or so, when the old woman spoke up.

"Turn off Sowwyn Road."

"No, Aunty! No can do. I have to keep to my route." I continued driving down the road.

The old woman spoke again. "Son. You need to listen to me. Turn off Sowwyn Road. It's better that way."

By then it was quite dark and tendrils of thin mist had begun to ooze up from the damp earth. There were potholes like craters, not to mention downed tree limbs everywhere. It took all my concentration just to navigate the road. The last thing I needed to do was hit one of those huge branches or slash a tire out there. So I didn't bother answering that time. I just continued picking my way down the road. The old woman spoke to me a third time: quietly, slowly, and clearly.

"Michael Anthony Lewin. Get off Sowwyn Road."

I stomped hard on the brakes right there in the middle of the road, turned and gaped at her.. How in God's name had that old woman known my name? I was wearing my uniform, but our names aren't written on them. I stared at her in confusion, then looked down at my uniform to double-check. She stood at my shoulder and looked directly into my eyes. I don't know how long I just stared back at her, my mouth hanging open. The woman said nothing further, just matched my gaze with an expressionless one of her own.

It was a sound outside the windshield that finally drew my shocked attention away from her.. There was a laugh. A sort of a high-pitched, wild laugh followed by a kind of a growl. I flicked the bus's high beams on and immediately wished I hadn't. There were people waiting for me on the edge of Sowwyn Road. A group of passengers stood where it had been empty only moments before. They were staring at me with unblinking eyes. In the harsh glare of the headlights, I could see a man dressed in a soldier's uniform from a war fought almost 70 years ago. Where his eyes should have been were black pits. Yet he saw me. He shook his head slowly from side to side, opened his mouth and flicked a black tongue at me. I saw a woman–she was dressed in a nurse's uniform. But the clothing hung on her in filthy, shredded rags. Her scarred and pitted face was emaciated; just skin stretched tight over sharp bone. A wriggling mass of something thick and dark and red erupted from her mouth, tumbled down her dress to the ground and began creeping toward the bus. A man—a boy, really—began climbing, spider-like, up a tree whose branches spread out over the road. He sped along as the branches bent under his weight until he was suspended over the middle of the road. Then he dropped down directly in front of me only to skitter on all fours back to the tree and do it again. I saw a man who was on fire. He was on *fire*, but he just stood still, staring at me while flames licked the sides of his face and the skin bubbled and turned black. I could smell the burning flesh. A woman stood next to him. She raised her hands and pointed to me. Even from where I sat, I could see her fingernails were manicured and polished a deep red. She lifted her perfect hands to her face and as I watched, paralyzed, she gouged her eyes out and held them out to me. Then she smiled.

And just like that, I wasn't worried about management or keeping to a schedule or following any damn regs. I threw the bus into reverse and practically stood up on the gas pedal. They–those, those *things* started howling and wailing and began to shuffle their way toward the bus. I rammed the bus backwards, the screech of its reverse alarm buzzer all but drowned out by the monstrous shrieks of those…*things*. I don't know how far I got, but I saw, almost hidden in the thick underbrush, a road off to the right. I screeched to a halt, jerked the wheel and skidded out onto the little road. It was even darker, narrower and more pitted than Sowwyn.

"Michael. *Hurry.*"

The old woman's voice was a thin mist in my ear. I could feel her breath on my neck, but I didn't dare take the time to acknowledge her words. Behind me, I could hear *Them*. Howling, shrieking, gibbering. Something was following me in the limbs of the trees that stretched out above me. Heavy branches rained down on the roof of the bus. I had no idea where I was going. I'd lost all sense of direction until suddenly, directly in front of me; the road came to an abrupt stop.

But I did not. I kept my foot on the gas and drove the bus onto a field overgrown with weeds, brush and even small saplings. The bus rocked dangerously from side to side but I kept going.

And those *Things* followed. I could hear them over the pound of the tires on the uneven surface, over the roar of the straining engine and over the swish of the grass (I hope it was grass) brushing against the sides of the bus. I could hear *Them*. Coming for me.

The old woman was quiet after that final whisper in my ear, but I was aware of her standing behind me as I drove the bus over the ground. I was about to tell her to sit down when I became aware of a terrible screaming from inside the bus itself. It was high-pitched, barely human and I almost died of fright before I realized that it was my own voice I heard. The bus was rocking from side to side as I barreled across the fields. My worry was that all that rocking would cause the bus to topple over onto its side. If that happened, whatever chased us out there in the dark would have us. I had to slow down. But then, just ahead, I saw the ground was broken by a small gully. I knew if I drove my bus into that it would never make it out. Buses are built for endurance, not for speed. The side-to-side motion meant a risk of overturning. But if I slowed down, I would never make it across that gully.

I had no choice. Instead of slowing down, I gunned the engine. In response, the engine roared its protest. Those that followed us roared back. I could hear the screaming and howling behind us. I heard the screeching sound of torn and twisted metal coming from the tail end of the bus. I felt the bus shudder as something rammed into its side, but I didn't take my eyes off the dip in the field to see what it was. It took every bit of concentration I had, every ounce of all my years of training. It took every trick I ever learned and everything I ever taught the new-hires to keep the bus from tipping over and slamming down to the ground.

"Aunty. Hold on!" All I could do at that point was floor it, steer it, and pray. All of which I did. The bus, belching foul-smelling black smoke, came flying up a slight incline just before the opening and then...I was airborne. The bus shot over that gully, wheels spinning uselessly in the air. For...I couldn't tell how long...there was no sound at all. I couldn't hear anything, not even the roar of the engine. I could feel the *thump-thump-thump* of my own heart. I could see the bottom of the gully, filled with mud and debris left from the storm. And I could see the gap was too wide. The bus would never make it across. The front wheels would make it. Probably. But the back end of the bus would fall short. I could gun the engine as much as I liked, but with my rear tires mired in the thick muck, it would go nowhere. And then *They* would have us.

Except that my bus's rear tires made it fully across. The bus fell back to earth with a huge jolt that jarred my spine and snapped my head forward. I was afraid we would stall out, but that didn't happen. I bore my foot down on the gas and kept her moving just as fast as I could make her go. And behind me, *They* followed.

Up ahead, through the dark and the mist I could make out the headlights of other cars: Commack Road, and to the right, the Long Island Expressway.

But I also saw the massive chain link fence that surrounded the hospital grounds. In the movies, the badass hero just rams his way through the fence, knocks it to the ground and continues on his merry way with nary a scratch on his vehicle. But this was reality, and if I slammed into the fence at the speed I was going, there wouldn't be enough left over for the things chasing us to bother about.

I had seen it on earlier runs as the route went along Commack Road–a gap in the fence. Many years earlier there might have been a guard's station in the space. But whatever building had been there was long gone, leaving a narrow gap that no county official had ever bothered to close. I steered the bus to where I remembered seeing the gap and fled towards it. I knew *They* followed. They were silent now, hunting, but I knew they were still there.

The gap loomed just ahead of me but there was this sick feeling deep in the pit of my stomach as I realized the bus was too wide. She would never make it through that narrow opening. I had no choice. I kept my foot on the gas and slammed the bus through the opening.

It did not make it through.

The entire bus did not make it through. I heard a bone-shattering crash of metal snapping and glass breaking. Both the left and right side-view mirrors had slammed into the steel posts of the fence and were torn off by the impact.. A hot-metal smell arose and sparks erupted in an arc on either side as the bus tore through the narrow opening in the fence.

I was through the fence but I was flying down an embankment at breakneck speed toward the traffic and other cars on the road ahead. I stomped *hard* on the brake, then eased the bus down, preparing to slip onto Commack Road. I was too scared to look back.

Until, with a jolt deep in my core, I remember the old woman. She had been standing in the aisle that entire desperate ride. Sick with fear that she had been hurt, I brought the bus to a halt and turned to help her.

I was alone on the bus.

That was impossible! I had spoken to her. I had carried and stowed her heavy cart. Turning the interior lights on high, I walked the full length of the bus and checked each seat. Twice. Three times. The pain in my back was like acid, but I stooped down and searched under the seats. The old woman was not there and neither was her old, rusted cart.

Only then did I look back at the hospital grounds. There was nothing there. The weed-strewn field I had just come barreling across was quiet and empty. A faint breeze stirred the grass, but other than that, there was no movement at all. A few yards inside the fence I could just make out one of the missing side view mirrors on the ground.The mirror's lidless eye winked at me; daring me to come back and pick it up. Or maybe it was just the reflected light from passing cars. I left it where it lay.

Besides the missing mirrors, I realized the left rear tire was badly slashed. By rights, a bus messed up that badly had no business in traffic. I should've radioed in for a tow, but there was no way in Hell I was waiting there. I limped the bus back to the depot where Ray had me fill out an accident report. I told him a huge tree limb, no doubt weakened by the hurricane, slammed into me. He looked at me a little queer, but in the end asked me only one question.

"Were there any passengers on the bus?"

"No. No." I said "It was a quiet run. I didn't see anybody."

The next day the flooding on the Sagtikos receded enough so that all buses resumed their original routes. Ulloa and the others were back on the duty roster, but I took a week off to deal with a badly wrenched back. It was good to relax at home and let Sylvia fuss over me.

If you see something…say something.

Unless you saw what I saw. In that case, you write it up in a story, change your name, and pretend it's fiction.

It's better that way.

FIVE

Leaving the Greenhouse

W.A. Ford

Clementine and Valencia faced each other over the loamy edges of the wide compost trench. Here, where the oldest layers of organic matter secreted a rich golden broth, the twins' experiment might go unnoticed.

"Concentrate," Clementine whispered, meeting the brown eyes that matched her own. "picture what you want."

Valencia nodded and concentrated on the space between them. She thought of the splat of raindrops on the domes of their glass-encased home and the clatter of runoff cascading from the gutters through the root filters and down into cisterns.

Once upon a time, before their people retreated to the haven of the greenhouse, powerful rainmakers held sway in their tribe.

"Good," Valencia's voice quivered as the atoms in the air coalesced into a light gray cloud that wept a few drops into the trench.

"Oh, great green!" Clementine exclaimed, "We're doing it! Mama O'Bethia will love this!" "Yes," Valencia struggled to hold her concentration. She loved her sister, but her aspirations were higher than becoming the queen's favorite. She wanted more out of life than the first fruit of a newly flowering tree or a personal bed of earth to ground herself. Valencia, bloom of the Lemon Vine, wanted out of the greenhouse.

"Val! Clemi!" Their brother, Pomelo, hopped from branch to branch in the trees bordering the compost trench. A woven bag hung from his shoulders and bulged with the daily harvest of citrus from the family's grove. "Time for lunch!"

The girls jumped apart at the sound of his approach. "Coming, Pomi," they called in unison.

"What are you doing?" He asked, hopping down and landing with a mild thud on the mulched ground, but the cloud was gone before he got close enough to spy it.

"We have a surprise for Mama!" Clemi announced with a dramatic flourish that indicated rain. "What?" Pomelo asked, drawing close and looking from twin to twin.

"You'll have to stay put at respite to find out," Valencia gave him a superior look, then hooked her arm with Clemi's and skipped away.

The girls made their way to the center of the greenhouse, hounded by a thousand questions from their brother.

They gave him no answers.

At the center of the greenhouse was a wide mossy common, crowded with people chatting and trading part of their daily harvests to put together a filling midday meal. It was a well-practiced ritual overseen by their queen, Mama O'Bethia, that fostered camaraderie, teamwork, and a sense of accomplishment and fair play.

"Pomi," Their mother, Navel, waved the boy over, "we have a few early trades to fulfill." "Coming!" he replied, but before he took off, he handed the girls two unblemished lemons and a fragrant orange. With a conspiratorial wink, he said, "You'll need these if you seek an audience with Mama O'Bethia"

Val sighed. The inside of her head was the only place secrets were safe in the greenhouse. "Thanks," Clemi offered, but he was already at their mother's side, ready to tease and posture with those who wanted their produce.

The girls looked at each other and with the silent accord, turned toward the petal-strewn boulder where the queen perched. They didn't get two steps before they were blocked by their grandmother, Mineola.

"And where do you two think you're going?" She was peach-skinned and rosy-cheeked like their mother, but with leafy green eyes that were sharp as nettles.

"To give these to the queen." Valencia held up the lemons and gave her best innocent smile. "You're the only child that would dare lie to an elder, Val," Mineola frowned, "I worry what blight that may bring."

"We have a surprise for Mama O'Bethia," Clemi grabbed their grandmother's hand and started towards the queen, "You'll never believe it!"

"Well, what is it?"

"What is what?" Mama O'Bethia turned away from the man bartering fresh herbs to smile at the girls.

This drew the attention of everyone on the common, causing the three Lemons to freeze. "These are for you, Mama!" Clemi blurted, rushing the queen and all but throwing the orange at her.

"Delightful!" The queen sniffed the orange and sighed.

Clemi gestured for Valencia to bring the lemons. Val approached with more deference and waited for the queen to take the fruit from her hands.

"Flawless," she said, holding one of the lemons up for everyone to see. She beckoned a handmaid over who quartered a lemon and added a few slices to the queen's water. The entire greenhouse held its breath as O'Bethia drank from the simple gourd.

"Ahhh!" She shook her head. "Great Green."

The crowd let out a collective cheer. "Great Green!"

"Something this wonderful comes with a price," O'Bethia handed the gourd back to the handmaid.

"We have a surprise!" Clemi bounced on the balls of her feet. There were audible gasps from those in earshot.

"I love surprises," The queen said in the tone adults use to humor children, "don't keep me waiting. I can hardly stand it!"

Clemi turned to Val, arms outstretched, but instead of joining her, Val looked Mama O'Bethia in the eye and declared,

"We wish to leave the greenhouse."

"No!" Navel appeared between the girls, a shoulder in each hand, "We do not joke about things like that!"

"Mother of the Green," Mineola had one hand to her mouth and the other to her heart in the traditional pose of apology. "They are at such a difficult age."

"And we require an audience with you," Val squirmed out of her mother's grip and knelt before the queen she'd no doubt insulted. "In Private."

"Very well," Mama O'Bethia rose to her feet with the help of her attendants. "The Vine of Lemon is granted an audience. All of you."

At this, she pointed to Pomelo and their baby sister, Tangerine, who was lounging on the far side of the green and who put down their plates to join them.

Mineola and Navel looked as if they wanted to protest, but they dare not contradict Mama O'Bethia. So, they followed in silence, Val and Pomelo first, Clemi and Navel, then the youngest who clung to their grandmother in terror.

Those left on the common went back to their meals or wandered off for afternoon respite whispering in fear-laden voices about Val's declaration.

No one ever left the greenhouse.

It was the only place they were safe. Perhaps once a week, when the doors in the southern walls were propped open and the stalls rolled out to sell the excess to produce, one of the elders ventured out to purchase gardening tools or request repairs. But otherwise the wider world remained a dull roar on the other side of the humidity frosted glass.

And rightfully so.

This was the horrid land of bondage that never seemed to end, but instead evolved into more insidious and torturous renditions that robbed them of their magic and of their earth honoring way of life.

No one ever left the greenhouse.

The glass palace was a concession. A treaty between the war-mongering old-world covens and their former bondsmen. Autonomy, protections, and building upkeep, in exchange for a world that could pretend they were happy farmers and that five hundred years of enslavement did not exist.

No one ever left the greenhouse. Especially girls.

The attendants hung back as the queen led them into the seedling area just off the commons. The Vine of Lemon waited patiently as the queen gathered tools and gloves then arranged herself on a workbench.

A few more minutes passed before she spoke.

"You will find no joy there," O'Bethia did not stop her work at the seedling station to look at the family before her. These seeds were water sprouted and destined for the greenhouse's newest venture, vertical hydro gardens. "But you are young and seek adventure."

"NO!" Mineola cut her off. "You must forbid it!"

"Not every sprout takes hold," O'Bethia held up a seedling, inspecting its roots in the soft light. "No matter how much you nurture it."

"Please, my queen," Navel threw herself to her knees and begged. "Don't let my babies go over to those wolves."

"We want to go west," Valencia stepped forward, "To the mountains." O'Bethia smiled, encouraging her to speak.

"To study with the air wardens," Val continued. "It will help with the greenhouse." "A little groundwork never hurt either," O'Bethia hummed.

"Tangi can stay here and learn the greenhouse," Clementine nodded, going along with the story. "And Pomelo."

"I'll take care of mom and gran," the little boy put a protective arm around his weeping mother. "And what knowledge would the air wardens give you?" O'Bethia finally stopped working to look at Val. "How will it help the greenhouse?"

The girls squared their shoulders and faced one another. As they had countless times before, they clasped hands, reached out for the minuscule points of moisture in the air around them, and shepherded

them into the tiny space between their thin arms. And just like before, the meeting of so many molecules caused a frenzy that created a dense, gray cloud.

The people around them gasped, and even the queen, who'd seen many things and knew even more, stared, mouth agape, at the spectacle.

"What nonsense is this?" their mother cried. "What have you done?" "It is a miracle," their grandmother clapped, tears in her eyes.

The queen remained speechless.

Spurred on by this silence, Valencia poured more effort into the magic until their usual little cloud grew to a swirling mass that extended far over their heads.

"Step back,' Valencia warned the others as she prepared to make it rain.

But the family wasn't the only person trying to get away. Although she could not see her, Valencia could feel Clemi twisting her wrist to break free.

"It's too scary," Clemi pouted. "Let's start over"

"Are you crazy," Valencia screeched, trying to keep a grip on her sister. "This is great!"

"I don't like this," Clemi broke Vali's grip on one hand and strained to free the other. "Something terrible is about to happen. I can feel it."

Valencia looked at the cloud expecting it to dissipate once their circle of two broke, but it still loomed above them.

"Clemi!" She lunged for her twin's free hand, "COME ON!"

"No!" Clemi screamed as a streak of blinding light cut across Valencia's vision.

Val covered her eyes, but that didn't protect her from the bowel-jarring boom that threw them both to the ground.

The world behind her eyes was unnaturally opaque. Her eyeballs flicked about erratically, searching for some point of light.

There was none.

However, she was not alone. A cold sickle tugged at the hem of her dress in light, gentle pulls. Hard enough to be felt, but not hard to send her sliding into oblivion.

How could you let this happen? Clemi's voice came to her over the dark expanse, a weak thread too soft and diffuse to reveal a location.

Where are we?

Val wasn't sure if that was her thought or a voice from elsewhere.

Take my hand, Clemi's voice wavered, growing even weaker than before.

I can't see you. Val clawed at the air around her in hopes of catching a hand, an arm, or some other part of her sister.

I'm right here.

Where? The panic grew in Val's gut and emerged as another thing sitting in the dark with them.

You're so close. Clemi's words came in choking huffs. *We can go together. Go where,* Val recoiled, horrified by the offer.

Home.

Home.

The word did not bring images of the tidy plots and neat rows under the glass dome. Instead, home expanded to sugary white shores, red clay roads, moist green foliage, and a kind yellow sun that reigned over peaceful lands where they'd be free to use their gifts.

Valencia sighed and relaxed beneath the weight of the sickle.

But she was too slow, and the gorgeous shores receded from her grasp.

She was drawn out of the oddly comforting darkness of her dead faint by blood-curdling screams. They surrounded her like a prickly fog and she had trouble distinguishing where one ended and where another began.

On second thought, it wasn't the screams that brought her back but the urgent smack of a work-calloused hand against her cheek.

"Val! Val, baby! Wake up."

Now more noise slipped past the muffled barrier of ringing that filled her ears. Pomelo cried freely, sobbing and sniffing in turn.

The queen gave orders in a sharp but calm voice.

And very close by, someone was begging Clemi to wake up, too. That's when Valencia felt it.

The nothing.

A gaping hole in the fabric of the universe occupied where her twin once stood. "CLEMENTINE!" Valencia roared as she sat up and looked around for her twin. "Easy!" Navel cooed, trying to soothe Valencia. "Easy baby!"

"Sh-she's," Val looked at Clemi's motionless form, but her vision refused to focus. The word death would not form on her tongue or pass the barrier of her lips.

Why?

Because no one left the greenhouse. Ever.

Val closed her eyes to return to the darkness to bring Clemi back, and when she opened them again, she was beneath the ancient canopy of vines that arched over the healer's quadrant. The sharp scent of dried herbs and bitter unguents told her she was in the eldering space.

There it was again.

Her twin no longer occupied a space in her awareness. Valencia reached out again, searching for a hand in opaqueness, but not even the death remained.

"Clemi, Where are you?" The words slurred their way out of her mouth and into the unnatural quiet.

She had not expected an answer, yet she received one anyway.

"You are alone, child," The chief healer's luminous umber face slid into her line of vision. His eyes bored into Val's, sending a spike of fear through her soul. "But not for long."

It was a threat.

The reality, hard and inevitable hit her. Even if Clemi were by her side, it would only be to face the queen, her advisors, and the council of elders for their crime.

The magic. The lightning. The disruption of the peace and ease of the greenhouse. The possible attention from the government that, despite generous compensation, still held them captive like butterflies under cloches.

All unforgivable violations.

Val rolled off the woven mat and into a crouched stance. Her drugged mind slogged through her memories, trying to find the penalty for murder.

She could not recall.

Was that part of the accident, or was it part of the greenhouse's stasis?

That strange cycle of eternal springs, the endless summers, the infinite autumns where death's wintry touch never drew near except in the compost piles. Where the golden afternoon of old age stretched for decades until the body slowed into a strange twilight like tulip bulbs but never perished?

"Here now, girl!" The elder hissed, "What do you intend to do?"

Val opened her mouth to sass her, but she felt a presence creeping up on her left, so she sprinted away instead. She broke more laws as she thrashed across neatly cultivated plots, her heavy legs tearing away at tender greenery and crushing juicy fruit.

To her amazement, no one called out in protests as she ruined their crops. The greenhouse appeared deserted except for the person trying to catch up with her. They stuck to the paths, giving her an advantage.

Val reached her family's citrus grove and skidded to a stop. She looked around, calling out to her family, but the area was deserted like the rest of the greenhouse.

"Valencia!" her pursuer was near.

Val took off across the plots again, aiming herself toward the common. This time her pursuer followed directly in her wake.

"Get back here, girl!" Certain death sounded very human. Val willed her spindly legs to move faster.

They ruined a few more plots then there it was, the common.
The atmosphere was decidedly less festive than the last time she approached.

Even over her ragged breathing, she could hear the sobs and other mournful noises in the crowd gathered at the queen's feet.

Val hurled herself through the crowd and directly at her mother. She wrapped her arms around the woman's soft waist, but the gesture was not returned. She looked up at Navel. Instead of a comforting smile or even an angry scowl, she saw nothing. The woman remained focused on Mama O'Bethia, tears streaming down her face.

As did Mineola. As did Pomelo.

Little Tangi looked frightened but still did not meet her eyes.

"Mommy," Val tugged at the woman's tunic. "I'm sorry. It was an accident." She waited a moment before trying again.

This time a deep hum rose from the crowd.

The tune was so rare, Val didn't recognize it at first. She laughed when she realized it was a farewell dirge.

"You find this amusing?" O'Bethia motioned to her attendants, and Val found herself forced into a painful bow at the woman's feet. "We are so few as it is. The centuries lost beneath the whip of the covens have thinned out the branches of our family trees. And now you, with your useless buffoon's act has taken another."

"It's not an act!" Val twisted in her captors' grip so she could glare at the queen. "You saw it. You saw us bring rain."

"I saw unripened talent from a blighted vine," An angry hiss slithered into O'Bethia's voice, "Doubled fruit on a worm-riddled seed. What good is your little trick here? We have no need for storms and lighting. We do not suffer rain and wind."

"Our magic was not for you," Val's voice broke and the anger burning in her chest surprised her. "I want to be free. I don't want to spend my life toiling for...for... this," she spat.

"Oh is that all?" O'Bethia stepped off her mossy dais. "Just a quick jaunt around this wicked land to satisfy your curiosity?"

"No one here can teach us magic," Val gritted out.

"And not one out there is willing to, " O'Bethia knelt beside Val.

"You don't know that. The aviary has teachers!" Val continued to twist.

"Don't speak to me of that dung-covered rock!" O'Bethia growled as her kind face collapsed into the sharp angles of pure hatred. "There is nothing for you out there." She inhaled, bringing her voice back into its usual pleasant range. "And now, thanks to your little light show, there is nothing left for you in here either."

Val heard the dirge grow louder as a strange pressure encased her chest and pushed outward from her scalp. She turned to glare at the attendants holding her down, only to find that they were no longer there. They stood, facing the crowd, guiding them in song and blocking their view of Val and O'Bethia.

"It's you," Val pressed her head to the ground, tears streaming down her face. Then the fight left her body and O'Bethia's magic flattened her into the moss. The dawning of the queen's power shifted all the oddities of life in the greenhouse into place. For a moment, Val considered letting O'Bethia win by falling on the sickle.

NO! Clemi's voice came out of nowhere. *If you die here, you can't go home.*

Home.

The white sand beach flowed before her again before disappearing.

O'Bethia will hold you captive forever.

Val scrunched her nose up to put space between her and the ground and to give her eyelids room to open. It was enough to get the queen in her sights. Val reached out to the air around O'Bethia's head and called the particles of moisture to the point between the woman's eyes. "Wretched girl!" O'Bethia screamed as the cloud engulfed her.

It was enough to break the queen's hold.

Val jumped to her feet, willing the cloud to engulf the entire common. She succeeded enough to get beyond the frightened, wailing crowd. "Let me leave!" She demanded once she was clear of her chaos. "What is the point, silly girl," the chief healer stood a few plots away. "How do I get to the aviary?"

The healer smiled.

"Come here, girl!" O'Bethia emerged from the fog, but Val was ready. A bolt of lightning ripped through the air and tore the ground between them.

"Let me out," Val raised her hand again, and the queen flinched.

"Wait," O'Bethia raised her hands in surrender. She exchanged a nod with the healer who reached in his robes for a piece of parchment and a carbon stylus. The elder brought them to the queen then stood there judging Val.

"Open the south door," O'Bethia ordered and turned to Val, "Clear out your mess." "Show me the way first."

"Go to this guild house," O'Bethia knelt to Val's level and quickly sketched a map. "They will happily send you to your doom."

Val reached for it, but O'Bethia snatched it away. "Your mess?"

Val eyed the queen and the healer as she ordered the clouds to disperse. She craned her neck to find her family, but she didn't see them on the common.

With no further ceremony, O'Bethia dragged her to the south door, placed the parchment in Val's hand, and shoved her onto the street.

Valencia did not let the wild contrast between the greenhouse and the bustling city block overwhelm her. She picked her way through pedestrians and across the slow-moving traffic in an effort to put some distance between herself and her former home. After a while, her feet grew heavy and her strides shrank. She was grateful to stumble across a huge green space. The large plot of grass was ringed by trees taller than any she'd ever seen.

Val hobbled over to one of many benches dotting the area and collapsed in relief.

She wasn't used to traveling. She thought as she wiped the fine sheen of sweat from her face. Her mouth was dry, yet the sun did not seem as bright as it had before. Perhaps the air was too thin out here as well.

No matter, soon, she'd be on her way to the aviary.

Valencia checked the map before setting out again. She stood up and nearly jumped out of her skin.

There before her, in the dappled light filtering through the trees, stood Clementine. "Clemi!" Val exclaimed, she intended to embrace her twin, but her body remained rooted in place. Val chalked it up to fatigue from her recent ordeal. "You're alive! You got out!"

"It won't be long now," Clemi smiled.

"Are they coming?" Val found she couldn't turn her head to look behind her. She didn't care. Her sister was back!

Clemi held out her hand, and as Val stepped forward, she felt a great weight fall away from her body.

When their hands touched, sugar-white shores rushed to meet her. She could feel the sand, warm and soft, beneath her feet and between her toes as she and Clemi ran hand in hand across the beach toward the red clay road that cut a perfect line in the tender green foliage. Four thousand voices rose in a joyful noise, beckoning them home.

It wasn't until a woman screamed that Valencia retrained her focus on the physical world around them.

A man knelt before her and bellowed to the gathering crowd to get someone from the greenhouse.

Val shied away from the man, ready to bolt across the square if he tried to restrain her. But he didn't.

His eyes remained on her limp body, mouth ringed in foam, cradled in his arms.

"No," Val wrapped her free arm around her waist in a delayed reaction to the healer's trick. "Come, sister," Clemi pulled her away from the growing crowd. "It's time to leave the greenhouse."

SIX

Sea Monsters

Mike Kloeck

A **Long, Long, Time Ago…**

The world suddenly went dark.
Her son had a glowing neck and chest.

"What? 'Oh no. Why did you do that?" She cried out in the dark.

"I'm sorry Mom, but I was really cold and hungry."

"You have to put it back."

"But I already swallowed it."

"Put it back."

"Mommmmmmmm! Really?"

"Yes, really. Now."

"Ok, fine." He burped. "But I'm still hungry."

Together the Sea Monsters slithered beneath the waves as the sea began to glow and the sun slowly rose.

A Little While Ago...

I first saw it in the morning after our last big storm. The waves were still rolling mahogany brown. The wind was pushing lines of fluffy sea foam across the flat wet sand. I was walking along the beach looking for nothing in particular, and there it was.

A dark hardwood window frame rose out of the sand. It was festooned with gooseneck barnacles, black mussels, and strands of seaweed.

Not knowing what to make of it I just shook my head and kept walking. It was still there when I circled back.

There was a dusty gray seagull pecking at the foam around the edges of the casement.
As I got closer, the bird skittered away from me and then, raised its wings, floated through the window frame and disappeared.

A few moments later the seagull poked his head out through the window, looked at me and asked me to follow him. I heard it in my head, "Follow me, it's better on this side."

I put my right hand through the frame. It was cold, and I could not see my hand on the other side. I pulled it out, but the hairs on the back of my neck were singed. I felt only cold, anger, fear and hunger, longing. I ran home.

Just Now....

As you fell asleep last night, I said, "I love you."

I lied.

Everything changed yesterday.

Sea Monsters do exist. He grabbed me, threw me down, snarling, dripping slime.

I was walking along the wrack line when I was snagged. He rose up half buried in seafoam and sand. Smirking, he offered me a deal. My immortality for you.

I'm telling this to you now while you are asleep because I am a coward.

He made it very clear. He is hungry for soul.

"Good Morning Babe."

"Let's go for a walk on the beach."

SEVEN

Starling

Erica Sage

There is a sound above her. Scratching. Star opens her eyes, stares at the ceiling.

The birdsong wakes her in spring and in summer. Before the full sun, before the man.

But there is something else this morning. More scratching, scuttling. Light feet.

The birds return with the rhododendrons' bloom. The purple, pink, white explode from the green stout trees, fireworks paused in the sky. The birds stay long after the flowers fade to brown, folding and crumbling, leaving skeleton hands begging the sky. The hatching comes then.

She has been here for four hatchings.

Star loves the orange-blooming rhododendron at the back of the property, the one that arrives late and stays long, on account of the sun only peaking into the shadows. It reminds her of the mother. There was a mother before. Star closes her eyes, finds the blue building with white trim, the seagulls, the orange ice cream dripping down the back of her hand.

A bird calls. Eager cries sound back.

A mother bird. Her babies hatched and nesting in the attic.

Star listens until it is time to feed the horse. She does this every morning before the man awakes. The door to her small room has been taken off its hinges. She descends the narrow stairs, opens the front door to the porch. She slips the boots over her bare feet. Her nightgown dampens on the tall, dew-burdened grass. The horse is waiting at the fence.

Hay, oats. Fill the bathtub with water.

Star walks around the stall to look back at the old farmhouse, tall and narrow. She peers up at the small window three stories above. Her room. She shields her eyes from the sun, spots the small, brown bird. Smaller than a crow, she sits on the roof above a hole. Something in her mouth. A branch, a worm. She swoops, she trills. The mother bird flies into the hole above her bedroom window. The nestlings' hungry chorus.

The first season, Star found a nest in the orange rhododendron. It rested high in the branches, under the dark green leaves, thick and mottled, like a witch's hands. She watched that nest all spring, but no bird ever came. She told the man. The nest wasn't there the next day.

That same season, she found a nest in the Wisteria, the trunk of the plant so thick, the vines so strong, it threatened to pull the shingles off one by one. It threatened to tear the whole house down. This nest had a bird in it, its yawning beak visible. Star had told the man. The next day, the nest was gone. The small, black bird lay on the ground near the side of the house. It wasn't broken, just on its side. Star had picked it up, touched its gray, downy feathers. The body was stiff, but no maggots or ants.

She buried the bird at the base of the old Wisteria, willing the vine to tear the whole house down. Every shingle. Every wall. Every beam. They would have to leave. They'd have to take Star from here. There was no other way.

She places her boots on the porch. In the kitchen, she fries eggs. She brews coffee. This is her job, no one else's, not even when there are other girls. Girls the woman delivers. Red-faced girls who cry and cry. Dark-eyed girls who've fallen silent. The other girls leave before Star ever finds the words.

Star has never left.

The man arrives first to breakfast. Star slides his eggs onto his plate. She pours his coffee. She does not mention the attic, the nest.

He eats silently, the fork loud against the plate. He has never left the property, only the woman.

The woman has been there for six days now. There had been a girl with her when she'd first returned. She looked older than Star. Angrier. Star could see in her that she would run, that she would not have listened to Star about the consequences. About the cement floor and the chain. Star would've had to hear the consequences through the floorboards. But the girl did not sleep even one night in the house. She was gone by evening. Headlights, two strangers on the porch. The man did not invite them in.

Star lamented the woman's return. Each time, she would bring a girl. Once there was a boy. But only once. There were scabs on his lips. Star wanted to bring him water. She didn't. The boy stayed two nights. He did not try to run. Star was grateful.

When the woman eats breakfast, she eats her egg in two bites. The second bite is the whole yolk and whatever is left of the white. She drinks her coffee in long pulls. The man sips. The man has time. He and Star do not go anywhere. Star remembers her legs are not fast enough. Star remembers the consequences.

She washes the dishes and sweeps the floor. The man and the woman are outside the house, by the truck. The front door is open. They are talking fast. Maybe they are angry.

Star leans the broom in its closet. It is time for her to be in her room. She sits on her bed, waits for the man. After, she will be allowed to bathe. To dress.

Only after.

But he has heard the scratching. The bustling and chirps above the bed. The mother's calls.

The man instructs Star to dress. He does not leave the bath towel on the bed. She will not be bathing. She feels the filth, the sickness on her skin. In her skin. Her clothes trap it against her person.

Outside, she must hold the hammer and wire mesh while he sets up the ladder. She must hold the ladder while he carries the hammer and wire mesh.

The mother bird cries. She dives. The babies say nothing because they do not know what has happened.

Star wills them to die fast. For the mother's sake.

Star wakes to the pecking, the beak on metal. Frantic. The babies cry, they shuffle. Soft talons on plywood.

Star puts her hands over her ears, but she can hear the pecking.

A bushel and a peck, Star remembers. *And I love you like heck.* Star closes her eyes, finds the mustard yellow carpet, the white sheer curtains, the long black hair and green eyes.

Star's legs were not fast enough.

She leaves early to feed the horse. She makes breakfast. There is only the man. The woman is gone. When she returns, there will be a girl. Never more than one. Star will feed the girl too, but the girl will not be allowed at the table.

. . .

Star wakes to pecking. You will break your beak on that mesh, Star thinks to the mother.

The babies chirp. They scuttle. Their mother cannot reach them.

You should have flown, she tells them through the ceiling.

It is only quiet at night.

The mother is there every morning. Maybe a nestling has died. The movements fewer, softer. But there is the pecking, there is the shrieking. Star swears she can hear it even in the kitchen, louder than the frying bacon. She swears she can hear it over the water when the man permits her to draw the bath.

The man had said it would take three days, but there is still something alive in the attic. It shuffles, but no longer chirps. The mother pecks at the mesh, but sometimes a whole minute goes by.

How long does it take to fledge, Star wonders.

Star visits the horse. Hay, oats, water.

She walks around the stall. The mother sits on the eave. She flits to the roof. Back to the eave. She pecks at the mesh. Her attention is fleeting. She eyes the chimney, another bird, a cloud, Star.

Star goes to the barn, finds the wooden ladder on its side. It is heavier than it looks. She lifts and drags it across the dirt and sawdust. She drags it across the dewy grass. She shifts, leans, hoists, maneuvers. She climbs till she faces the mesh. The mom wails and fusses above her on the roof. She does not peck her, but Star would understand.

She has the hammer. She wedges it under the nail. She pushes the handle against the eave until it gives and a nail drops to the grass below. She does this a second time, then peels back the mesh.

One small bird stares at her with black eyes. The other three are dead.

"You have to fly away from here," she tells the bird.

The mother cries. She dives.

44

Star pulls out the last two nails. She does not reach in to touch the bird. The mother might finally abandon it. She does not reach in to remove the dead. That's between the mother bird and nature. Star doesn't know what the mother will do now with only one left. What she will do with the dead.

Star does not want to know.

The man shouts her name. He is in the yard. He is at the horse. He rounds the stall. He is three stories away.

Star closes her eyes, finds the mother with the blackbird hair.

Her legs are lead on this earth.

Star must fly.

And so she does.

EIGHT

Tempesta

Jordan Nishkian

Fate, a small sandstorm,
keeps direction—
change, chase,
the storm adjusts.

Give in to the vacuum.
Step inside, closing eyes,
plugging ears;
be swallowed by lacking.

Abraised by sand cutting through
flesh, pulverizing bone—
grasp without aim
hands catch only blood.

Fling far the chain of being mortal,
scream, head thrown back,
throat to stars—
capable, destructive, glorious.

Rip the veil of
bellowing night—
consuming, devouring,
unstringing our history.

NINE

The Grassmarket Butcher

Stephen Mills

B lood was in the air. Most wouldn't know it, because the hard balance of Edinburgh's denizens trudged their way from one tragedy to the next, *living* just a byword for survival's miseries. Yet it was there, all the red iron stink of it, and Wooly Bunnet drew its familiar scent deep into his lungs. Morning had come with the blood, though most couldn't tell if it was dawn or dusk or even high noon, such was the gloom of the choking smog. Sea breezes did little to cleanse the reek of burning coal and humanity's waste from the city's air, and with that stench came the cloying grit of filth that clung to everyone and everything. Noxious coal smoke clogged the city's squares and alleys, so thick and black that a rare morning sun struggled to punch lifesaving holes through its dense, gray clouds.

Twice Wooly Bunnet had seen the dingy port from a distance, once as the great sailing ship had sailed off into the Firth of Forth, and again on its return.

He remembered the pall of smoke and grime that formed a gray, hazy dome over the place of his birth, he remembered the first lungful of cleansing sea air that he'd ever breathed in his life, and he remembered the wonder of such sensations as they coursed through him.

Bunnet's eventual return to Edinburgh was as a changed man. War changes a soul, and he had numbed to the horrors of the world. Edinburgh wasn't Wooly Bunnet's home any longer. It had become just another place to fight and survive, and he found that fighting and surviving were the two things that he was good at.

Two years had melted away since his return, and the horrors never strayed far, but though the familiar smog still choked the alleys and the Leith waterfront was as dangerous as ever, Wooly Bunnet's eyes narrowed as the familiar tang singed his nostrils. It was an unmistakable scent, he had experienced far too much death in his life to be fooled. There was blood in the air. He was certain of it.

Winter had been bitterly cold yet thankfully dry, and that was a welcome respite from the usually sullen and spitting rain, but then the air had grown stale and gritty. Wooly Bunnet almost wished for a bit of rain to cleanse the city's filth and sin as he pushed through the Wheatsheaf's peeled, creaking doors.

"Whit'll it be, Bunnet?" the one-eyed tavernkeeper slurred through smiling lips. His teeth looked like the many ruined buildings that dotted Edinburgh's Old Town - brown and decayed and shot through with massive gaps.

"A tuppenny, Sonsie," Wooly Bunnet graveled, his gray woolen bonnet pulled low to obstruct any unwanted attention. The name "Sonsie" was a joke between friends, one the unlucky tavernkeeper took in stride.

"A tuppenny it'll be, Bunnet. Eyes down then, there's Bloodyback 'round."

Too late, Wooly Bunnet heard the expelled air of a groaning sigh and a skinny Redcoat sat heavily in the chair next to him. "Tam Baird!" the man smiled, his tongue flicking to taste the air. "It's been a wee time since I've seen ye 'round. Ah heard ye be going by name a' Wooly Bunnet, then."

Bunnet turned his head slowly, gray-black irises smoldering like coals. "Last time I saw ye, ye were stripin' a man's back, ye gristly pintle," the big man growled with feral savagery. The sergeant had proudly absconded with the name Old Bloodyback on account of his ruthless glee at flogging privates, no matter how trivial their infractions. Old Bloodyback was also a wee strip of a man whose only authority came from the King's rank and the whip's leather thongs.

"Watch yer mouth, ye traitorous bastard," Bloodyback snapped back. The sergeant reminded Bunnet of a wee yapping dog. Snatching up his beer, Wooly Bunnet stretched from the chair and turned to rid himself of the little man but Bloodyback kept crowing at the retreating Bunnet. "Ye can't hide forever, Tam Baird. We'll get our hands on ye yet, an' when we do, me whip'll be singin'!"

Bunnet felt no fear of the little man. Crimea had stripped him of humanity's falsities. That is what battle did to a man. Wooly Bunnet had been called to fight in a war he had no understanding of, to kill Russians by the bushel for his King. He found that he was good at it, too. Killing came naturally to Bunnet, and in consequence, Crimea had peeled back every layer of the *old* Big Tam Baird until nothing was left but Wooly Bunnet. Save for the rare few, love and dread and worry and every other emotion had been scoured away until all that remained was an empty, self-loathing husk.

And hate.

Self-loathing and hate, they gobbled at the core of his soul, and Old Bloody-back embodied the worst of it. He was the distilled liquor of all the wrongs that had drummed against Bunnet's soul his entire life, and as Bloodyback pushed past the hulking, fuming man, he let loose a shrill laugh. "Ah'll see ye soon, wee jimmy. Me an' me whip 'll see ye soon."

Behind Sonsie's tavern was the piss-yard where patrons drained their waters, and Old Bloodyback pushed through the door, his last laugh singeing Bunnet's ears so that his hands clenched into fists before they started the familiar quak-ing. He had fled the army once the gangplanks dropped, the bile of Crimea's terrors still burning his gullet, and Bloodyback's red coat and barking laugh made the old rancor rise again.

On the other side of the door was a hard-packed dirt courtyard that stunk of urine and was filled with Edinburgh's choking, coal-smoke filled air. Leith was rough. Another scream would be just another scream, another wail in an endless cacophony of misery and violence. Not a single scarred soul would be surprised or troubled by such a common sound, and as Wooly Bunnet consid-ered the piss-yard door, he let a hidden blade slip from the worn tweed's cuff into the palm of his hand.

Bloodyback couldn't be allowed to live. Bunnet had built a life since deserting the King's army and he wouldn't let some self-important prick threaten what little peace he had found. Those few that he still cherished in this cold world were reliant on him to support and protect them from the decaying alleys that consumed unwary souls. Wooly Bunnet resolved not to fall prey to the Sergeant's threats. Expelling a breath to ward off the impending finality of a wasted life, Bunnet slid his bulk through the door, his eyes squinting momen-tarily against the hazy light of day.

Urine's ammonia-perfume seared Bunnet's sinuses, yet such a reek was expected. The shock he felt wasn't from the foulness of the piss-yard, but rather that Bloodyback was nowhere to be seen. The sergeant had just pushed his way, grinning and laughing, through the door, but the skinny, diseased man in his government redcoat was gone. Instead, the sergeant had somehow been replaced by a half-dozen hardened toughs, all scarred faces and broken teeth. Not a single man smiled, though one dribbled saliva between toothless gums, his mental faculties obviously long-since sacrificed to the bottle and crime.

"Thomas Baird," a slender man called out, his accent marking him as one unused to places like Sonsie's piss-yard. "That's yer name, is it not?" He was tall, well dressed, with nary a stain on his waistcoat or a scuff on his beaver-fur top hat. Even his leather shoes positively glowed from what little light burned its way through the coal-smoke gloom, such was the sheen on them.

Wooly Bunnet took a step back, every sense shrieking out in danger. Whoever this man was, his formidable sociability easily trumped any dirty trick the streetwise tough could dream up. His scruffy lackeys guaranteed that.

A chuckle slipped from the neatly trimmed hedge that crowned the stranger's face. "Ah'm not here t' see ye apprehended, Thomas. Neither am a' here t' bury ye."

"Wit th' fook are ye after, then?" Wooly Bunnet growled ferally, his body tensed in a half-crouch, ready for any attack. Snarls sounded at his curses.

"Easy, easy, jimmies," the man said to his pack, manicured hands gesturing for calm. Those jet pupils turned their piercing stare back onto Wooly Bunnet, who swore the spirit within them was devoid of life, devoid of emotion. They were cold eyes, as cold as winter in the Gàidhealtachd. They were a killer's eyes, just as Bunnet saw when he stared in the ancient brass mirror that he used to trim his beard. "Ye've a reputation, Mister Baird. Ye an' I ken those who run in th' same circles, or near enough. Ye an' I both ken 'at foul things are about, we both smelt th' blood in th' air, ye ken?"

"Ah ken wit yer on about," Wooly Bunnet snarled through squinted eyes, his body still poised to launch a savage attack. Trust wasn't easily gained for someone like Bunnet, and no matter the sweet words out of this pampered stranger, the wary man wouldn't let down his guard.

"Ah know of a job fer ye, Thomas, if ye'll take it," the mysterious stranger grinned, and his threadbare companions milled about nervously.

Bunnet's hard eyes narrowed further under the soft wool of his cap. Honest work was difficult to find in Edinburgh's hardscrabble tenements. Some men were manual laborers on the waterfront, while the lucky few that were skilled tradesmen plied their wares in the markets that dotted the city. Still others were merchants or traders, lawyers or doctors. To the uninitiated, there certainly seemed to be opportunity in the hustle and bustle of Scotland's capital, but those born and raised in the rotting flats and closes knew better, so men like Wooly Bunnet made their own way in the world.

His was a difficult life, living in the shadows and walking the thin line of lawlessness, but he reckoned it was better than laboring to an early death for meager scraps. "Ah werk fer no man, y' ken?"

With a deft move of his hand, the stranger tapped the brim of his top hat and dipped his head in a nod. "Ye say that, Mister Baird, but yer mind's a'ready been made up. Ye just don't know it yet. Blood is in th' air, ye know it just as I do, an' soon enough ye'll happily agree t' th' terms of employ."

Bunnet growled, but his hands began to relax and he stretched to his full height, a straight-backed giant who towered over the rough-edged men that eyed him back warily. Something was wrong about the slender killer who unflinchingly returned Wooly Bunnet's stare. He was dressed as a well-off man, aristocratic even, but those black eyes had seen nightmarish things so that the soul beneath had become hard and uncaring - if there was even a soul there at all. "Why me?" he demanded simply. Edinburgh was filled to no end with murderers and thieves and all manner of undesirable filth that would sell their own children for a shilling.

A sound like a steam whistle streamed from the man's mouth, and Bunnet realized it was a laugh. He went on like that for a long second, the humorless whistle eventually evaporating into the city's gloom, and Bunnet nearly let out a mirthful laugh of his own but bit back the bark of it. Instinct told him that this man valued fear and respect, much as any back-alley man does, and that one was the byproduct of the other. Bunnet knew that, because he himself cultivated grudging respect from the fearful dregs of humanity that existed in his own tenement. The figure that opposed him may look like a polished aristocrat, but Wooly Bunnet realized that he wasn't that far removed from Bunnet's own life.

"Ye've raised an eyebrow o' twa', Mister Baird. Ye've skills 'at 'ave value fer m' employer an' he has resources 'at would keep men like you an' me safe."

"Ye assume 'at ah need t' be kept safe."

"Ach, I 'ave no doubt 'at you can tak' care of yersel, but yer sister an' niece may hae 'nother opinion entire."

At the mention of his sister and her daughter, Bunnet lurched forward with a menacing step, the blade whipping out in a blur. "Th' fook ye say?" he raged, the target of his wrath within range for a quick strike of the needle-thin steel. "Th' fook did ye say about m' sister?"

The ring of toughs collapsed as a noose, a dozen hands grabbing hold of Bunnet's arms, the nook of a wiry arm hooked around his neck to choke the words off. Grunting like an animal, Wooly Bunnet fought their strength but succumbed to their numbers as a bull tires before the bullfighter, until he sank, immobilized, into the stink of the urine-soaked dirt. Still he fought, with snot and white saliva streaked across his face, and that steamwhistle laugh grated him again.

"Ah din't mean t' distress ye, Thomas," the man winked as he crouched next to the pile of men that struggled to hold Bunnet's wrath in check. "Ah would'n' 'arm a hair on their 'eads. But 'ere's blood in th' air, and money t' be made in th' trade of it." He stood and stretched, a keen eye taking in the mountain of a man that still shivered with uncontrolled fury. "Let 'im go, jimmies. Ah can see in Mister Baird's eyes 'at he won't do nothin' now, anyways."

One by one, the men climbed off of the prone Wooly Bunnet, just as the layers of an onion are peeled back to expose the rank core. Eventually, he heaved himself to his feet, the slabs of his hands brushing piss-sodden filth from his gray trousers. Every ounce of Bunnet's strength was consumed with harnessing the rage that threatened to consume him, but with great effort he swallowed it back to train his own eyes on the black soul of the man. "If anything 'as 'appened to 'em, ah'll come fer ye. Mark me," Bunnet seethed through clenched jaws.

His opponent flashed a smile of tea-stained teeth, themselves the same color as the Edwardian sandstone buildings that surrounded them in the piss-yard. "Ye mistak' me, Mister Baird. Ah've come here t' help ye. Someone 'as an axe to grind against yer millstone, but it ain't me. Th' terms of th' employment, then, are t' yer favor."

"Wit is it yer on about?" Wooly Bunnet frothed. He was sure the stranger represented a threat, and the comment about his sister and niece had sealed that argument.

Yet, he still had a job on offer?

"Listen carefully t' me, Thomas. Someone is stealin' bairns an' cuttin' 'em up. Pairts of 'em are bein' found in th' Grassmarket. Th' Grassmarket Butcher, some 'ave taken t' callin' 'im. Th' Grassmarket Butcher, ye ken? It's upsettin' th' community, which is affectin' business an' things fer m' employer. Ye 'ave skills 'e needs, an 'e pays a handsome coin for th' right skills. Meet m' tonight at Saint Giles after evenin' prayers. Don't dally, though." On the last word, the man spun on his heel and stalked from the yard, his train of lackeys filing out behind him with bilious eyes and curled lips. Wooly Bunnet cursed, spat, then let loose another curse. The last orders he had taken were from a sergeant before the gangplanks fell, and he had sworn never to take another order again, but God had a way of making a joke out of the most solemn of oaths.

"Why should I?" Bunnet shouted, his voice a phlegmy growl, his voice echoing off the stone walls.

The reply shot back immediately, a blade of words that cut Wooly Bunnet to his core so that the blood leaked from what was left of his desiccated soul. "Go home and talk t' yer sister," the mysterious man said. "Unless ye desire yer sister's bairn t' be th' Butcher's next victim, ye best hurry, 'cause her precious little Bet hasn't been seen aw day!"

Bunnet's heart clenched in his chest as his brain tried to process the awful words. Suddenly the yard's piss-stained walls closed in on him, the coal-dark sky pressing down, and a rising gorge scorched his throat. *How did the stranger know that Bet was missing?* It was a haunting question, but one that could be answered in time.

First, he would find his niece, the only bit of illumination in an otherwise dark and bitter world.

Failing that, he had a man to meet at Saint Giles' Cathedral, because blood was in the air, and he was determined to ensure that it wasn't Bet's.

TEN

The Locket

Matt Micheli

Madison swung away on her swing-set—back and forth—pointing her toes out and leaning back, getting higher and higher with each pass, her dad's lawnmower humming along in the background. Her parents wanted to get rid of that old playscape they insisted she had outgrown, but Madison loved that thing, sometimes still spending hours at a time on it, swinging, sliding, climbing like it was her seventh birthday all over again.

The late morning sun broke through the trees, illuminating the healthy, green lawn that Madison's dad Robert so assiduously and proudly cared for. He mowed in perfect rows, sometimes more than once to ensure the clippings were mulched from existence and the yard was completely flat and uniform, rivaling the greens of the most prestigious golf courses around and earning compliments from other lawn hobbyists in the neighborhood.

Madison's swinging slowed to a stop as she watched the speeding Lincoln come roaring through the fence, an explosion of broken pickets flying over the hood and into the air. The car bounced and swerved, tearing through the lush lawn, finally smashing head on into one of the large oaks on the property. The crashing steel and shattering glass breached the loud purr of the mower, snapping Robert from his robotic trance. He looked up and released the handle, cutting the engine. It took him a second to register what was happening, and when his brain finally sparked, his first instinct was to look for Madison who was safe and walking toward the wrecked car.

"Madison! Stay back, baby!" Robert said, watching the smoke rise from the busted front end of the Lincoln and hearing what sounded like a boiling tea kettle on the verge of combustion. He hurried toward the car as the driver-side door creaked open, and a man fell out onto the ground. The man crawled only inches with something clasp tight in his hand before his heavy head hit the earth and his grip released, blood seeping onto the freshly cut lawn.

"Holy shit!" Robert said as he raced to the driver's aid. "Sir! Sir! Are you alright?" He nudged the man who lay motionless, a puddle of blood expanding around his head. He looked back to the house. His wife Samantha stood on the front porch with her hands on her head, eyes wide and mouth hanging loosely open.

"Honey," Robert said. "Call 9-1-1!"

When she didn't move, he tried again. "Honey! Samantha! Call 9-1-1!"

Finally, the words registered with her, and she raced inside for her phone.

"Help's on the way, sir! Stay with—" Robert's words were cut short by the woman in the passenger seat, her head hung low from a loose swivel. Robert walked from the man and peered inside the car. "My God," he said, horrified by the amount of blood and viscous, lumpy fluids that had only moments prior been contained within her skull, now splattered around the cabin, still oozing from the gunshot wound in the side of her head. Chunks of burrowing windshield bulged from her face like blisters ready to pop. Robert gagged and turned from the vehicle, hunched over, fighting back the acid that tried forcing its way up his throat. With his hands on his knees, he caught his breath and wiped the excess saliva from his mouth.

Madison stood completely still about twenty feet from the accident, quietly observing the carnage, her face lacking any expression, her ten-year old brain not developed or mature enough to process the horrific images.

"Maddy," Robert said. "Go inside, now."

It had been several days since the accident and things were beginning to normalize again. Robert put in an insurance claim on the fence that would be fixed the following week. He raked out the tire tracks in the lawn and re-seeded the bare patches. With a little time and some water, his lawn would soon be back to its lush, uniformed appearance.

The brakes on the school bus squealed as it pulled up in front of their house. Madison and her older brother Maddox came off the bus, both hoisting their backpacks. Maddox walked directly to the house, intent on getting something to eat for his unceasingly hungry and growing teenage body and speeding through his homework so he could get online with his friends and shoot every-thing in sight. His life consisted of eating and gaming. School and everything else were just in the way. The screen door shut behind the determined teenage boy on a mission.

Madison slowed as she walked past where the accident occurred, visions of the dead man's and woman's bodies flashing through her mind like a cursed old film projector. While her family seemed to have moved on from the traumatic incident, or were at least pretending, Madison couldn't get the questions out of her head. *Why did the man shoot her? How did they end up in our yard?* She stopped where the man had crawled from the vehicle and bled out, still seeing remnants of the rusty color coating the ground, despite her dad having put the hose to it several times. The afternoon sun reflected from something in the dirt, the shimmery object catching her eye. She bent down and picked up the unfamiliar silver locket, looking it over, assuming the man must have dropped it as he fell from the car. She noticed a soft reddish glow leaking from the seam and wondered what could be inside. *Maybe a jewel or crystal,* she thought. *Definitely something red and sparkly.* She held the chain and tried prying the locket open with her fingernails, but it wouldn't budge. The glow from within softly flickered—brightening and dimming, the locket like ice seeping into her fingertips. As if in trouble, she looked around for a moment to ensure there were no witnesses, before placing the locket in her pocket and walking inside the house and up the stairs to her room. She set the mysterious locket on her nightstand next to her bed, whatever contained inside still emitting a gentle ruddiness through the seam.

Madison woke the next morning to yelling coming through the walls. She couldn't make out the words, but she didn't need to. Her parents were obviously upset and arguing about something. She looked at the clock showing it was before six a.m., let out a frustrated sigh, and fell back into the pillow that felt cold and damp. The sheets were also damp. Madison had apparently sweated half her body weight throughout the night, the mattress and pillows nothing more than a big sponge. The yelling continued as she covered her ears. Her parents didn't fight very often—actually they hardly ever fought—but sometimes they could be so stupid, she thought. *Annoyingly stupid.*

Madison tried closing her eyes and catching that last half hour of sleep before having to get up for school, but it was no use. The assault from the other room was too much. She threw the blanket off and got up from bed, noticing the shiny locket she placed on her nightstand spread open. *Weird,* she thought. She wasn't able to pry the thing open yesterday, yet there it was. She anxiously picked it up to see what was inside. There was no glow, no jewel or crystal, nothing. Just an empty old locket.

The front door of the house slammed shut, vibrating the walls. An aggravated Madison looked through her blinds to see her dad rev up his truck and back out in a rage. *What is wrong with these people?*

———————

Madison felt off all day at school, like she was watching her classmates from a distance. Her normal happy, boisterous self had been replaced by a quiet, annoyed child who just wanted to get away from there, away from everywhere and everyone. Madison's best friend Sofia tried engaging with her, but Madison offered nothing more than one or two word replies, uninterested at best.

That evening was more of the same from her parents. Constant bickering and yelling over this and that, capped by Maddox's in school suspension for getting in a fight. That seemed to send them over the edge as both parents stormed out of the dining room in opposite directions, abandoning their plates half eaten, too angry to be in the same room with Maddox or each other any longer. Cabinet doors slammed from the kitchen as curse words flew around the house like wildly-thrown daggers.

Madison couldn't deal with these idiotic people any longer, taking only a few bites from the chicken and macaroni and cheese that tasted awful and was hard to swallow before stomping up the stairs, slamming her door, and locking herself in her room. She lay in bed, staring up at the ceiling and the spinning fan, frustration percolating through her tensed fists. She couldn't pinpoint or focus on any particular thought as her mind spun round and round and round with the blades of the fan until she finally fell asleep.

———————

The next morning, Madison *really* didn't feel well. She didn't get much sleep, the deadly accident haunting her dreams along with some other strange images she couldn't quite place. She remembered an old woman in a long, flowing, dark red dress from her dream, but couldn't recall any facial features other than her deep-set black eyes like two infinite tunnels. Madison felt uneasy as something turned over in her belly and her pores released more sweat upon the already drenched sheets. She held her hands to the sides of her head that throbbed from her first headache, a new sensation she would rather have not discovered.

There was banging from the hall.

"Maddox!" her mom said. "Get your ass out here, right now! You don't talk to me that way!"

The yelling and banging intensified the pounding pain in Madison's head. She covered her ears and rocked back and forth, wishing she could get far enough from her terrible parents and annoying brother to where she'd never have to see or hear them again. She was beginning . . . to *hate* them.

"Now, Maddox! You little asshole!"

Maddox yelled something back. Then came heavy clomping up the stairs.

"No, Robert," Samantha pleaded. "No!"

Then there were two loud bangs that shook the house followed by the door slamming against the wall and yells between her brother and dad, while her mom begged, "No—No—No!"

A heavy thud in the hall silenced her mom's pleading, followed by a loud slapping sound that could only be her dad's hands or fists pummeling her thirteen-year old brother. Maddox cried and squealed like something from another planet as the pounding continued for what seemed like forever. Then it all stopped, except for her mom's panting and whining and her dad stamping down the stairs, the door slamming on his way out. Madison peeked her head from her room, seeing Maddox's game system smashed on the floor, and then her mom's troubled face, wide eyes angry and full of tears.

An unknown rage grew in Madison as she closed her door, the only release being a cracking scream at the top of her lungs that lasted several seconds.

Within a matter of days, the house that had been home to so much love was now filled to the brim with an overwhelming hate. Spite and anger bled from the walls. The lawn that Robert spent so many tedious hours perfecting was now untrimmed with new weeds reaching toward the sky, sucking the life from St. Augustine. No one in the house spoke to each other, other than verbally assaulting or yelling in passing. Maddox stayed locked away in his room, nursing the beating at the hands of their father. Samantha did her best to stay preoccupied with reality TV or romance novels, but even the fluffiest, emptiest forms of media made her blood boil, sending her into random bouts of screaming and shouting obscenities at anyone within earshot. Robert would make his presence known by slamming every door in his path and calling his wife every name in the book from the other end of the house, loud enough for everyone to hear, even their elderly neighbors over an acre away.

The Clemons, who lived in the next house over, were beginning to worry but weren't the nosy type so felt it best to mind their business and keep to themselves. They assumed whatever was going on with the nice family next door who they'd known for years would work itself out.

That night, Madison again dreamt of that old lady in the long flowing red dress. There was something weirdly comforting about her, despite not possessing any facial features other than her eyes that were two endless black holes. Weird or not, Madison embraced any comfort she could get, which was a welcome escape from the anger she felt for her horrible parents and loser brother. She climbed from her bed and followed the old woman down the stairs and out of the house. Outside, Madison looked back and forth, surveying the yard for the woman who had suddenly disappeared and then reappeared next to the shed. She was facing Madison. *How'd she get over there?* That's when Madison noticed there were no feet below the red dress. As if being summoned, Madison walked over to the woman who moved into the shed. Madison followed, noticing her dad's mower that he loved more than his own children, and the gas canister next to it. A sudden rage filled her along with a fiery desire to burn that damn mower, destroy it to hurt her asshole father. The old woman had no mouth to smile but Madison could *feel* her smiling. The woman drifted softly and slowly toward the house and around it. Madison circled the house with her. Tortured screams and cries for help echoed in the distance which seemed to please the old woman, which pleased Madison.

Madison opened her eyes to the violent popping of the fire that had engulfed the house in a blinding blaze. The sounds of sirens grew louder and louder until they were splitting the air, and flashes of red and blue lit up the sky like the fourth of July. Countless uniformed men and women ran every which way, a blurry ocean of first responders.

"Little girl!" said an approaching voice. "Are you okay?" The man turned and called out for a medic. He then faced Madison, placed his hands on her shoulders, looked directly into her eyes, and compassionately said, "You're going to be okay. I promise."

Madison watched vacantly as the reaching fire consumed her house and everyone inside. With her stupid parents and idiot brother out of her life, she believed what the young officer said. She *would* be okay.

The man with the fluffy blonde hair—Trevor—opened the car door for Madison who climbed in. He and the slender, dark-haired woman called Beth couldn't stop looking at each other nor control the giant grins on their faces.

Once in the car, between smiling at each other, they'd both sneak peaks at Madison through the rearview mirror.

"We've waited a long time for you, Maddy. Can we . . . can we call you Maddy?" Beth said.

Madison hated the idea of being called Maddy, but she nodded anyway to play along.

"Well, Maddy," Trevor said from the driver's seat, looking back through the mirror. "We're new to parenting, but we are going to do this together. And I promise–" he looked over to his wife, "*We* promise . . . that we are going to do our absolute best to give you the best life possible."

Madison stayed quiet, blankly staring out the window at the passing buildings and cars, her previous life getting farther and farther away.

"Do you like horses?" Beth asked, overly excited. "Because we made your room look like a horse stable, full of horses and sunshine." The woman smiled but then doubted herself when Madison didn't answer. "Well . . . if not, we can change it, right, honey?" she said, looking over at her husband. "We can change it?"

"Yeah, of course," Trevor said. "It's your room, Maddy. So whatever you want is what we want."

Madison continued gazing out the window, the sun warming her face. This was the first moment since the fire where she wished she could see her parents again, her brother. She felt something from deep inside, trying to surface. She almost . . . *missed* them. Within a matter of seconds, those feelings were gone, pushed back inside and locked away.

"Hey, Maddy," Beth said. "That's a beautiful locket you're wearing. Who gave it to you?"

Madison didn't answer.

"I bet there's something *really* special inside it," said Beth.

Madison stayed quiet, staring off.

Beth smiled, sincerely. She couldn't even try to imagine what Madison was thinking; what this poor girl had been through. "You can tell us about it when you're ready."

Beth's words bounced off of Madison, as she rubbed the locket that hung from her neck, feeling the smooth cold texture, the red glow from inside a soft flicker that chilled her fingertips, comforting her.

ELEVEN

Tomorrow and Tomorrow and Tomorrow

Megan Speece

I stood in the living room of a house filled with boxes, breathing in the new paint smell, cherishing those few quiet moments. I had spent the past several weeks packing up my childhood home, the home I'd lived in for twenty-six years. When I was nineteen, my mother had a stroke. I was barely an adult, but it fell to me, the only child, to take care of her in the years after that stroke. My father had left when I was young, no doubt driven off by my mother's high expectations. She never regained all of her strength and wasn't able to care for herself. So, I stayed, and I became the mother.

I had thought she stifled me as a young person, never allowing me to dress in the latest styles, or wear my hair in ways that were "unbecoming of a lady". She'd been strict, overbearing, and judgmental of any friend I dared bring home. She did it all out of love, of course. She would tell me that I was her precious diamond, and I deserved better than the friends I brought home, or the fast fashion that wouldn't last the year. I was her entire world, and she never let me forget it.

All of that was nothing compared to what she was like after the stroke. She became even more critical of me, asking me why I was a spinster, sitting at home taking care of an old woman, rather than married and taking care of children of my own. She'd point out the clothing that I was wearing as the reason I couldn't find a man. Never mind the fact that I was wearing sweats because I was staying home with her where a man would never see me. If I dared to go out, if I got dressed up and went anywhere, even if it was just the coffee shop where I could read in peace, she'd guilt me for leaving her alone. She would accuse me of not caring for her, of only being interested in myself. I was simultaneously a bad daughter for being a spinster and not having run off to get married and start a family of my own, and a bad daughter for not being at her beck and call every waking minute of every day.

In the end, as I sat in a chair next to her bed, reading to her, she would tell me that she would always be with me. That I was hers, forever. Since I was little, she would tell me "I will love you tomorrow, and tomorrow, and tomorrow." It's a sweet sentiment, something to be put on greeting cards, and one every child should hear. I just never thought she meant it literally.

The day after she died, she showed up at the foot of my bed. I thought I was dreaming, my grief trying to work itself out in my sleep. But then I'd see her in the living room, in her favorite rocking chair. Or I'd see her in the garden she had cultivated to perfection. The dead are supposed to rest in peace, and she wasn't resting. She was disrupting my peace. The first chance at peace I'd had in the seven years since her stroke.

I'd begun to go out, to meet people. I made friends; I brought home men. But they would always leave, saying that my house made them uncomfortable. Or that things fell off of shelves every time they walked by. One man, called Andrew, was covered in tattoos and rode a motorcycle. I found him funny and thrilling and he stuck around, coming to the house every weekend for roughly two months. But he seemed to be plagued with bad luck every time he set foot in the house. His foot went through a stair, though there'd been no previous sign of rot or damage. The dryer caught fire when his clothes were in it, despite him just having cleaned out the lint hose for me. The bed broke beneath us one night; a sturdy old metal thing that had seen its share of prac-ticed baby making over the years. We'd laughed about that and had continued to practice, undeterred by the angle at which the bed now sat. It was when he sat down in my mother's favorite rocking chair and flipped backwards, spilling him onto the floor, that he finally gave up.

"Look, I like you. A lot," he'd said as he rubbed the goose egg on the back of his head. "But I can't keep coming around here where weird things are happening to me. It's going to get me seriously injured or killed."

So, I packed up the house. I sold off the furniture and her life's collection of things I didn't need, and I bought a little house of my own one town over. It was only one bedroom on a tiny lot in the back of a rundown neighborhood, but it was all mine and I already loved it. Andrew helped me load my modest number of boxes into a small rental van and then helped unload them into the new house. He smiled at me, a lascivious glint to his eye, as he helped me set up the bed. We christened my tiny little house before we'd even unpacked, relieved to be in a place that didn't attack him from every direction.

I set out to unpack the boxes the next morning after bidding Andrew goodbye for the day. I was placing the dishes into their new homes in the sunny yellow cabinets in the kitchen when I heard it: the familiar wooden creaking sound of the rocking chair. I walked into the dining room, dragging my feet, dreading what I would find in my small living room. There, in the corner, was the rocking chair, moving slowly back and forth, seemingly of its own accord. I cast a furtive glance around the space, trying to determine what could be making the rocking chair move. But, then, as I came to terms with the fact that there was nothing in this house but me, the sound of the rocking chair changed and it seemed to speak. A barely audible sigh, but truly words coming as the rails rocked over the hardwood floors: "tomorrow and tomorrow and tomorrow".

TWELVE

Two Bridges

Shannan Chapman

"I think we're lost, Mawmaw." Aria huffs as she slaps another mosquito dead on her arm. "13" she whispers under her breath. She has noticed the tiny dirt path they started out on has all but disappeared under the weeds and bushes and tiny pinecones that lace the edges of where they are stepping. It feels as if the trees are closing in on them, trying to suffocate them.

"I told you to wear a long sleeve shirt. And we're not lost child."

"It's like 200 degrees out. If I wore a long sleeve shirt, I would melt."

"I'm wearing a long sleeve shirt and I'm not melting. Not yet," the old woman tells her, not looking back, not breaking her stride. Aria hears the humor in the old woman's voice and rolls her eyes for perhaps the 100th time this afternoon.

To take her mind off her misery, she mimics her grandmother's walk, taking great big steps but still falling behind. She watches the way her long red hair bounces with her steps. Red like hers, like her mom's. But Mawmaw's is also streaked with bright white lines, tentacles, she thinks, scattered haphazardly between the deep red. She doesn't look like other grandmothers Aria knows. Well, actually, she doesn't really know any other grandmothers. Only the ones she's seen on TV and in movies and they certainly don't look like Mawmaw. *Mawmaw.* She stops just short of snorting and rolls her eyes again instead. Why does she have to call her Mawmaw anyway? Why can't she call her Granny or Gramma or even Beatrice? Since she doesn't really know her. Mawmaw is such a baby name. Maybe if she was five. But she is eleven. Almost 12 and the kids in New York would have a field day if they heard her say *Mawmaw.* A field day. That's what her mom used to say. *If I let you go to school like that, your teacher will have a field day. If I miss work again, my boss will have a field day.* And then, to take her mind off her mother, she changes the subject. As if there has been a conversation all along.

"Are there bears?"

"Of course, there are bears."

Aria stops and peers cautiously into the woods where it goes dark. The green eaves hang low, reaching towards the forest floor. A perfect hiding spot, she thinks and quickly runs after her grandmother, slowing just shy of catching up.

They round a bend and the trees suddenly give each other a little more space, and she can better see the sky now. But the light is still dim. There is no blue above them, only a dreary gray pushing down on her and she feels the full weight of it. Looking at her feet, Aria wonders again if they are really lost and Mawmaw doesn't want to admit it.

Slap! "14" she says, louder this time. "How much further?"

"Just around the next bend."

But she said that three bends ago. And Aria just wants to go home. Not her new home. Her *home* home. Back to the apartment in New York where she lived with her mother. And more than anything, she wants her mother to be there with her. She hates the woods. The trees. The mosquitos and the flies. She hates the crunchy needles under her feet, and the birds. She especially hates the birds. Maybe more than she hates the mosquitos. Always singing as if the world is wonderful. The birds in New York don't sing. They know better. There are trees, but they are in the parks, where they belong. Not out here in the woods, hiding the bears and who knows what else.

Wiping the sweat from her eyes with the hem of her t-shirt, she remembers that her mother had once been happy; when they used to dance in the dim light of their tiny apartment, twirling round and round until Aria was dizzy. And then collapse in a fit of laughter onto the couch where her mother would light a long white cigarette. In between puffs, she would drink from a small glass that tinkled with ice and Aria remembered that sound most of all. She would inch closer as her mother wrapped them both in a fuzzy blanket. In awe of her long, tall beauty, smoke swirling round her like a ghostly aura, Aria would say a tiny prayer that she would grow up to be like her. And it was good.

But the laughter had stopped. The dancing gave way to stillness, an unbearable and oppressive stillness. No more music. The only sound was the tinkle of the ice and her mother's soft breath as she puffed on those long white cigarettes, the smoke still swirling and ghosting.

"Here we are Aria," Mawmaw says, stopping so suddenly that Aria runs right into her and has to catch herself. Mawmaw turns around and looks at her and for a moment so brief, Aria sees her mother. And then it's gone, flitting away into the soft, stillness of the woods.

Aria looks away, past Mawmaw, at the river suddenly stretching before them. Not like any river she's ever seen, although she hasn't actually seen *that* many rivers. This river is green and blue and brown and yet, she can see all the way to where small rocks sleep peacefully and content on the sandy bottom. The water is so still that she catches sight of tiny creatures swimming around the sleeping rocks. Tadpoles? Minnows? She doesn't know. But she sees them.

And then she notices the shadow reaching across the river like a bridge. Looking up, she sees that it *is* a bridge. But not like any bridge she's ever seen, and she has certainly seen many bridges in her life. No. This is a bridge made from…from the earth itself, she thinks. From a huge rock that stretches towards the sky. And there are trees growing out of the rock. She didn't know trees could grow from rocks.

"What is this place, Mawmaw?" she whispers, afraid she might disturb the magic she is seeing.

"This is where your mother used to play." Mawmaw pauses, and Aria sees in her eyes what she feels in her own heart. "It's where I used to go when I was a child. I first brought her here when she was just a little thing. She didn't like the mosquitos either." She paused again, the memory bright across her face, as if somehow the sun had gotten through the trees. "When her daddy died, this was her place. She said it was magic."

"Did she ever cross it?" Aria points to the top of the rock, stretching her neck. She tries not to think about the other bridge. The one in New York. The one they pulled her mother's body from under only a few weeks ago.

"She never did. She was too afraid." She follows Aria's gaze and then quickly looks away. "Sit child." Mawmaw guides her to a rock. They slip off their shoes and dangle their feet, their toes touching the cool water. Aria breathes in the mossy scent of the river. The bridge provides shade. And comfort somehow.

"Mawmaw?" Aria tries to find the right question, but it doesn't come. Mawmaw stays quiet, as if she knows. As if she may not have an answer anyway.

"Mawmaw?" she tries again, looking not at her grandmother, but at the bridge that looms above their heads.

"Yes, child?"

"Why?" It comes out now. Under the shadow of this bridge that her mother could never cross.

Mawmaw reaches over and takes Aria by the hand and Aria can feel the softness in the folds of her skin. "When your mother was, oh, maybe your age, she said she wanted to cross the bridge. That she was no longer afraid. But only if I would go with her. So, we hiked up. She stood right there." Perhaps remembering, she points up to their side of the bridge. "But she couldn't bring herself to cross it. She said she had decided that we should just stand on our side. I tried to show her that there was plenty of room. I even crossed so she could see that it was safe. But she wouldn't follow. She was so frightened." Mawmaw pauses, and Aria sees that she is crying.

"So, I came back," Mawmaw continues. "And we stood together, looking across to the other side. But then she said something I'll never forget."

Aria looks up as her grandmother hesitates. "What did she say, Mawmaw?"

"She said, 'I just can't. What if I get to the middle and get stuck? What if I'm too afraid? What if I have to jump to save myself?'"

Aria squeezes Mawmaw's hand and inches in closer, resting her head on her shoulder, and closes her eyes. And thinks of her mother up on those two bridges. And knows.

THIRTEEN

Two Days

Rebecca Carlyle

The way the moonlight streams between buildings and illuminates a small section of the still pool nearby is idyllic. Steam from the hot tub soaks into my hair, saturating me in the strong scent of chlorine and mascara runs from the moist air. The lamppost only lights up one side of your face and the smile that flits at the corners of your mouth. That smile is perfect. I live for that smile. Goosebumps prickle my shoulders and I completely submerge myself under the water. Heat burns my face more than I thought it would; I can feel my cheeks turning bright red. Waves slosh around the edges when I break the surface again. You catch me watching the way the water laps at your muscles, the water making your smooth skin look flawless.

Embarrassed, I stare into the water, "Can we go back to your dorm?"

I hear the water dripping off your lanky body onto the cement and see your feet in my peripheral vision. I listen to the towel rub across your glistening skin as you dry off. You offer me a hand and you help me out of the water and into the towel that you fold around me. My wet, stringy hair sticks to my face, but you envelop me into your arms anyway, squeezing tightly and I breathe in your warmth. I shiver from a chill running down my spine, but it's not from the cold. I press my face into your neck; being this close to you is never short of amazing.

"I wish we could stay like this," you whisper to my forehead, kissing it after.

I do too because it's perfect. I peer up into your face just so I can see that smile. That smile that I love. Slowly, you drop your arms and lace your fingers through mine. You always do this. You always need to be touching me somehow. A hand on my shoulder, on the small of my back, or the nape of my neck. It seems like you have to check to make sure I'm still there.

As we make the trek from the common house back to your room, I dream back to the first time it all seemed so perfect, back to when we were actually a couple two years ago. Just the way a first love is supposed to be. The stars are shining, ocean breezes caress our faces with the scent of salt. The Dream Inn harbor's sand that's a perfect combination of soft and firm to support our bodies in just the right places. It's everywhere; in my hair, between my toes, and grinding against my skin under my clothes. We lay there in moments of silence with a level of comfort that only people who have known each other their whole lives could have. Laughter fills the air with thick contentment. And other moments we are running, sand tossed into the wind behind us, my shrieks causing lights in the hotel nearby to flick on. We try to stifle our laughs and fall back into that soft, firm sand; bliss emanating from us.

It's amazing how everything about us seems to match. From the way I fit nestled up against your side, to the way your personality brightens mine to the point of bubbling over.

The once-blooming roses you hand-picked from your yard are wilting at my side from the lack of water. My eyelids start to droop with sleep as fog settles over the bay, hiding us from the prying eyes of the hotel.

It was almost perfect; the silence uninterrupted by the cell phones we left in your car. My mind pushed the endless voicemails from parents away from my thoughts and I let myself completely feel the amount of happiness a person's heart is able to hold.

How was I to know it wouldn't last?

Two years later and everything is different and I am trying so hard to fix it. To fix us. I haven't seen you in months, not since I last saw you in our hometown. You invited me to visit when I told you I was interested in going to the same school as you. I had made it clear we were friends, a moment that I regret now, but your affection doesn't seem to dissipate.

Your room looks as if someone with OCD lived here, a fact I hadn't known about you. I am in awe of how clean and organized it looks. The bed is made with your sheets pulled tight, not a wrinkle anywhere. Even the corners were tucked under with military precision. All your books are on shelves in alphabetical order and your laptop is open with your half-written paper. Not a thing is out of place on your desk and your clothes are hanging in the closet and folded neatly, waiting on the top of your dresser to be stowed away; not even a sock on the floor. Two glasses of fresh water are on the bedside table. You have the incessant need to wipe the condensation off the glasses every few minutes. Then there's my suitcase at the foot of your bed, my clothes spilling out and onto the floor; the only messy part of the room. My hairbrush sits on the desk awkwardly next to your pens and my make-up bag is placed on a bookshelf near the door. I feel like the sand of your world, seeping in everywhere and making a mess, getting into all the hard places. Maybe I thought you would fix me; gather up all the little grains of sand and make a castle.

I'm perched on the edge of your wrinkle-less bed in baggy sweatpants and a shabby, large t-shirt, the opposite of what I'm striving for. At least I had washed my face and scrubbed the mascara off. You gingerly sit down next to me and your hand is rubbing my back, trying to get me to relax. It's not working. My hands are gripping the sheets, and I'm shaking. You're murmuring things like "it's okay" and "we have all the time in the world." But we don't. I'm only here for two days. Two days to say I love you, and to convince you that we should get back together. That we were at our best when we were more than friends. That we should go back to laying in that soft, firm sand. That I was wrong and you were right those two years ago when you said that we were perfect together.

Your free hand gently turns my face towards yours and you gaze down into my eyes. You lean over and slowly, softly kiss me. For the first time in two years I know for a fact that it was a mistake to break up with you. But then you become more urgent and I don't recognize the person in your eyes when you pull away for a moment. It's not what I remember. I squirm and try to push you away. This isn't what I want. It's not what I meant by coming here.

"Let's try to sleep. Maybe talk tomorrow," I whisper, trying to divert you from your current course. You know this isn't what I want. You watch as I climb under the covers and hide. Here. In your bed. How perfect. Last night you slept on the couch. But tonight you went to lock the door. I thought you were leaving the room, but when I heard the click I knew. When you turn back towards me your smile is distorted in the light of the lamppost through the blinds. That's not the smile I love.

Now your shirt is off and I'm torn between wanting to touch your smooth skin and wanting to disappear. Your muscles ripple as you move quietly towards the bed. You tear your eyes away from me and I follow your gaze. The drawer of your bedside table is ajar and inside is a box of condoms. I want to crumble and drift away like sand in a sift and I'm trying to disappear, trying to get to the other side where everything will be okay.

I squeeze my eyes shut. I can hear you opening the drawer farther, the mechanics of the wheels in the tracks. I want to be back on that beach. To breathe in that salty air. To feel that sand between my toes. I now know you won't make a castle, but you will destroy the small tower I have made all on my own. And I know you will walk away, leaving me to clean up the mess.

You will come back here, to your perfect room, and forget all about me and my massacred tower.

I hear a package being ripped open and slump farther under the sheet. Why didn't I listen to your best friend yesterday when he told me that you weren't the same as before? He was right. You used to be my home. You used to keep me grounded. Now I don't even recognize you. The sheet is pulled back but I still refuse to open my eyes. Your hands are on my thighs and I can feel through my sweatpants how rough your fingers are. One hand sneaks up under my shirt and slowly your fingers brush along my waist, ribs, and-

I finally open my eyes. You're wearing nothing. I'm in sweats and my shirt is hiked up, showing more skin than I'd like. I'm covered in goosebumps and you're no longer emanating warmth.

"Can't we just talk tomorrow?" I try to stealthily pull the sheet back up, like the slow ebbing of an ocean tide on the shoreline, back and forth.

"What do you want to talk about? This? What we're doing? Or us?"

I'm clutching the sheet to my chest now and whisper a quiet yes. You just stare at me with cold eyes. Your smile is gone. You look like you have something to say, but you hesitate. "You know I loved you."

A tear streaks down my face, "I know."

You move to pull away the sheet again. You smash your lips to mine and your hands are all over.

"Stop it." The words come out sharper than I meant as I turn my head to face the wall. Anywhere but face you and your anger.

"No. You stop. You flew down here to see me. I thought you knew what that meant. I thought this is what you wanted."

"I missed you. I luh-" I broke off, a sob cutting off my voice.

You stroke my face and I turn back. The coldness in your eyes is evaporating and sympathy warms them. "I miss you too. I've always missed you, you know that." You lean down and gently kiss my forehead. I scoot to the side and make space on the bed beside me and you lay down closer than you need to be. One hand is still on my waist and I shift nervously. We fit perfectly on the small bed and you tilt your head to look at me with that smile. Your fingers slowly pull the sheet away and your rough fingertips scrape my sides. No, no, no. My mind wanders, wondering how your fingers got that way when the rest of you is so smooth. It's the only way I can stop myself from thinking about what's happening.

"You ready?" you ask.

"No."

But you pay no attention to me.

I try not to look at you and stare out the passenger side window, watching the dry, brown farmland pass by. It's as scorched as I am. Two days have gone by. Two days I want to forget.

You sing along with the radio blaring, but it doesn't block out the buzzing in my head. For once, you aren't touching me. No hand on my thigh, no fingertips searching for my hand. I am grateful for this. I no longer want your shining blue eyes on my body. I don't want to see that dimpled smile. I don't want your sun-kissed flesh invading my space.

I thought I was a mess when I had arrived and hoped that seeing you would fix me. Now you're taking me home with more baggage than I had left with. Your rough fingers tap in time with the beat on the old, cracked leather steering wheel, forever ruining my favorite song.

Loss | Loneliness

Part Two

Blooming

By Alisa Hartley

FOURTEEN

Imagined

Alisa Hartley

Morning sunlight filters through closed blinds
nudging its way into her bedroom
a warm abstract painting decorates the wooden floorboards

she pretends the sunspots are lightning bolts shooting down
from dark and moody skies
as she rises

and lets the little girl she once was
imagine
dust particles that sparkle in the streaky
haze
like raindrops
on the ocean

thunder echoes in the distance
as she senses the pregnant clouds above

even though today

the first dawn

is open to skies
as crisp

Imagined

and as blue
as the sea

her fingers dive
into the pool of beams
casting shadow creatures
onto the wall made of stone
in front of her

a wolf
a deer
a mouse

frolicking there
together in the golden light
imaginary forest friends
now tucked away safely in dress pockets at her side

ten tiny toes tap dance
in tune with
the old songs
of the worn out planks
sleeping at her feet
as she journeys down the long and narrow tunnel

toward the garden

FIFTEEN

A Twinkle in the Dark

Shannan Chapman

Out the window, she sees the lights in the jars just beginning to twinkle against the approaching darkness. Like clockwork, they begin with a bit of a falter, fighting against the dying light, struggling to break through the tension between dusk and nightfall. She watches, as one by one, they proclaim victory.

Except the last one. Tonight, the jar on the end, the one closest to the decaying fence, is giving up and she wonders if she should retrieve it or just let it sit.

If he were still here, she would tell him to go give it a shake. Maybe check the batteries. He would sigh, as if it were a big deal, but as he walked out the sliding glass door, she would catch his eye and he would smile. And he would head for the jar, the one hanging on the last tree, next to the fence. But he would stop along the way.

First at the bird feeder, now empty and hollow, the glass murky, dirty, brown like the dust. If it was running low, he would look back at her through the glass doors and remind her. And then he'd fill it, dropping a few handfuls on the ground, in the flat spot next to the rocks.

And then he'd walk to the fence and straighten the ceramic lizard she used to love so much. And make a comment about staining that old wood soon.

And finally, he'd take hold of the jar, the one with the dimming lights, and give it a good shake. And slowly, as the twinkling filled the desert outside the door, he'd walk back in, kiss her hand, and wheel her outside where she could see it all.

SIXTEEN

Blue Lake

Clara Olivo

I t's 5am and the sun is just beginning to rise over the Cascades. Dawn in the Pacific Northwest is something else, nothing like what I've seen before. The darkness makes way for day, a deep blue as rich as midnight and stars melting into amber tones of red and gold. It happens quickly, the switch from night to day and the beauty of sun and moon teasing each other in the heavens. I don't always get to see it, sleeping late is more my thing but I knew today would be different.

We've been planning this trip for over 6 months, doing all of the training and conditioning needed to ensure we can make it to the top of Blue Lake. We got all the right gear this time, even the Lifestraw in case things got bad and we needed to drink from the streams. It wouldn't but, you never know.

Do you remember that time we were camping in …what was it, McKinney Falls, I think?

Anyway, do you remember drinking water from the river during our hike to the falls? You were all freaked out about it thinking you were gonna die or something, haha

Yeah, it was the first time I've ever had fresh water like that. And pleeeease, don't act like parasites aren't a thing. But yeah, it was pretty dope actually

We did it right this time. All our gear is ready and staged by the door. Lunch is packed in the cooler along with a couple of White Claws for when we reach the top. I threw in a couple of those MRE's you like in case we decide to head home tomorrow instead. Oh, and enough water to get us through the weekend if we really want to make a thing of it.

You're always prepared aren't you?

Yeah but you like that. It's why we do what we do.

There used to be a time where I was bold enough to go out alone. I knew of the dangers that came with being a Brown woman in rural areas. The dangers of nature are unforgiving but it doesn't discriminate the same way that people and their dangerous nature does. I've had a few close calls driving through Snohomish county; I remember driving to visit a new client and as soon as I pulled up I immediately began to panic. Their next door neighbor had two confederate flags flying high in their front yard. I didn't stay long enough to find out how friendly they'd be, I just kept driving until I got far enough away to pull over. Safely. White knuckled and shrouded in fear, I remember fumbling through my bag looking for my meds. I didn't have to take them until I moved here. I've always been an anxious person but something about this place *really* brings it out of me. I guess being the only Brown person in most places I step foot in really heightens my fear. I hate being looked at….

Zarahi! Adonde estas, nena??

I've always loved how you called me by my actual name. Growing up, most folx had a hard time pronouncing it properly. I gave up as a kid in school and relented when teachers would just call me "Sarah" during roll call. I've never felt like a "Sarah" but it's how I was forced to introduce myself to the world. It wasn't until I met you that someone took the time to see past the "Sarah" facade. I think the first time I heard you say *Zarahi*, I immediately knew you were legit.

You okay there? You zoned out for a bit…we're still going right?

Yeah, for sure…let me just grab my coffee and we're good!

The drive to Blue Lake is long and though the first couple of hours are spent driving out of cities and into sprawling farmland, we soon begin to embark into the forest and onto the mountain. The road is rugged and curvy with rocks, gravel and dirt churning underneath the car. There's a luscious canopy of trees shading our path, shining wisps of light into our view. The golden hour is every hour when I'm with you and in this drive especially. The elements and their power washes over us, anointing us in their grace. I smile slightly thinking back to a time before nature and I got acquainted. When I was still so new at facing my fears and doing things that felt bigger than me. Blue Lake is my way of reclaiming all those fearful moments and showing us that yes, I *can* fucking do this and yes I *will* keep going.

Why you looking so happy, huh?

Just thinking about you again…that time you were teaching me how to belay at the rock gym. Man, you were hella brave to let me practice on you.

Yo, that first time especially!

I hear you laugh, your beautiful face looking down and off to the side, as though maybe you're holding back. I see you blushing through your smile, your radiance expelling the joy that drew me to you in the first place. Except for the gravel crackling underneath us, there is silence holding us together. Our smiles speak louder than any words we can release.

I've always felt safe with you, Antonio…I don't know if I've ever told you that.

Nah. But I kinda figured, hehe. I mean, most homies don't go thru what we've been thru and if they have, it's not shit they talk about.

You saying we trauma bonding?

Yeah fam, that's it! Pero mira nena, es more like trauma healing, no? I mean, look at how far you've come.

Yeah, I guess.

You ever miss climbing?

All the time man. My body just isn't what it used to be though, no matter how I condition or treat it. Fibro sucks fam!

I tease as though I had a choice in inheriting this illness. Still, it isn't stopping me from reconnecting with nature and the world outside. Training just looks different and going out and about is few and far between. But I still do it.

I keep my eyes on the road, there are no signs and its wide enough for one car to squeeze through. There're no buffers on the sides either, just a 2000 foot drop into the side of the mountain and a rocky ditch on the other that'll probably fuck up your day. Blue Lake is an alpine lake so we have a ways to go before we can hit the trailhead. It's a different kind of climb but it's how I'm still able to feel the rocks and the wind, everything that Mother Earth shares with us.

I always hate driving up mountain roads. I'm still trippin from the time we got a flat looking for a campsite in Shasta. I've never seen you so shaken before, all the beautiful color from your face washed away and the fear in your eyes is something I'll never forget. Still, you moved quickly and after shoving rocks and logs underneath the wheel we were finally able to jack up the car and change the damn tire. We didn't get to camp that night and had to stay an extra day in a hotel while they serviced the car but since then, we decided this ain't gonna happen again.

The new tires get us through the forest service roads and its precarious terrain. We finally made it to the trailhead. There's a little camping spot to the side and I back into it just barely missing the fire pit. We pull out our gear, set up a hammock and double check my backpack to make sure everything we need is at hand. As we walk towards the trailhead, we stop to read the trail info and notice a sign-in sheet with the names, dates and a message from previous hikers. They let us know that the view from the top is worth the steep climb, that the lake promises beauty unparalleled. One person wrote "you'll want to give up but don't! It's worth all the effort!".

The hike gains over 1000 feet of elevation within 2 miles. "Doable for most people", or so the trail website says. 10 years ago, my body may have been able to do it in no time but we'll see what it can do today. It's a perfect day for a hike too, not another person on the trail and the picture-perfect PNW weather that people move across the country for. I used to think that places like this were only real in magazines and postcards. Now I live in one and I can't say that it's everything it's cracked up to be or as pristine as the pictures make it seem.

The trail is steep right off the get-go. I'm out of breath within the first 10 minutes of the ascent and Antonio reminds me that it's okay to pause and breathe, there is no rush to the top. We're at the end of a switchback ready to turn the corner onto the next level but I can't. I reach towards a large branch hanging over the trail and pull myself towards its trunk, wrapping my arms around it tightly. I'm holding on as I catch my breath, hold back the tears and notice the throbbing discomfort in my knee. I slowly slide down, one arm still clinging to the tree, stretch out my right leg and breathe.

Ugh, Fuck this knee!

It hasn't been the same since the move. It's too cold here for my bones but on summer days like today, it almost feels like we're back in Texas. But the evergreen trees and the way the breeze gently cools the sweat on my brow, rather than making it sweatier, reminds me where we are. I release the tree, turn and look out from the trail and into the thicket. Past the pine trees you can see the mountain exposing its grandeur over the streams cutting through the forest. We've already ascended so much and I feel so small. I inhale the bounty of life growing before me, accepting the offering of relief this place brings. I exhale, releasing my fears and expectations of perfection and remember that the journey is just getting started and we have a ways to go.

I'm sorry fam...I'm good, I just can't move like I used to.

Aqui tu mandas mami, we go when you're ready.

We continue forward, getting past the narrow, rocky ledge, pressing our bodies close onto the mountain, so as not to lose our step. I don't look down, keeping my eyes forward and onto the rock, letting my hands and feet almost glide through the path. I always feel like I need to control everything. Right now though, treading lightly and precariously upon this part of the earth, I feel like I've let all that go. Losing control has never felt so good.

Finally, some dirt! We step back onto the soft, brown, forest floor where pine needles, mossy branches and even some lichen unrolled before us. For a moment it felt like we were in a procession of melanated glory. Look at us, taking over the mountain, the forest and now the stream. I can hear the rushing water of the creek and its invitation to come cool off.

The trail is this way!

Yeah but the water is this way!

Oh you gonna pull out that Lifestraw?

Nah son, I'm gonna get my feet wet

Without any hesitation, I made my way through the thicket and scrambled down some rocks to finally have a place by the water. It's rocky but I didn't come here expecting a beach and at this point, I'm not so sure I'll even make it to the lake. It's past lunchtime anyway and I honestly can't think of anywhere else I'd rather break bread with you today.

So we just gonna chill here for a bit?

For a bit.

There isn't much sun shining through this part of the trail, the trees shading much of this area of the mountain. This spot though!? Here, on top of the rocks there's a break in the trees that shines so bright, you'd think you're in a different world.

Remember that time at the Pedernales when we figured our way up that boulder on the river? I fell so many times trying to get up there. But man...I'll never forget how beautiful the river looked from up there. The way the sun just baked our skin on top of that rock and how you were just glowing. We were the color that made this world so bright and your smile was the light that made it shine.

I'll drink to that.

I pull my mango White Claw from my backpack along with my koozie and some Tajin, and start settling in. I'm surprised it's not hot from being in there so long, and I instantly feel refreshed as its coolness travels through my senses. I slip my feet into the water and let the stream's icy rush flow through my dusty skin. Cleansed.

I thought we were gonna drink those at the top?

Well, this one is mine. We can have yours later.

The trail winds upward through a wide footpath with tall thin trees overlooking from all directions, the mountain just barely peeking through. I can't help but look up and shrink into the grandness of it all. My physical therapy, cardio and strength training came into play and brought me so close but I know my body better now than ever before. I'm not pushing it any further, especially when I know I have to hike down and then make the long drive back home.

The way down is always easier. I pack it all up and retrace my steps back onto the trail, replenished and restored after our time in the water. The swelling in my knee has gone down and the pain seems to have washed away along with the dust and debris from my journey. I finally make it back to the trailhead and decide to sign it:

Zarahi y Antonio 05/25/2021

I head back to my car, drop my bag in the trunk and slip into my chanclas. I take your drink onto the hammock and sway back and forth, reveling in our accomplishments. I crack it open, I spare you the Tajin, I know you don't like that shit. I take a sip. Still cold. I smile, you always find a way to make things feel right. To let me know you're here. We've come so far fam, it's not easy for folx like you and I. It hasn't gotten easier since you left either…a whole year gone by and it hurts just the same.

I raise up your drink and look into the sky, its infinite reach holding me still in your presence. Your absence. I bring the drink to my lips.

I miss you everyday Antonio.

I know fam.
This one's for you.

SEVENTEEN

Great White Buffalo

Jordan Nishkian

I.

Dearest Lena:

It is true, and I find you to be the one who understands what I've been trying to expel from my mind;

generally, people are stingy with their love.

Fact is, I love you, too, with such tenderness and care and though it may seem as I am careless beneath this "cool and calm" exterior of mine, you notice, lies worry and wonder beyond belief.

Continue, Lena, as you are you. Define the line.

I, too, hope we get to share many more times together as we have before. I enjoy them, and I enjoy you.

Yours– Jason

II.

When I arrived at Jason's place, he was creating a backdrop with an old painter's tarp. His shirt lifted while he reached up to nail one end to his wall and let the excess drape over the bed.

I set my bag down. "First time over and you already have me on your mattress?"

He took a nail from between his lips. He tossed the hammer onto a chair and sat down on the creation. In the low light of the bedroom, I saw a cloud of dust fly off the tarp and attack him. He didn't seem to notice.

III.

I fell in like with the back of his head. We didn't have assigned seating in Coach's U.S. History class, but I always sat behind him: I made him laugh, he made me nervous.

Jason hated my boyfriend because he bit my arm and left a huge bruise on it. I didn't have the heart to tell him I kinda liked it.

For the rest of sophomore year, I'd always peek over his shoulder and see which fine-tip millimeter pen he was using for his drawings. He was so serious about his doodles. Mine never went past the margins.

IV.

"What are you wearing underneath that?" Jason asked as he got the camera ready.

"What I normally wear." That was a lie.

"They match?"

I nodded. He invited me over to his place. Yes, of course they matched.

He set the Nikon down on a chair. "Good. Undress."

Chills pricked the backs of my arms and he turned away from me.

I took off my shirt and watched him pick up a tube of black acrylic paint while I stepped out of my jeans. I kicked them over to my bag and started walking towards him and the tarp-covered bed.

V.

The black and orange bleacher creaked beneath my feet. He sat alone on the center row overlooking the empty tennis courts, back hunched over his well-worn Moleskine notebook.

I stood there for a while, hoping he'd look up at me, but he didn't. He was adding the details to a man with a long, looping neck.

"Why didn't you come to me?" I asked. He needed a haircut so badly.

I fought my damp eyes. "April Fool's Day. Really?"

He added another couple pen strokes, reached out to touch the back of my knee, and said, "It would've been funny."

VI.

The cold push of black paint traveled up my arm. He was using his fingers instead of a brush, and it was the first time in a long time that I'd felt his hands on me. He put three vertical lines on my bicep and two horizontal rings on my forearm.

"Hold your arm out for a bit," he said. "It won't take long to dry."

I lifted it, feeling the acrylic stiffen and tighten up.

He brought his face close to mine, studying my skin. I shut my eyes, knowing that he could hear how hard my heart was pumping.

VII.

When he came back he surprised me outside of the sushi bar I was working at. His skin had gotten dark and weathered; his chapped fingers handed me a smushed quarter. I could barely see the outline of the eagle.

"It's for you," he said. "While I was sleeping next to the train tracks someone left a quarter by my head. I put it on the rail."

I still have it somewhere, that souvenir from him finding yourself, from me filling out missing person reports, thinking the worst. I can't see the eagle anymore—it's smoothed out since then.

VIII.

I watched Jason tap three black dots along my cheekbones before he dipped his index finger back into the paint.

"Close your eyes," he whispered. "Try to relax, please."

I nodded and shut them tight, flinching at the cold press of his fingertip on my cupid's bow. I felt him drag his finger down my bottom lip and stop at my chin.

He tugged my hair and tipped my head back before trailing the line from my chin down my windpipe.

I thought he paused to get more paint until I felt the heat of his breath on my collar bone.

IX.

We sat on a beachside bench with my head on his lap—there was a kite festival that day.

"Why did you keep looking for me?" he asked.

I shrugged. "I told you I loved you."

My hair blew across my face and into his open hand. He tucked it back behind my ear.

"It would never work," I said, tapping the samurai belt buckle his mom gave him.

"I know."

"I mean it would for a little while."

"You don't have to explain. I'm still here."

I kissed his rough palm and watched a box kite dip with the breeze.

X.

After we photographed my face, he asked me to turn around.

"Do you trust me?"

I nodded and switched my position to face the nailed-up end of the tarp. I was used to his hands by then, but my shoulders tightened when he unhooked my bra.

"You don't have to take it off." He was nervous. "I just want to paint your back."

"Jason?"

"Hm?"

"Why haven't we?"

I felt him looking. Soft exhale: I let the black lace fall down my arms and into my lap. Painted fingers on my waist, he pressed his lips to my cold shoulder.

XI.

I woke to "Crimson and Clover" and the scuffle of my suitcases wrestling with each other in Mina's trunk. The song's psychedelic sounds rang in time with the dull ache of my legs' healing sunburn—not a desirable souvenir after three years of successful tanning in Sydney.

"Hey there." Mina smiled at me, keeping her eyes on the 405. "Have a nice nap?"

"Yeah, I'm sorry I fell asleep." I leaned my forehead on the chilled window, glazing over the unreplicable network of Southern California freeways.

"It's ok, you're jetlagged." She turned her blinker on to get out of the carpool lane. "How does it feel to be almost home?"

I smiled. "I don't know, it's been a while."

Ah when she comes walking over

Now I've been waitin' to show her

The two of us passed a huge, sprinkled donut just on the other side of the freeway wall. The old donut sign was a local monument, a reminder of the functional parts of Pacific Coast Highway, a symbol that meant nostalgia was just a generic pink box away. "That's a Dunkin's now?"

"Yeah, recently I think."

"That sucks." I picked at a few flakes of dead skin on my thigh. "Jason and I went there a few times when the Vietnamese family owned it. The maple bars were good."

Mina went silent, pretending to be too busy driving. Hard-hitting drums poured out of her stereo.

"Shit, I'm sorry." I sat up and rested my elbow on the center console. "He's been on my mind. I actually DM'ed him a few days ago to meet up but he hasn't responded."

She took her eyes off the crowded lane just long enough for me to see her confusion.

"What?" I asked.

Mina's jaw shifted: two tectonic plates grinding at the faultline of her teeth.

What a beautiful feeling

Crimson and clover over and over

"What?"

"He died last year," she said. "I thought you knew."

Fresh, exposed flesh stung from under my fingernail.

"It was an accident I think—I'm sorry, I really thought you knew about it."

Crimson and clover
Over and over
Crimson and clover
Over and over
Crimson and clover
Over and over…

"Oh," I said and pressed my head back onto the cool glass, chattering with the relentless rattle of asphalt.

EIGHTEEN

In the Void

Jordan Nishkian

Despite echoing splashes and the dive team's buzzing chatter, the quiet of the cenote was almost impenetrable. For the past hour, the six had been able to keep their heads above the surface and reserve their air supply, but the deeper they traveled into the underwater cave, the lower the cavern ceiling had become. Now, there was only a foot of space between the clear, abyssal water and crumbling limestone.

Aliyah waited for their lead, Rafael, to instruct them to get ready to submerge for the scuba portion of their expedition. Her sight lined up with the direction they would be continuing down, wondering if her eyes would ever be able to adjust to the darkness.

A flash of light burst from behind her and briefly illuminated the wet, jagged stalactites. Aliyah's chest tightened and she twisted her neck to find the source.

Paloma, the videographer and photographer, was behind her, finger ready on her camera. "Sorry, I was testing the flash," she said.

"You scared me."

"Nervous?" Paloma fidgeted with a few settings. "I thought you did this all the time."

"I'm focused." Aliyah adjusted the neoprene under her chin. "It's definitely my oldest case."

Paloma offered a smile, even though the scuba mask stunted her cheeks from rising. "Everything will be fine," she said. "Just give me good footage and don't break anything."

"Ok, everyone," Rafael's voice boomed against the low, craggy ceiling. "Here's where we all go under. We still have an hour there and back to go, so let's stick together and keep talking at a minimum to conserve our oxygen."

With her hand grazing against the rough rock above her, Aliyah steadied herself as she turned on her oxygen tank. She glanced at the rest of her team, but her eyes couldn't help but notice how the downcast light from Paloma's camera caught the pedaling movement from her fins. Aliyah's eyes followed the path of light straight below them, thinking perhaps she'd see the floor or the glistening scales of fish, but the illuminated stream continued, unin-terrupted.

"You good?" Paloma asked.

"Yeah," Aliyah answered. Even in the low light, she could see Paloma's huge brown eyes and where her mascara had caught in her waterline. Her mom was like that too—always wearing eye makeup regardless of the activity.

Rafael's words clicked into their headsets. "Can everyone hear me?"

The team answered into their mics.

"Alright, let's go," he said before plunging his head below the surface.

Aliyah followed suit, letting her underwater scooter propel her forward until she was behind Rafael. She paced herself, pairing her legs to the rhythm of his kicking flippers to stay warm in the chilled water.

Most of her work as an underwater crime scene technician took place retrieving evidence and bodies from lakes and large rivers, but she'd done archaeological dives in the ocean as well. Even in murkiest, most open water—the kind where only the bubbles from her mask could tell her the direction of the surface—there were still traces of sunlight. This was like pushing through ink, like floating through the dark matter of an unborn universe. She focused on slowing her breath, on feeling the individual muscles working in her legs, and on the loud, continual stream of her thoughts. It would be too easy for her to feel devoured.

As grateful as she was for the opportunity, nerves gripped her belly. She'd signed up for excavations at Yucatan's ancient sinkholes for the quick dives and the chance to study prehistoric animal fossils like sabertooth cats and giant sloths, but the last thing anyone expected was the discovery of an anatomically modern human skeleton by one of the AI diving drones.

"Aliyah," Dr. Burke had approached her last week at her workbench while she was brushing sediment off the lower mandible of what she thought belonged to a short-faced bear. "You have experience excavating human remains?"

"Yes, I've been an underwater crime scene tech for five years and earned my forensic science certification last year," she answered, trying to hide her confusion. As a summer volunteer, Dr. Burke had only spoken to her once or twice before, so all she could manage at that moment was a recitation of her resume.

He nodded. "Good. Could you join me, please?"

Aliyah followed him to his workstation: a canopy tent where four men had gathered around a thick, blocky laptop. "One of the drones found human remains in a remote part of the cenote," Dr. Burke explained, pointing at fuzzy photos pinned to a corkboard. "Female, I think, and presumably around ten thousand years old, give or take—but we won't know for sure until we see it in person. We have a dive team and guide to help you get there, but I was hoping with your experience, you could retrieve the bones."

"Of course" popped out of her mouth before she could process the situation—how she wouldn't get any credit, how dangerous it could be, how she'd traveled here for the summer to specifically get away from handling dead humans.

After a week's worth of preparation and a shaky walk into the cenote this morning, her team of six was ready to embark. Aliyah stared at the overhead opening of the sinkhole while three of her younger, more eager teammates waded into the water. After studying the drone footage, she knew it would be the last bit of sunlight she'd see until they returned. From where she stood, she couldn't see much of what was happening on the surface. There was a rough ridge of shadowed earth, and beyond that was pure blue sky. It made her think of the time her mom took her to the roof of her apartment building to sunbathe.

Dr. Burke's body came into view, silhouetted from the bright sky behind him. She strained her eyes to focus on his weathered face, but all she could make out were the wisps of hair that peeked out from his hat. He gave her a thumbs-up, which she returned, then walked away from the overhead ledge.

Now, a couple of hours later, she was cutting her way through cold, hermetic water where other than the occasional, raspy check-in from Rafael, the only noises Aliyah heard were the flood of bubbles from her apparatus and her all-too-obvious heart rate.

Dr. Burke was expecting a near-complete skeleton, which was why every diver's scooter was equipped with a padded box for safe transport, but Aliyah was unconvinced. The cenote was rife with the skeletons of predators, and any other bones they found had evidence of teeth marks or scraping. What were the chances that all 206 bones had stayed near each other over the course of multiple millennia? Even when she was retrieving relatively recent corpses, intact bodies were few and far between thanks to currents and hungry animals.

Still, it was the first time Aliyah had seen a total absence of marine life. As far as she could tell, she and her teammates were the only living things that had been in this cave network in the past ten thousand years. Without the torches and movement from her team, she thought the cenote's primordial belly would swallow her—that she would lose her light and her air and she'd become another fish in the school of drowned ghosts.

Her heartbeat pounded in her ears and her breath fought its pacing. Keeping her light on Rafael's tank, she tried to ease the muscles she didn't need and allow the jets to do the work.

"Let the bike do the work," her mom's voice muffled the sound of her pulse. "You're pedaling too hard."

In a vivid flash, her memory of trying to keep up with her mom during that afternoon bike ride rose to the front of her mind. It was her first bike, and despite being eleven, it was only a week after she'd learned to ride it. Her mom paced next to her on the winding park path.

"When you pedal that fast, you can't feel any resistance anymore, right?"

Aliyah nodded, trying to keep her helmet straight on her head.

"That means you can stop working so hard," she continued. "That's as much work as the bike will let you put in so it's no use wearing yourself out."

Aliyah nodded again, slowing her feet and letting the wheels spin. She gripped the handlebars and fought for her balance, but had to smile when her mom said, "Good job!"

Watching her pedal ahead, Aliyah tried to soak in the image of the mid-summer sunlight catching her mother's hair and the sounds of her teal zip-up flapping behind her. Capturing the memory was worth it, even after she fell and scraped her knee through her jeans moments later. For weeks after, Aliyah fought her grandma when she tried to dab honey on the cuts to keep them from scarring, but eventually, time and sunlight had erased the marks she tried to treasure.

"Halfway mark," Rafael cut through her thoughts. "One."

"Two," Aliyah answered. Paloma followed third, then dive assistants Shelby, Miguel, and Cassandra as fourth, fifth, and sixth.

Memories of her mom didn't come up much anymore, but in the sensory vacuum of the cenote, it was easy for Aliyah's mind to wander toward her. Her mother, Ida, was beautiful with caramel skin and ink-black hair she always kept at waist-length. When Aliyah was younger, she was curious about her father, but after years of being raised by a grandmother who avoided the subject, that curiosity dimmed. She looked so much like the women in her family that there was no doubting where she came from anyway.

Ida was a talented healer, and Aliyah always marveled at her gift for it, even after she realized that the only pain Ida's antidotes could heal were the ones her cutting tongue caused in the first place. She was personified chaos, and loving her was like having to swim into a wave to avoid being toppled. Aliyah pressed her torso into the scooter, thinking of the times she would be lying face down on her bed after Ida's voice finished shaking the walls of her grandma's home. A few minutes of quiet would pass, then the next things Aliyah would hear were the turning of her bedroom doorknob, light footsteps to her bedside, then the creaking of the mattress as Ida sat down beside her. Aliyah always pretended she had slept through her mom and grandma's fighting—that she didn't hear her name get volleyed and flung across the room downstairs. As a seven-year-old, Aliyah wasn't a talented actor, but Ida always played along and rubbed her back until she fell into true sleep, telling her how loved she was and how she would always be there when she needed her.

The latter turned out to be false, but Aliyah never doubted the former, even when her mom's presence would ebb and flow into her life sporadically. Aliyah wasn't surprised that these memories were cropping up—Ida's frequent absence and eventual disappearance were what inspired her career choice in the first place.

"It's been too long," Aliyah reported after months of not hearing from her.

"She has a history of disappearing," a young officer in the police station told her.

"Yes, but she wouldn't miss out on things like this: my birthday, prom, graduation?"

"She has before," her grandmother retorted from her recliner, not looking up from her magazine. "She's only ever done what she wants to do."

"I haven't heard from her at all," she pleaded with a ranger at a national park in the neighboring town. "But I know her boyfriend liked to take her to the lake here."

"When did they last make a trip here?" the khaki-clad man asked while stirring a mug of instant coffee.

"I don't know, but he was abusive. She said he tried to drown her in the bathtub once."

"What's his name?" the officer asked, fingers ready at the keyboard.

"I don't know."

"Why do you think she's in the lake?" The ranger took a sip of his coffee.

"I don't know."

"Why can't you accept that she's gone?" her grandmother challenged, scraping dried rice from a steel pan. "Don't you think you'd be happier if you stopped trying to find out what happened?"

"I don't know."

"When can you start?" her interviewer at the lab asked as she extended her hand.

"Next Monday," Aliyah answered, returning the handshake.

A chill climbed up her leg as Shelby accidentally brushed into her. She had recurring dreams that went like that: she would be searching for her mom along the cloudy bed of the lake, then feel a hard, unforgiving grip on her ankle. The image of her mom's pale, peeling face and the sound coming from her screaming, unhinged jaw would scare her so much that she'd wake up kicking.

Two months after getting her CSI job, Aliyah started spending a few hours every Sunday morning at the ironically named Clearwater Lake in her own scuba gear to comb through seaweed with plastic baggies and a cheap water-proof camera. Ida was legally presumed dead by that point, but Aliyah strug-gled to accept that her mother's life had an ending that was open to interpretation. For almost a year, she would return to the sandy banks empty-handed, exhausted, and emotionally depleted, then cross off sections on the grid map she made of the 70-square-mile lake. Her investigative work honed her abilities to swim and identify evidence faster, but handling bloated, decomposing corpses and learning how to identify dismembered body parts through unopened trash bags killed her hopes of finding her mom in a pristine or recognizable condition.

"You'll have plenty of time to miss me after I die," Aliyah's grandma told her once after she saw her scribbled map resting on the passenger seat of her car. "But I'm missing you now." After that, Aliyah's weekly trips to the lake became monthly, and then quarterly. Now, most of their Sunday mornings were spent together at her grandma's favorite pancake diner a few blocks away.

"Finally," Paloma said into her mic. There was a collective shift in energy once the six streams from the divers' torches illuminated a pale limestone wall ahead of them.

"Almost there, team," Rafael's words filled her ears. "Let's descend about ten more meters and we should be able to see it."

Aliyah took in a deep inhale. The waiting and diving were unnerving, but the real pressure was encroaching. The bones were going to be brittle after being submerged for this long, especially the all-important skull.

She stayed focused on Rafael as they all steered their scooters downward. After a few minutes of scanning the ledges and nooks of the wall, Aliyah's eyes caught what were, unmistakably, human bones.

"I see them," Aliyah said. "Headlamps on, everyone. Follow me but give Paloma space to work."

Smaller lights flicked on as Aliyah shone her torch onto the remains. Paloma swam by, documenting the bones and surrounding area. While she worked, Aliyah looked to the surface. It was a long, long way up.

"We're in a deep gorge of the cenote," Miguel said. "Whoever that person was didn't end up here on purpose."

She nodded. The drones had performed a topographic analysis of the site earlier in the week, and after examining that data, she theorized that this prehistoric person had gotten lost in the network and fallen into the gorge. Now, after thousands of years of rising tides and resting in place, they would be seen and touched by another human.

"I'm ready for you, Ali," Paloma said.

She made her way to the bones and Paloma fit her into her camera's frame. "Cassandra, keep your lights over here, please," Aliyah instructed. "Shelby, I'll need your help as I place the bones in your container, and Miguel, I need you to stay below me with your container open in case anything drops."

They all swam to their positions and Aliyah unclenched her hands while surveying the pile and plotting the order of recovery. She was skeptical when Dr. Burke was excited by the prospect of a complete skeleton, but after seeing the bones in person, she was beginning to see it as a possibility too.

When the group was ready, she reached for the right femur. She allowed the water to do most of the work and let the brittle bone rest on her hands as she maneuvered it into the container. She repeated the task for the right tibia and fibula, then the left tibia, fibula, and femur, all while trying not to disturb the smaller tarsal and metatarsal bones. From her quick glances at the femur, she noticed that the growth plates had fused together, a likely sign of them being a teenager or adult.

"Close your container, Shelby, and switch with Cassandra," Aliyah said. "You'll head back over when we're working with the smaller bones in their knees and feet."

The two switched as Aliyah positioned herself to grab the pelvic bone. Using only her fingertips, she lifted the bone and watched as two pieces fell away from a deep crack in the ilium.

"Paloma, did you get that?" she asked.

"Yes, I'll zoom in," she answered.

While waiting for the pieces to settle into the sediment and for Paloma to get the shots she needed, Aliyah studied the pelvic bone. There was no evidence of that crack healing, so it could potentially be what led to their death, which made sense with her falling theory. Judging by the wide subpubic angle, the skeleton was female. Aliyah fixed her eyes on small pockmarks on the inside of the bones—she had given birth.

"We've got a Jane Doe," Aliyah announced while resting the pelvic bone in the bed of the container. "Rafael, did the drones capture any more visual footage lower than this or was that just topographic mapping?"

"Both, why?"

"She gave birth, so we may want to look out for a child or a baby."

"We didn't see anything else, only her," he answered. "But I'll make a note for another sweep just in case."

"Why would someone bring a child in here?" Miguel asked.

"She might not have. She could have been alone," replied Shelby.

"You think she would leave her kid?" Miguel debated.

"Let's save the discussion for when we're not on a limited air supply," Aliyah said. "Cassandra, I'm going to have you carry her scapula and clavicle too."

One by one, she placed the two scapula in Cassandra's container, but as she was reaching for the left clavicle she noticed some bone remodeling. She'd seen injuries like this from past cases. Out of habit, she glanced over to Jane Doe's ribs and forearm, where she saw more remodeling in one of her ulnas.

"Paloma, can you get some close-up shots here?"

Paloma approached, zooming in on the places Aliyah was pointing to on the bones. "What does this mean?" she asked.

"Signs of abuse or some sort of domestic violence, but I can't say for sure."

"That's really rough," she said. "Her life definitely didn't seem easy."

Aliyah nodded and began to work on retrieving the bones again. When she was swimming through the cenote earlier, she was wondering how many animal skeletons were settled on the rocky floors around them. She envisioned

Jane seeking shelter in the cavern, then wandering deeper into the network seeking food or water. It was only a theory, but Jane had to have known about all the predators that lived there. Someone or something scared her more than potentially facing a bear or sabertooth cat. Aliyah felt her chest tighten. Jane's situation must have been pretty bad if she thought she had a better chance of surviving in here than out there. The idea of finding her child with her or nearby was beginning to seem less likely.

After clearing some of the larger bones, her hands now had an unobstructed path to Jane's cranium. "Ok, Miguel. Go ahead and bring the skull container to me," Aliyah requested. She closed her eyes as the dive assistants rearranged and prepared themselves.

After she crashed her bike, it took a few minutes for Ida to notice that Aliyah wasn't behind her anymore. Even though it was broad daylight and she was only suffering a scraped-up knee, those moments alone scared her so much that she couldn't find the breath to call out for her mom.

She inspected the slopes and angles of Jane's skull, thinking of what her last seconds must have been like; in pain, in the dark, in silence. The light from her headlamp shone through her eye cavities, and Aliyah could see the intricate web of cranial bones. Holding her breath, she placed her fingers around the skull and lifted her carefully, letting her lower mandible stay behind on the limestone. She could picture deep brown eyes looking back at her as she turned toward Miguel and the box.

By the time Ida rode back to her, it only took a few seconds for her to leap off her bike and scoop Aliyah into her arms. Aliyah didn't start to cry until she could smell Ida's rose-scented lotion, and she remembered curling her body to make herself as small as possible.

"I got you, I got you," Ida whispered, rocking her and placing a hand onto Aliyah's helmeted head.

"I got you," Aliyah murmured, letting her palm cradle Jane's delicate temple before laying her onto the container's soft, safe surface. "I got you."

NINETEEN

Night on the High Desert

Joseph E. Hopkins

Night settles on the high desert. Rolling clouds rest over the towering mesas, and briefly the moon cuts through and illuminates the distant valleys in brilliant light. Normally on a clear night the stars would cascade across the sky and move in flowing patterns, much like the Rio Grande - a river of lights stretching out to meet the horizon. On nights like these however, the desert is unwelcoming. The light of the stars is dulled and hidden away, like the embers of a fire behind a veil of smoke.

It is under this blanket of night we find Katomatuk sitting by his fire. Nursing a boiling pot of found things. He pushes a wooden spoon to the bottom of the pot, forcing the burnt pieces of food stuck to the bottom to float to the surface. Katomatuk breathes in deeply and looks out into the night. He was hoping for some company and thought the smell of found things would attract a guest, perhaps a lost traveler in the desert.

It had been so long since he had a conversation with the living. So often these days strangers would avoid a welcoming camp and the promise of a warm meal, electing instead to push on through the night, traveling vacant roads to unwelcoming darkened towns. However, Katomatuk was patient and soon that patience was rewarded. The light of his fire did attract a young man who was lost and very hungry. Out past the dancing light of the fire the young man wondered, skirting the light so that no normal man with normal eyes could see him.

But Katomatuk could see him.

He sat by the fire and looked out into the night with dark, unblinking eyes and waited for the young man to approach.

As the man stepped into the flickering camp light, Katomatuk bellowed a welcome.

"Please sit!" said Katomatuk. "You must be thirsty, drink with me!" and he quickly pushed a bottle into the young man's hand and led him to a seat. "I will fetch you a bowl of my found things" said Katomatuk. "You will eat well tonight young man."

And the boy did eat well. And drank well. And soon he found himself telling Katomatuk all about his life, where he was from, his family, and the secret things that only he knew-he and Katomatuk that is.

Katomatuk remembers all secrets that are shared over drink, on dark nights, and in confidence.

Soon Katomatuk knew everything about the young man. The young man was afraid to go home, his brother had passed away some time ago and his parents pleaded for him to return and be their son. He wanted desperately to do that, to go home and see his family and mourn his brother and to be a son again. But he had become lost somewhere on the way back home, and while he admitted that yes, he was lost and that this was frightening to him, the fear of going home and not being welcomed was far greater. So...as if almost on purpose, he stayed lost. And so he had been lost for a very long time.

As the young man continued to speak, Katomatuk would refill his bowl and cup. Katomatuk nodded to the man and patted him on the back as an assuring gesture.

He was a good friend to those lost and far away from home he thought to himself.

The young man stared into the fire and let the smoke wash over him. He sat now in silence and glanced up at the rolling sky, looking for the moon to see what time it was. But he could see no moon, no stars, the night was too dark for those things. The young man went to stand but found that he could not, the drink had made him sleepy and the food had turned to rock in his belly. He found that he could not move. He turned his head to Katomatuk to ask for help, but found the creature now stood above him holding a knife of deer bone.

"It is something" said Katomatuk, "to be so young and so hungry. Yet look at me child...I am so old and I hardly ever eat." With that he lifted the young man's arm and slid the blade along the inside of his armpit. The blade cut away the stranger's flesh as it made a full rotation around the young man's shoulder. Slowly and with care, Katomatuk began to roll the young man's skin down his arm, until at last the skin had gathered at the young man's wrist. Katomatuk placed his palm in the young man's...almost as if to shake hands and in a quick and gentle movement, pulled the skin free from his arm.

The young man looked on in wonder and confusion as Katomatuk continued the process with the rest of his body, taking strips of flesh and laying them near the fire. At last...the young man laid skinless on the cold desert floor. His blood pooled and ran into the pit where the fire now burned low, meeting the coals, and turning to steam in the chilled night air.

Katomatuk rose and dusted his hands, looking proud at a job well done. Moving to the strips of flesh, he started to slide the young man's skin over his own...until he wore the young man's face.

"Your face is now my own" he said. "It is good. It is a young man's face. It will welcome me into many homes I think...maybe even yours."

"It will not work" the young man said. "My family will know that I am different...that I have changed. They will not welcome you."

"You are so young and have been gone for so long" said Katomatuk. "It is well known that the desert changes all men."

With that, Katomatuk turned his back on the young man and ran into the cool night, yelping as the stray dogs do, and calling out to distant flickering lights.

TWENTY

Slow Motion Crash

Mae Wagner

T he waiter sat their drinks down in front of them, attempting to slice the tension with a chuckle and an "oops!" as a splash of her cocktail escaped the glass.

It did not work.

As the waiter walked away, it was the husband's eyes who attempted to cross that chasm mistakenly labeled *a table for two*. He wanted to reach for her hand, but they were folded in her lap. As he watched this life-worn woman who seemed a million miles from him, he became overwhelmed by all that hung between them…

Stark white, blinding hospital rooms in place of lavish vacations; blood-soaked sheets followed by ambulance rides and wordless grief as sisters and friends gave birth to healthy babies while the two of them shattered upon the floor again and again.

They'd attempt to piece their relationship back together, but each time the glue became less reliable and the cracks wider.

He couldn't reach her anymore, even reaching across the table would not change that.

The heat within her was sweltering, and she hadn't even brought the cocktail to her lips yet.

She could feel his gaze searing into her.

Why was he just staring at her like that?

She couldn't bring herself to look back at him, instead, her gaze was burning a hole in the tablecloth connecting them. It was fear that kept her frozen, and she knew this. She was terrified of no longer having this man fill the space across from her– she didn't know how to lose him.

Nor how to face *him*. She didn't want to look at him, because she hated the sight of his face– the sound of his voice… him.

She allowed her mind to drift to the stalactites hanging between them, cloaked in invisibility to the rest of the world, while visible and growing to her…

So many times, he'd left her broken, because work had called.

Work.

Work named Sheila, and that was just *this* time. *Had there been others?*

Kisses and indiscretions made up these earthen spikes threatening to destroy her.

How many kisses had there been?

How many women?

He'd lied to her so many times, she knew to ask would only frustrate them both.

The waiter returned, smiling far too widely as he placed their meals on the table. First, her roasted chicken, followed by his veal parmigiana. She knew she could not give this man the satisfaction of watching her enjoy her dinner, though it did smell divine.

Her stomach begged for her to reconsider, but she sat firm. A fleeting thought questioned whether she was successfully punishing him, or only hurting herself.

She lifted her gaze to him, hoping he'd be lost in his food, too distracted to notice.

He wasn't even sure what he wanted.

Some minutes allowed him to think about his wife and who she used to be– who they both used to be, *before*. He couldn't deny the other minutes though, which left him longing for the ease of a life with Sheila.

· · ·

I wish she would just look at me. See me. Please, look up.

As her gaze rose, connecting with his, a jolt shot through him. In flashes, like a fragmented slideshow of deep shadow and white light, he saw it all– the candles and kisses, the wedding cake, the honeymoon sex, their laughter, the blood on her fingers as she screamed she'd lost the babies... the fights, the way her personhood eroded more and more with each loss, and how he felt himself stepping farther and farther away. He knew he had hurt her, and he couldn't do that anymore.

"I love her." Did he mean Sheila, or had he accidentally spoken out loud as he'd thought about his wife? He wasn't sure.

Could both be true? Was he running?

Why is it so hot in here? He could feel sweat pooling at his collar.

"Ok." It was the absence of emotion, the complete lack of change in the pools of her eyes which decided it for him.

He would divorce his wife and go to Sheila.

As he shifted in his chair, his napkin fell to the floor.

TWENTY-ONE

Snapshot

Thomas Leventhal

Morty sat in the window booth closest to the door. The light was better here, he thought, easier to read the fine print of the classifieds. Carefully, he took his fork and poked the egg yolk, letting a little bit drip out. Taking a piece of toast, he dipped it in the yolk, and nibbled on it as he scanned the paper.

He would start his day in Silverlake, at an estate sale high up in the hills overlooking the reservoir. From there he would work his way across Los Feliz to the Griffith Park area and then head down to Hollywood. Last week he'd been through Long Beach, Lakewood and Bell Gardens.

Morty picked through the hash browns, separating the dark crunchy pieces and ignoring the rest. These he consumed one at a time, savoring them. Refolding his paper napkin, he wiped his face, dabbing around his mouth in small circular motions.

Reaching over, he noticed his coffee cup felt cold. The non-dairy creamer floated in oily swirls on top of the tepid brown liquid. The service was slow here, even if you were a long time regular. He looked around for the waitress and couldn't see her. Must be on break, he thought. He picked up the check and saw that it was the same as always. He left the same tip as always, gathered up his papers and left.

The first stop on his list was a wash. There was nothing there that interested him. A folding table on the front lawn was covered with souvenir coffee cups, old mismatched dishes, a single book end, paperback books, and a couple of beat up pots and pans. All had prices written on masking tape stuck to them. There were no personal items, nothing that told anything about the person who had owned them. Morty gave the table a quick glance and then looked over at the house

"See anything you like?"

Morty turned toward a youngish man wearing shorts and a t-shirt. His hair was long and pulled back into a ponytail.

"Do you have any photographs, albums, old family portraits?" Morty asked.

"Gees, I don't think so", he replied," I think all of that stuff was thrown away. Didn't figure anyone would want it. This was my great aunt's place. I'm trying to clear it out so we can sell it. Got some nice furniture, though. If you are interested, I'll take you inside for a look."

"No thanks," Morty replied. "I'm just looking for photos and family portraits."

"Are you a collector?" the guy asked. "Is stuff like that worth any money?"

"Just a hobby", Morty said and walked down the driveway to his car.

He had better luck at his next stop. The door of the house was open. Morty walked into the living room and looked around. Most of the furniture was gone. What remained was dark, heavy looking. All the windows were covered by thick velvet drapes, casting the room into long shadowed darkness. A small bird-like elderly woman sat at the dining room table, sorting through odd pieces of silverware. She turned and looked up at Morty, but didn't speak. He nodded hello and walked down the hall to the first door. Inside was a bedroom with two twin beds, a dressing table and a mirror. The walls were covered with pictures. Some were religious scenes, others old family portraits.

Morty walked over and ran his hand absently across the ornate carving on one headboard while studying the picture hanging just above it. The old woman walked into the doorway and stood for a moment, waiting until Morty turned and noticed her.

"Well, what do you think?" she asked. "Did you want to see the rest of it first?"

"I beg your pardon", Morty said. "The rest of what?"

"The furniture", she replied. "Before you make an offer. Isn't that what you called about?"

"That wasn't me", he said, smiling softly. "I am interested in the pictures, though. Do you have any others?"

"The pictures", she asked, shrugging her shoulders. "Why not? Come with me. I have more over here." She walked down the hall to another bedroom and went in. When Morty followed he saw that the room was filled with boxes of books, photo albums and small china figurines. He picked up an album and opened it. It was old, the heavy paper pages covered with scallop-edged snapshots carefully held in place by small triangular corners. Most of the photos were black and white.

"You want it?" she asked. "Take them all."

"I just want the pictures," Morty replied. "These and the ones on the wall in the other room."

"Take all of it", she said."Take it all for ten dollars."

"I don't want all of this", he said, "Just the pictures."

"Take it all," she replied. "It's all or nothing. I want to be finished with this. I want to get rid of this stuff already."

"It's a deal", he said, handing her two five-dollar bills.

She watched as Morty carried the boxes out, one by one and loaded them into the trunk of his car. Looking back, Morty could see her still standing in the doorway as he drove off. On his way home, he stopped at the Goodwill store and unloaded the boxes. Carefully sifting through them, he kept the pictures and photo album and left the rest.

Morty stood in front of the small apartment-sized stove and watched the pot of water come to a boil. He waited until the bubbles were really popping and threatening to boil over and then tore open the box of macaroni and cheese. He took out the silver pouch of cheese sauce and put it aside. He then poured the noodles into the pot and turned down the heat. He would wait seven minutes exactly. He liked the noodles to be firm, not overcooked. Stirring occasionally, he kept his eye on the clock and waited. At exactly seven minutes he lifted the pot off the stove. He held a plate over most of the top of the pot and drained the water, careful not to get too close to the steam. Damn, he thought, as he watched some noodles evade his trap and fall into the sink. Shaking the rest of the water out of the pot took a certain amount of skill. There was always a little water left at the bottom of the pot and that made the cheese sauce too soggy. Carefully, he shook it out and prepared the sauce. Out of the fridge came a half cube of margarine and a quart of milk. Morty eyeballed the necessary amount of each and added them to the pot. He tore open the cheese sauce packet and blended it in. Taking his time, he mixed it thoroughly, covering all the noodles with the orange powdered cheese. He worked to break up the lumps, to smooth it together with the milk and margarine.

He picked up the pot and carried over to the small Formica topped table that sat next to the window. There was not much furniture in the small studio apartment other than the unmade single bed that was pushed up against the wall. The room was quite unremarkable except for the photos and snapshots that covered the walls, some hung in ornate frames, others pinned to the wall with thumbtacks. Morty flipped open the album and went through it page by page, carefully, so as to not spill any of the macaroni and cheese on its pages. After going through the entire album he returned to the beginning and scrutinized each photo in turn. Mid to late Fifties, he thought, maybe early Sixties. This was good because it filled a void in his collection, the early years, when he was just a young child approaching his teens, just the age of one child in the photos. This boy sat in the background, hiding behind the others, a chubby kid with a moon-shaped face and unruly hair. A slightly disheveled appearance, not quite put together correctly. As painful as it was, he recognized himself in the child's demeanor, though he was not the image of Morty's fantasy about himself at that age.

There were no photos of Morty at that age to compare this one to, no photo albums, studio portraits, snapshots of birthday parties, baptisms, or wallet-sized school portraits of a fresh faced child full of promise, smiling crookedly at the camera. He was a blank, growing up in a succession of good intentioned foster homes, always the extra place at the table, afraid to eat until the "real" members of the family had filled their plates.

Flipping back through, he stopped at a picture of the boy sitting with others in a canoe. All were smiling, their paddles dipped into the placid waters of a large lake. Closing his eyes, Morty imagined himself in the canoe. The sun felt warm on his shoulders, the bright light reflecting off the rippling water. He would put his paddle into the lake, feeling the pull of the stroke move the canoe in concert with his buddies. The canoe would gently rock, bob and weave through the waters as the young paddlers learned to coordinate their efforts. Later, an adult in shorts and a tee shirt would blow a whistle to summon them back to shore. They would splash the other kids as they attempted to dock alongside the old wooden pier. There would be a campfire, songs, marshmallows, and ghost stories later that night.

Carefully, Morty removed the picture from the album and searched the walls for a space. He scanned those already hung up: pictures of infants, toddlers, pre-schoolers, until he found just the right place next to a group shot of a junior high track team. This is about the right age, he thought, as he pinned another event onto the chronicle of his life.

TWENTY-TWO

Swim or Sink

Ariel Kay

My arms crack down against the unforgiving, unyielding surface of the ocean as I swim towards safety. I can't see the shore, but I can see lights from boardwalk casinos and high rises. My north star.

As children, you and I came to this beach every summer with our families. We dug holes we thought could make it to the other side of the world if we worked for long enough, plucking mole crabs from the safety of their burrows into our sandy buckets. You cried when you realized they'd died.

Saltwater burns my eyes and bitter, briny mouthfuls of it fill my lungs as I dive beneath the heavy waves. I kick and kick and kick. Did you kick?

Grief compels and propels me forward time and time again on this Sisyphean journey. Tonight I've made it two miles from shore, to where it happened. This time maybe I'll find my answer.

Why were you even out this far?

Every time I've followed your path, I hear you shouting over the roaring of the sea, "Do you want to die?"

"Did you want to live?" I counter. We're both asking the wrong question.

The sea yanks me backward. A welcome relief, in a way, to experience that power firsthand. You struggled against it, I tell myself, you must have.

My body rages against the current until my feet can touch the pebbly ground. Soon I'm crawling the rest of the way from the shallow end of the waves to the safety of shore where I collapse with exhaustion.

Shivering and gasping for breath, I gaze up at the stars above, cold air burning my throat. The bittersweet tang of survival salty on my tongue. If I made it back, could you have too?

The Carpenter's Daughter

Jacqueline Layne

Deep in the cloudless canvas of sky, black-and-white warblers flew in aimless circles. They had traveled thousands of miles to get here, but now they looked unsure. The thought left me with an empty feeling so I rolled to face the earth.

The hammock swayed as my shirt bunched uncomfortably beneath my hip. Some women relaxed with elegance, like recumbent figures in a Renaissance painting, their soft expressions a lesson in unstudied grace.

I was not one of them. I could never quite get comfortable. My limbs tangled; my skin sticky from the heat. I loved the idea of relaxation- the romantic airiness of being lulled to sleep by a gentle breeze- but my brain denied me the luxury. It refused to be silenced.

Suddenly, a memory rushed to the surface of my thoughts, like a small scrap from the roll of yarn I had been unraveling all day. He sat across from me. His large arms rested on our scratched dining room table; his hands were as gnarled as the oak trees he tamed into furniture. His bright red hair had softened to a strawberry blonde, although flecks of white had begun to spring up around his ears.

"Where is your head?" He asked. His voice surprised people. It was too soft- too kind-for a man so large.

The sound startled me-lost in a world of my own design. He was always pulling me back from far-off places, grounding me.

He gave me a lopsided smile, amusement dancing in his misty blue eyes. "What is it they say, quietest people, loudest minds?"

The memory evaporated as a single hot tear rolled down my cheek.

For a moment, it was so real that I could almost smell him. He carried a small plume of sawdust everywhere he went, the cedar scent of freshly chopped wood. I inhaled deeply through my nose, just to be sure, but all I came away with was the smell of grass.

The sun had journeyed to the sky's midpoint. My body was divided. The sun splattered up my thighs, my hands dappled by light, my face shadowed by the mossy oak looming over me. I could feel my feet burning, but I did not budge.

I had begun the day with an irrational belief, a blind conviction based on nothing but my simple need for it to be true.

If I stayed here, nestled in this hammock, I did not have to face the day. I could pretend the last twenty-four hours never happened. I could pretend my life was not upended.

So far as irrational beliefs go, this one had merit, but the sun's steady climb up my body highlighted the major flaw in my plan.

It was nearly two o'clock, and no one else was going to pick up my kids from school. How could I do it? How could I look his granddaughters in the eyes-the same misty blue as his-and tell them…

The minutes crept by, but I was no closer to reconciling the truth.

Somehow, a man that had loomed larger than life was no longer living.

And the world was so much worse for it.

TWENTY-THREE

The Scent of the Scattered

Ted Morrissey

P hinn took a sip of rye. He wasn't inclined toward hard spirits but he hoped it would quiet his thoughts, blunt his worries. He wanted to go out but the snow would make it difficult, if not impossible. Still, he wanted to be near her, to be near them.

Little Elizabeth—Bitty, they called her—was an able student, especially when it came to her letters, but her brother Bobby was slow, people said, couldn't read, they said, barely write his own name, they claimed. He was probably too old for the schoolroom, but Phinn may be able to tutor him—teach him to read simple sentences, do some useful arithmetic. Phinn had taught such students in Cincinnati, at Woodward High School No. 1, and some had made progress. Before he'd been compelled to leave. He replied to the advertisement in The Enquirer, that this godforgotten place—ironically named for the site where Jacob witnessed angels—was seeking a schoolteacher. The ad's appearance seemed serendipitous, maybe even a matter of fate.

Phinn rented a horse from the livery, a red-chestnut mare named Huldah, and visited Bobby Frye's parents to see about Bobby and offer his assistance. Mr. Frye was aloof, or mortified, and found something to do besides sit in the parlor and discuss his son. Mrs. Frye, Roberta, was welcoming to Phinn and to the idea. She made tea, served with a plate of shortbread biscuits. Her hair was tucked behind her ears, a style he associated with cities—the two he knew. A strand fell loose as she poured his tea. She smiled, self-conscious. Phinn smiled too, meaning: It's no matter. Thinking: It becomes you, as does the brushstroke of gray. There was a spice coming from the kitchen. Cinnamon.

———

He set down the book he'd been reading, in hope of distraction, and swallowed the last of the rye in his glass. It felt hot and thick in his throat. He listened for the snow. It'd been falling all day, and now into the night, which had come early. It would be hard in the snow, yes, but not going was harder.

———

At first they spoke of Bobby and what a chore reading had always been, writing more so—he was near nine before he could draw his name, that's what it seemed, more drawing than writing, mimicking the look of it, not under-standing the letters and how they operated one with another. Talking of her son and her worries for him—possibly articulated aloud for the first time, and to someone who also cared—released a rockslide of words, held back in her heart for years; and others, not about Bobby, slid free with them.

———

He was in the living quarters of the schoolhouse, a small set of rooms connected to the classroom. The quarters were comfortable enough. The bed, with its lumpy feather mattress, was nearly too short; he suspected that previ-ously the village had only hired female teachers: young women who had a tendency to be courted, marry, and resign their teaching post. Perhaps the board believed they could interrupt the pattern by employing him. Chalk dust permeated everything.

———

Phinn looked at the bed, with its head and foot of iron, and imagined her there again—the feel of her body beneath him, the release of her taking him in, absorbing him, as needful as he was. Her hands held his neck and back. They were rough, calloused, from her labors on the farm, but he wouldn't have traded their toughened texture for the polite hands of any other—and he wanted to feel them on his skin now.

———

Phinn's nearest neighbor was Old Man Bishop, and at night Phinn could hear him playing his violin. He'd been accomplished, people said, but now his rheumatic fingers could only claw a piercing dirge, the wayward tune barely detectable among the heartbroken, illegitimate notes. Now and then Phinn could catch a glimpse of Vivaldi or Paganini crouched between the cracked and sinking crypts.

He called her Helen because he'd recited the poem for her, to her, and told her the story of Poe's Helen. Helen he would call her after, my Helen, holding her, caressing her in the closefitting bed.

She'd wanted to be an artist, a painter, she told him one day, afterward, as they lay together. Being a painter had been her childish fantasy. Her father had taken her to an exhibition in Chicago, practically by accident. He was looking for the Innovations in Agriculture show. The pictures bewitched her. The New Woman, the exhibition was titled, she remembered it vividly. There was an artist who especially captivated her, Mary Cassatt. One of her paintings gave the exhibition its name.

For a time she drew sketches and colored them with natural pigments she collected from the farm and the countryside and the woods. She dreamed of being taught art. But farm life didn't make space for such dreams. Then she was being courted, then she was married at seventeen, then there were children, including the lost children, a twin, Bobby's twin, and later another baby —in between came Elizabeth, Bitty she was nicknamed because she was so small, itty-bitty. Then the stillborn baby, another girl. It was Christmastime, and heavy black bunting replaced the bright colors.

She thought there must be something wrong with her, something sick, misshapen, inside. Tears trailed across his bare shoulder, dampening the pillowcase. He held her tighter. She seemed, slightly, subtly, to resist the comfort, the refutation. Old Man Bishop's melancholy chords were in the wind.

Normally he would skirt Hollis Woods to reach her farm, keeping to the road, except for a shortcut here and there along the edge of the forest. He felt the need, the longing every night, every night since she told him the news and stopped seeing him. He was rarely able to resist.

Tonight the darkness that was coming was too dark, the caul of pain too suffocating, and drink was only making him more morose. He hoped to see her, literally that was all, to catch a glimpse of her in a window, or coming and going to the privy. He would stand at the corner of the henhouse, in its shadow if the moon was out, and watch. Only watch. Until the last lamp had been extinguished.

The walk would be difficult, due to the snow, but the difficulty appealed to him. He deserved the trial. He took an accounting of every action, frequently, obsessively, and each appeared rooted in a pure impulse, a Christian impulse —even the act that changed everything was attached to love. But in sum, all the actions taken together amounted to wickedness in the ledger. The final tally was inescapable.

If instead of skirting the woods he cut through them, the route may be shorter, and easier in a way, the snow less deep. He'd never taken a path through the woods. Almost from the moment he arrived people warned him of Hollis Woods: they were dangerous, a place of paralyzed luck, the home of hopeless souls. His students told him the story of the Hollis children, whose disappearance, one after another, gave the woods their name—how from time to time hunters would spot one at the edge of the forest. Except the Hollis children disappeared more than fifty years before.

He took a final sip of rye, for the cold, then bundled into his fur-trimmed coat and hat, pulled on his deerskin gloves, and set off. He carried a lantern, cumbersome but necessary. Because of the storm there was no moon or stars. The falling snow was all but invisible. He felt it against his face and heard it adding to the depth already on the ground—heard it between his snow-crunching steps. He tried to tread lightly, quietly even though he was alone in the cold white world.

It would be a long hard walk indeed. The lantern cast a yellow circle on the white ground but did little to light the path before him. It occurred to him that the walk was like the way forward with Roberta and the baby—except the walk, even with its difficulties, was at least possible. No matter. He wanted it still, that life. He had a cousin in Coffey, Kansas, and a former teacher, a mentor, somewhere in Wyoming, Casper?—perhaps these were places where he and Roberta and the baby could begin anew. She would of course want to bring Bitty. Maybe Bobby would prefer to stay with his father, on the farm? He knew the rye helped to paint such fantastical pictures, like the picture of Roberta at her easel painting a panoramic Wyoming landscape, a vista Phinn had only seen via words.

Ahead was the path into Hollis Woods. The place to enter was plain, even with the fallen snow, so maybe the way through would be just as clear. Maybe a path would present itself, like a chain of epiphanies.

Stepping into the woods was like stepping into another world. He thought of Lewis Carroll. The wind fell, instantly, along with the storm's intensity; the shortcut may prove prudent after all. There was a path, an imprecise pattern of clearance between the trees. The way remained discernible mainly due to the hunters who ventured into the forest but it was first cut by the Shawnee, he imagined, who had lived on the land for centuries, or by an older people still.

Whoever laid the track, Phinn appreciated their perseverance. He tried to think only of his good fortune, and not of the forest's darkness, which gathered around him and pressed against the lantern's weak dome of light. With the wind halted and the snow less deep, Phinn's sense of hearing was heightened, and the woods were alive with things. He thought of the Hollis children whose ghosts were said to haunt the woods. And there was the other creature, the local goblin—Plague, the children called him, part man, part crow. He came for them at night, they whispered. To snatch them from their beds.

Old Man Bishop's mournful notes seemed to have been caught in the tallest trees, and from time to time a malformed phrase would fall to the forest floor.

He thought also of Evangeline, buried in a family plot outside Cincinnati. Could her shade follow him here? Why not? Memories of her, of them together, harassed him still.

———

Some said no less than the devil himself denizened these dark woods.

———

Phinn's love seemed a punishment, a kind of plague itself. First Evangeline, victim of diphtheria, and now Roberta, who rumor said was struggling with her pregnancy. He tried to pick up news of her wherever he could—gossip really, including the wonderment that her husband could still seed such a situation (some said it was a miracle, they'd been touched by the beneficent hand of God). Mr. Frye was older after all, and in imperfect health, though his specific complaints were unclear. That was the talk, coming in dribs and drabs, from here and there.

———

He anticipated the looks, the unspoken accusations, the change in the way others addressed him, the edge of disapproval in their voice, their eye—as it had happened in Cincinnati. Not a scandal. Evangeline was nearly sixteen after all, and always serious for her age. Not a scandal, but a lapse in judgment on his part. She was impressionable, with her father having passed just the Christmas before, and she was Phinn's student. Not a scandal, but a breach of decorum certainly. The gossips were harder on Evangeline and their whispered barbs hurt. She claimed not to care, but he saw. Her eyes, as gray and as turbulent as the Ohio before a storm, always spoke more plainly than her lips.

———

He was in turmoil; what to do until the situation came to a sudden end. He heard Evie was sick; then he learned she was dead. If she'd asked for him, no one delivered the message.

———

A sound in the darkness, beyond his sphere of light, woke him from the past, a disturbance of dead leaves, a thump of fallen snow, a twisting snap of twig. He kept moving, trying to disregard the sound. He thought of the book he'd been reading as a distraction, and of the unearthly, androgynous sisters who accost the Scot on the road. They in turn recalled for him tales of witches, the sort that inhabit black New England woods, Hawthorne's woods. Witches and their misshapen familiars. Two-headed snakes, toads with six legs.

He was attempting to replace the disquieting images with more pleasant ones when something crossed the path before him, just at the edge of the lantern's anemic light. He stopped. Then something else, again at the edge, almost sheer movement detached from physical form.

Phinn took a few cautious steps and examined the uneven forest floor, where there appeared to be fresh prints in the newest snow. Poorly defined paw prints, wolfish.

He peered back along the path but saw nothing beyond the sphere of light. His instinct was to turn around; recalled returning were as tedious as go o'er.

Perhaps he was close to emerging from the woods if he pressed on. The fog of drink had been clearing in the cold and with it the reasonable rationale for entering Hollis Woods in the first place.

He kept hearing sounds beyond the continual cascade of snow. They may have been real or only the warble of his tightly wound imagination.

Phinn continued forward, supravigilant for the sight or sound of anything. The sense came to him that there were images just beyond the border of lantern-light. People, phantoms that looked like the cinema figures he'd seen in Cincin-nati. He had attended two moving-picture shows in the lobby of the Sinton Hotel. The Nihilist and The Miller's Daughter. Gray-tone ghosts moved fitfully on the canvas that workmen had stretched between cream-painted columns. Meanwhile the Sinton's piano player improvised accompaniment, adding an incongruent score to the barely comprehensible scenes. Each time, Phinn had the feeling he was viewing someone's unsettling dream, made visible by the cinema-machine's magical projection.

Such figures inhabited the woods beyond the lantern's reach. He could almost see their silent, achromatic shades. First there was Evangeline, her gray ghost pantomiming scenes from life: sitting politely and properly in Mr. Folger's classroom, then waiting anxiously for his approval or dismissal of the poems she had proffered—there was in fact something substantial hidden among her schoolgirl rhymes. Then in the cold woods played the spectral spring day he and Evie confessed their feelings—he felt the electric current of their clasping hands, and the jolt of their first kiss. Evie had just eaten a butterscotch and it would forever flavor the moment's jubilation. All along, the tormented lamentations of Old Man Bishop's violin wept as if a grief-stricken wind. Evangeline's image faded and flickered away, removed from his classroom by her uncle and then from life by disease. The Enquirer's obituary notice brought the bitter news in fourteen precise lines of print, like lead-gray furrows in a fallow field.

Invisible things moved among the trees pressing in upon the narrow path.

The cinema image of Roberta materialized beyond the sphere of precious light, first in the parlor, self-conscious of hosting a man, a younger man at that, she confessed later, an educated man, but her husband preferred to find chores in the barn to discussing his son's slowness. Phinn felt her isolation, her unhappiness even at their first meeting. It hung upon her like a haphazardly given hand-me-down, yet couldn't disguise her beauty. An ember of her true self still smoldered within, wanting, needing to ignite before it died entirely. Then Roberta's ghostly gray-tone image was in his rooms at the schoolhouse, against her sounder judgment but she was sick to death of sound judgment. Two lonely beings embraced across a void that seemed too far, too deep, but was instantly vanished, vanquished. Age and long-hidden despair dropped from Roberta like the workaday clothes of a farm wife she shed upon his bare floor, cast alongside his loneliness and gnawing sense of worthlessness, of being unworthy of love. Old Man Bishop's accidental dirge wailed on.

Phinn sensed something was behind him on the forest path. He turned and it scampered into the woods at the extreme edge of the lantern's influence. Perhaps he saw it with sufficient clarity, or his perception was prodded by the wolfish tracks he saw earlier—but he believed it was that kind of creature. He supposed it was possible there were still wolves in this part of the country. More likely a coyote: smaller but still a worrisome presence.

He faced forward again. Where was the terminus of this interminable path?

He hurried on, and shortly new cinema-apparitions arose beyond the lantern's timid light. They seemed his pupils, standing, staring at him with vacant eyes —except he didn't recognize the children, five in all, of varying ages. And their clothing: especially old-fashioned, coarsely homespun, ill-fitting. Phinn knew them: the Hollis children, disappeared, dead these many years, long enough to be mythologized into local legend—the inspiration for this envisioning, for their unwelcome visitation. Broken and betrayed notes rained down more savagely than the storm's merciless snow.

To his relief, the children dissolved as quickly as they came, and he thought surely the path, too, must conclude soon.

He began hearing more movement, more beings here and there in the dark, their indeterminate steps mixing with the unremitting snow, their undefined shapes blending with the black trees.

He switched hands and held the lantern higher, which did nothing to project light farther into the dark. The only revelation was how low the lamp-oil had become. Phinn looked up hoping to see some stars through the canopy of naked limbs, a sign the storm had run its course, but there were none. Snowflakes picked at his unshaven face and spotted the lenses of his spectacles.

He hastened his pace among the uncertain sounds that surrounded him.

Old Man Bishop's crippled fingers clawed upward toward a dreadful crescendo, a devastating climax. Old Man Bishop, found dead two months before.

The fog of rye had fully lifted, and with its evaporation came the coldblooded clarity of his recklessness, his foolishness. What was he doing here? What was his nightly vigil at the Frye farm meant to accomplish? The baby would be born a Frye and be raised a Frye—and one day enter his schoolroom a Frye, with no connection to Phinn whatsoever. Mr. Phineas Folger, who had taught the child's siblings.

Phinn gave up the hope of finding his way through and turned to retrace his steps. The lantern illuminated their eyes. On the path before him. And everywhere in the woods.

Love | Adoration | Jealousy

Part Three

Striking Out

By Robin Chapman

TWENTY-FOUR

Courageous Creative

Mae Wagner

My creative foundation is built on the moments, statements, and memories of those bigger than me who found me lacking.

It was never *good enough*, the things I'd dream to life. Be they the color scape from my *Looney Tunes* coloring book, or free hand love affairs with Crayola on blank page.

The best of moments found it *fine* but deeply lacking in worth compared to…

Those bigger than me eventually evolved into the better than me and I surrendered my willingness to try.

I chose instead a preservation of self-mediocrity.

If I decided to be the one who could not, then I would always be the one who would not disappoint. Seeking hole-filling love and acceptance, not disappointing felt like approval–at least for a while anyway.

This chosen way of life would surely encounter less embarrassment, less shame, less rejection…

Less…

In time I became the ego fanner, tending the flame of those around me. The saint encourager of *his* sketching and *her* dabbling with paint. The cheerleader of creativity while the veins feeding my own inspired life source held only air.

Less than less, it would seem.

Once seeking hole-filling, I began to realize my emptiness when it came to feeling whole.

Where I lacked in self-worth, others bloomed.

To be a courageous creative, for me, looks a lot like revisiting those once deemed bigger and better than me and seeing them through healthy adult eyes rather than the perspective of an aching child. To answer the question: *What made them need for me to be kept small?*

The truth is no one breaks a child because they feel whole and worthy themselves. In seeing this, roots began to take hold.

Tiny seeds sprouting of something akin to inspiration–something being watered and warmed by a dawning belief that I can.

I will...

And truly, I always could.

TWENTY-FIVE

Epitaph

Billie Spaulding

T he Cecropia Moth is North America's most giant moth, the granddaughter read off of the screen of her phone. The image of a sizable autumn-colored moth with crescent moons on its wings glowered near her face, and she stared back, hoping to understand the fascination. It was the same moth in the photo on the table before her. Although it took on a grainier, black and white color, its size was emphasized by the smallness of her grandfather's hands. Her grandfather's face was turned toward the *Saturniidae*. His dark, hooded eyes glanced down, and his long eyelashes made winged shadows on his cheeks.

"I wonder if he hunted all of those," her brother said nearby. He gazed down at the photo motioning towards the various boards with moths pinned to them. It was a vast collection comprised of Peppered, White Witch, Gypsy, and surprisingly the Death's-Head Hawk moth, which both the granddaughter and her brother recognized from *The Silence of The Lambs*. "I didn't know he liked moths let alone collected them," she said as she zoomed in on a picture of the Death's-Head Hawk moth, *Acherontia atropos, Atropos relating to the nightshade plant*, she continued to read.

Her grandfather never seemed like a man intrigued by something so myste-rious and macabre. He was a pious man, a man who watched Spaghetti West-erns while he looked at stocks in the local *Pantagraph*. He was committed to providing for his family and passing on his principles to his children and grandchildren in the typical Eisenhower fashion. They wouldn't have consid-ered him a boring man by any variation of the word. Yes, he was prone to telling tall-tales and liked to collect coins, as well as antique guns. Maybe he fancied himself the Clint Eastwood of Bloomington-Normal. Yet, the romance of the photo betrayed his descendants and their collective opinion of him. It seemed they placed him snuggly in a box of archetypes, leaving very little room in the urn sitting on the dresser to contain all that he was, and it wasn't more obvious than in this moment.

"Do you think he killed them or collected them while they were already dead?" her brother asked. He was reading something on his phone, scrolling quickly, scanning it robotically. "It says that it's better to kill them yourself before mounting them to better preserve their beauty." *Killing them to better preserve their beauty,* the granddaughter mused inwardly.

She couldn't imagine her grandfather killing something to admire it better. He enjoyed growing things with a gentle, firm hand just as much as he enjoyed nurturing them. He planted daffodils in his yard since their grandmother cherished yellow flowers and the raspberry bushes that lined the driveway for many years, providing them with sugared raspberries with milk in the Mid-Western summers. She'd watch him shoot BB's at wild rabbits from time to time, but that was the extent of his outward malice. He was eternally patient with each and every grandchild as if each child was another flower in his garden.

Her brother began to rummage through his grandfather's drawer. The sound of jostled objects disturbed her for reasons she didn't know. She thanked the sudden silence when he paused.

"What's the *Blood Beast Terror*?" he asked. She turned around and saw him holding a yellowed ticket stub in his hand. "It's dated 1970 at the Avon Theater in Decatur." She took it in her hand as if it were an antique or family heirloom. She tried imagining her grandfather being one of many faces in that audience. Perhaps he watched that movie with the same whetted interest he paid to all the other things he liked and admired. Was it his love of collecting moths that brought him to the movies or was it this movie that inspired him to collect moths? How often did he stroll down the avenue of inspiration and interest? More importantly, why didn't his family get to meet the man who snuck off to midnight viewings of gothic horror B-movies?

She typed in the title of the movie on her phone, "It's a movie about a were-moth drinking people's blood," she said to her brother. The image of their young grandfather staring at a movie screen, entranced, began to materialize like a phantom. Black was usually his shade of choice and he would, no doubt, be wearing a black collared shirt with matching pressed pants. His lean body could have been the edge of a blade and he would absorb the moment with his hands in his pockets. It began to dawn on the sister that her brother and her grandfather were similar in this way and that made this arcane romance seem genetic and molecular. Her brother had the same specific interest that ranged from Kurosawa films to collecting tintypes that he hunts for in thrift stores.

The difference was her brother wore his passions like a garment while their grandfather kept them under the floorboards.

They tried to fathom the clues in front of them, of the mystery that was their grandfather, his hidden complexities, and the passions that bore them. They were so glad to meet this person, officially, but the memories they had of him were becoming mired by a moth-shaped shadow. It would have been easy for them to take his need to be private personally. They were of a different generation after all; they would have been more tolerant and appreciative of these things. All they simply could agree on is that their grandfather had their reasons to leave behind this person and they had no choice but to accept it. Maybe there wasn't a tunnel of white light that met their grandfather at the end but, instead, a box office and the smell of buttered popcorn. Her brother was smiling to himself while he looked down. "What's so funny," she asked. His index finger outlined the shape of their grandfather's expressive mouth, "we would have been friends in high school."

TWENTY-SIX

Freak Show

Maggie Friedenberg

"Well, that's not something you see every day."

Del was used to hearing phrases like this one by now. In fact, at this point she could predict the entire series of events that would take place whenever a healthcare professional entered her brother's hospital room.

First came the curious look – they'd been warned what to expect. Next, the wide-eyed stare as they beheld the thing they'd heard about. Then, the polite turning away, putting back on the benign, expressionless face they'd been trained to present, asking the same questions she'd been asked a thousand times already. Finally, when they left the room, the hushed tones in the hallway as they discussed what they'd seen with their co-workers. The monster. The freak show. *Come one, come all. Step right up.*

Del sighed and sat back in the ugly vinyl recliner, hands resting upon her swollen belly. As if in response, the child within her nudged the spot where her hands lay.

These people didn't even see her brother. Didn't see the human being right there in front of them. Nash, six years her senior, once her fierce protector and strongest ally, and later, the person who'd hurt her most.

He'd practically raised her on his own. After their mother left – which wasn't an identifiable event so much as a gradual realization that this time she wasn't coming back – it was just the two of them. Nash dropped out of high school, scraping together enough money from two or three part-time jobs to pay the bills and keep them fed. Some days all they had was a bag of microwave popcorn to share. When they didn't have enough money to pay the electric bill, they lit candles, played cards, and told spooky stories in the dark. Nash made every hardship seem like an adventure.

Then one day, the police knocked on their apartment door. Del opened it, unaware that her life was about to change. Her brother was led away in hand-cuffs, and she was left alone. She was only fourteen, and he was all she had in the world.

"I'm sorry, Del," he said. She stared after him, speechless.

Later that night, another police officer came back to collect her. She spent the next four years in foster care, until the system spit her out at eighteen. By then, Nash was out of prison. He tracked her down at school, trying to apologize, but she was full of anger. Before yesterday, she hadn't seen her brother in more than fifteen years.

The cancer had robbed him of his muscular physique. The dark hair that still fell past his shoulders had lost its shine and was now streaked with silver. And, of course, there was the tumor, the source of all the curiosity and disgust, that had disfigured his neck and the lower right side of his face. But Del could still see the young man he had been, handsome and strong.

Del's phone vibrated, jolting her back to the present.

Lindsay: Still at the hospital?

Del checked the time. It was almost six. She'd been at the hospital since noon. She shifted in the chair, stretching her arms out in front of her.

Del: Waiting for the social worker.

Lindsay: Be there in 45 minutes.

Del sent back a heart emoji. Things would be easier once Lindsay got here. She always knew the right things to say, the right questions to ask.

Lindsay had come with her to the hospital last night, after she got the phone call from Nash's neighbor, Alice, who told her he'd been taken to the hospital by ambulance. They needed his next of kin to come make decisions. She didn't tell Lindsay that the same neighbor had called her twice already.

The first phone call was about a month ago. Alice identified herself and said Nash asked her to call. He needed to see her. Del said she needed time. It wasn't until the second call, a few days ago, that Alice explained time was something Nash didn't have. They arranged a meeting, which was supposed to take place the day after tomorrow. Del guessed she could delete it from her calendar now.

Nash was in surgery when they arrived, and Del had to wait several hours before she could see him. Although Alice had prepared her, she was still taken aback by his appearance. For a few seconds, she almost doubted it was the right person. Maybe she was in the wrong room, or maybe Alice had made a mistake. But when her brother opened his eyes, she recognized him right away.

She stood up from the chair and wandered over to the window. Nash's room overlooked the hospital parking garage. A car made its way down the incline towards the cashier's booth. Del envied the driver, no doubt on their way to a home-cooked meal and a comfortable bed. She pressed her forehead against the cool glass of the windowpane.

"Knock, knock," she heard someone say from the doorway. She turned. A middle-aged woman entered the room, wearing khakis and a blouse. Del watched her eyes widen as she took in the sight of her brother, then quickly looked back at Del.

She introduced herself as the social worker. Now that Nash was stable, she explained, they needed to make a plan for his continued care after being discharged from the hospital.

"We have a couple of options," she said. "Because his condition is terminal, he qualifies for hospice care." She explained that he could receive care at a skilled nursing facility or at home.

"He can go home?"

"Someone would need to be there with him."

"I think he lives alone," Del said. How in the hell was she supposed to make these decisions? She barely knew this man. She didn't know if he'd ever been married, ever fathered a child. She knew nothing about what his life had been like or who had been in it. He'd left her when she needed him most. Her head swam.

She closed her eyes and swallowed. She only knew two things: he was her brother, and he was dying. Did anything else matter?

"What about bringing him home with me?"

The social worker's eyes flicked to Del's pregnant belly. "It's a lot to handle," she said. "You've obviously got your hands full already. When is the baby due?"

"Five weeks," Del said.

"I spoke with his caseworker. We can try and arrange a bed for him at a state facility. Talk about it with your family," she said, patting Del's upper arm. "Let me know what you decide. Then we can start the paperwork."

"Thank you," she answered.

The social worker left the room. "How do you let it *get* that bad?" Del heard her ask someone in the hall.

Del rolled her eyes. As if everyone had the time, money, and insurance to go get things checked out when they first became a problem. She knew Nash had been working a handful of odd jobs, mostly under the table, when he'd gotten sick. This much, Alice had told her. She said he'd been in and out of the hospital several times in the past year. A couple of months ago, he'd come home with the tracheostomy in his neck, and had been on disability ever since. Ironically, now he qualified for health coverage, when it was already too late.

Del got up from the chair. Her back ached. She reached back to rub it with the heel of her hand, taking a step towards her brother's bed. She put her hand on top of his, as she had several times in the past few hours.

"Nash," she said, softly. "Open your eyes."

He didn't stir. She watched the rise and fall of his chest as he breathed.

"Del," Lindsay said, sounding out of breath as she breezed through the doorway in a light gray pantsuit and three-inch heels. "Sorry it took me so long." She gave her a kiss. Del noticed she kept her eyes averted, not wanting to look directly at the disfigured man in the bed.

"Has he woken up yet?"

Del shook her head. "They say it's because of the pain meds. I don't even know if he knows I'm here."

"I'm sure he does," Lindsay said, flashing her a reassuring smile. "Did the social worker come in yet?"

Del nodded. "I wish you had been here. These people all talk to me like I'm a dumb kid."

Lindsay glanced sideways at Del's outfit. Basketball shorts, pink tank top over a black sports bra, athletic slides on her feet. "I wonder where they got that idea."

Del laughed and elbowed her. "Stop. It's so hot outside. I just want to be comfortable."

"You have all those cute maternity clothes."

Del wrinkled her nose. Lindsay shook her head.

"So what did they say?"

"We can put him in a facility or he can go home."

"Home?" Lindsay raised one eyebrow at her.

"I know," she said. "I wish I knew what he wanted."

Lindsay's phone buzzed. She looked at it, frowned, and tucked it back into her pocket.

"What if I brought him home to stay with us?"

Lindsay's eyes widened. "Are you serious?"

"I was thinking, that might be the best thing to do," Del said.

"Babe, take a minute to think about it," Lindsay said, putting her hand on Del's belly. "We have a lot going on."

"I don't want him going to some state facility."

"No, no, of course not." Lindsay's phone buzzed again. She rolled her eyes, pulling it out of her pocket. "We'll pay to have him stay someplace nice." We, of course, meaning Lindsay. Del had already taken leave from work in antici-pation of the baby's birth, but her own salary was meager compared to what Lindsay made as a project manager at a pharmaceutical company.

"I'd rather we pay a nurse to come in and take care of him at home." Del's eyes filled with tears. She blinked.

Lindsay's face softened. "I'm sorry. Come here." She wrapped her arms around Del and kissed her forehead. "You look exhausted. Have you eaten?"

Del shook her head.

Lindsay opened a food delivery app on her phone. "What do you feel like? A sandwich? Pasta? Ooh, there's a Thai place nearby," she said, scrolling through the options. "Drunken noodles? Papaya salad?"

"Are we allowed to order delivery here?"

Lindsay shrugged. "Who cares? My baby needs to eat." She smiled. Del's heart flipped over in her chest. Sometimes she still couldn't believe this gorgeous, brilliant, irresistible woman was hers. Lindsay was fearless, self-assured, assertive – qualities that had never come naturally to Del. Her childhood was the polar opposite of Del's. A supportive family, a big, luxurious house, private school. Her parents were kind and gracious, welcoming Del into the family with open arms, but sometimes she still felt like an outsider.

"I'll go down to the lobby to wait for the food," Lindsay said after she placed the order. Del listened to the clicking sounds her high heels made against the floor of the hallway.

The social worker came back into the room, along with another woman in a white jacket. The social worker introduced her as the coordinator of the hospice program.

"Nice to meet you." Del shook her hand, wishing Lindsay hadn't stepped out.

She handed Del a folder with the hospital's logo on the front in raised, gold lettering. "I understand you're considering taking your brother home to stay with you," she said.

"I am," she said.

"You understand your brother has a tracheostomy and a feeding tube."

"Yes, but I don't really understand what that means," Del admitted.

"The tumor is completely obstructing both his trachea and his esophagus. The tracheostomy allows him to breathe through a surgical opening in his neck. He can't eat, so he has to be given liquid formula and his medications through the tube in his stomach." The hospice nurse began to explain the details of what caring for Nash at home would involve, crushing his meds, flushing the feeding tube, caring for the tracheostomy site. Del listened, trying to follow along, eyeing the clock on the wall, hoping Lindsay was on her way back.

The social worker gave her a checklist of medical equipment they would need to order. Some of it could be rented, she explained, like the hospital bed and wheelchair, but most of it was what she called "single-use."

"And his insurance covers all of that?" Del asked.

"Most, but not all," the social worker said.

Lindsay reappeared with the bag of take-out food, her heels clicking as she strode into the room. A wave of relief washed over Del as the two women's heads turned in Lindsay's direction.

"Hello," the social worker said to Lindsay, sounding more like she was asking a question than offering a greeting.

Lindsay introduced herself, smiling and extending her hand. Each of the women shook it.

"My wife," Del said.

"Oh, I see," the nurse said, exchanging a sideways glance with the social worker.

Lindsay set the bag of food on the tray table near Del's seat. The savory aroma made her stomach growl.

Lindsay motioned to the paper in Del's hand. "What's this?"

"A list of medical supplies you'll need at home," the nurse answered.

"At home?" She looked at Del, tilting her head to the side. "I thought we talked about this."

"For about a second," Del answered, her brow furrowed. "I want to bring him home."

"We'll let you two talk it over," the social worker said. "He'll be here for another day or two at least." She reached into her pocket and handed Del a business card. "If you have any questions, let me know." She and the hospice nurse left the room.

Lindsay turned towards the bag of food, setting containers and utensils on the narrow tray table. "God, I'm starving," she said, opening a container of dumplings. She popped one into her mouth and offered the container to Del.

Del took a dumpling and chewed it slowly, not looking at Lindsay.

"Look, why don't you let me call Reed and see if he can pull a few strings? I'm sure he can find a bed for Nash at one of those really nice assisted living places right outside the city. You can visit him every day." She handed Del a container of noodles and a plastic fork.

Reed was Lindsay's older brother, an emergency surgeon at one of the top hospitals in the city. He'd won all kinds of awards and been profiled several times in the local newspaper and lifestyle magazines. Del wasn't sure what kind of strings Lindsay thought he'd be able to pull, but maybe it would be worth a try. Maybe Nash wouldn't even want to come and stay with them. After all, their apartment only had two bedrooms, and the nursery was already set up for the baby.

"Okay," she said.

"Great." Lindsay flashed her a smile and ate another dumpling from the container. Her phone buzzed again. She looked at the screen, sighed, and began tapping out a reply.

Del looked down at the food, her appetite suddenly gone. When had she become such a pushover? Back when she was a teenager, growing up in one foster home after another, she'd quickly learned that if she didn't speak up for herself, nobody else would do it for her. She learned to push through the fear, working her ass off, making sure she got all A's, earning a full scholarship to college, graduating with high honors. But somewhere along the way she'd begun letting Lindsay call the shots, deferring to her because she was older, smarter, had a better upbringing.

"Hey. Del." Lindsay said, laughing.

Del shook her head, realizing Lindsay had said something she'd missed. "Sorry."

"You were in outer space."

"Just tired, I guess."

"Why don't we go home and get some sleep?"

Del glanced at her brother. "You go ahead," she said. "I want to stay just a little longer and see if he wakes up."

"Don't stay too late, okay?" Lindsay kissed her goodbye, leaving the remnants of their dinner behind.

Del packed up the containers, threw away the trash, and sank back into the chair she'd been in for most of the day. When she left late last night, Nash was still in recovery. The surgery to repair his tracheostomy had gone well, and the doctor said he was stable. Del didn't want to leave him, but Lindsay convinced her to go home and sleep. She'd missed the brief period this morning when he was awake and alert, according to the nurses. She didn't want to miss it if he woke up again.

If he ever did.

As if he could hear her thoughts, her brother's eyes fluttered. He turned his head to the side.

"Nash?" She stood, putting her hand on his.

He opened his eyes, squinting.

"Sorry, I know it's bright in here," she said. She walked to the door and shut off the overhead light, leaving only the light from behind the bed.

Nash looked at her face, his eyes filling with recognition. He put his hand on his heart.

"Hey, big brother." She leaned in to kiss his forehead.

He took a quick look around the room. Not seeing what he was looking for, he held one hand out, palm-up, and used the other to mimic the action of writing.

"You want paper and a pen," she said. He nodded. She fished in her purse for a pen. The only paper she could find was a long receipt from the pharmacy. "Will this do?"

He put his hands out for them. Del moved the bedside table over so he could lean on it.

I'M SORRY, he wrote, in all caps.

"What are you sorry for?"

EVERYTHING.

Del's eyes burned. "It's okay," she said, putting her hand on his again. He raised it to his lips and kissed it.

"How did you know where to find me?"

He laughed silently. *INTERNET.*

"Of course." Del laughed.

Nash extended a hand towards her belly, his eyebrows raised as if to ask, *May I?* Del nodded. He put the palm of his hand on her swollen middle. The baby shifted, stretching. Nash grinned.

"It's a little boy," Del said. "Due at the end of August."

Nash reached for the pen. *I'M SO PROUD OF YOU, DEL.*

Del smiled. "Listen," she said. "They need to know what you want to do when you get out of here. You can go to a nursing home, or I can bring you home to stay with me."

There was a knock at the door, and a new nurse walked into the room. "Hello," she said, introducing herself in a cheerful voice, taking a quick glance at Nash before looking away. She took a marker and wrote her name on the whiteboard on the wall.

"How long has he been awake?" the nurse asked Del as she checked Nash's IV line.

"Just woke up a few minutes ago," Del said. She backed up from the bed so the nurse could check him over, asking Del all the standard questions. Del answered as best she could, annoyed that the nurse seemed to be caring for and ignoring Nash at the same time.

"How's he doing tonight?"

"He's right there," Del said, pointing at her brother. "Ask him yourself."

The nurse glanced at Nash again. "How are we feeling?" she asked, loudly, as if his hearing was impaired along with his speech.

Nash gave her a thumbs-up.

"Any pain?"

He nodded, holding up ten fingers. He reached for the pen and paper again. BATHROOM, he wrote.

"I'll have the aide come in and help you," she said, "and then I'll bring you your pain meds. Sound good?"

Nash nodded.

"Can he get some blank paper, too?"

"Of course," she said.

Del rolled her eyes as the nurse walked out. Nash gave an exasperated exhale through his tracheostomy tube, making her laugh.

Nash pointed at the nightstand next to the bed. Del opened the drawer. Inside was a plastic bag with the few things he'd had when he arrived at the hospital. Wallet, phone, keys. She handed it to him. He opened the wallet, removing a folded piece of paper and handing it to Del.

She unfolded it. "What is this?" The paper felt slick, like a page from a magazine or catalog, but had clearly been folded and refolded many times. She looked down at it and saw herself and Lindsay on their wedding day, more than two years ago, smiling at each other in matching white dresses. The page had been torn from a local magazine that had featured them in their annual wedding issue.

It hit her then that if Nash had come to her when he first knew he was sick, he might not be dying now. She would have been able to help with his medical bills, his living expenses. If she'd given him the time of day when he came to see her after he got out of prison, or if she'd bothered to look him up at any point in the past fifteen years –

Her eyes spilled over with tears. "I'm sorry I was such an asshole. I didn't know – I wasted so much time – " Her voice broke. Nash had given up his teenage years to take care of her. He was the only family she had, and she had pushed him away, made him feel like he couldn't approach her when he needed help. She wasn't any better than these nurses, treating him like something less than human. Disposable.

Nash pulled her hands into his again, squeezing gently. He shook his head.

Del sniffled and reached for a tissue. "I want you to come home to stay with me and Lindsay," she said. "Our place isn't big, but we can set up a bed for you, and have a nurse come and look in on you each day."

Nash shook his head and picked up the pen. *YOU DON'T HAVE TO DO THAT.*

"I want to."

BABY? He looked at her belly, raising his eyebrows.

"He'll be lucky to get a chance to meet his uncle," she said, smiling.

He smiled back, but his face turned serious again. *I DON'T WANT TO BE A BURDEN.*

She put her hand over his. "Let me take care of you. Nash. Please."

Nash pressed his lips together and nodded, not meeting her eyes. When he looked at her again, his eyes were wet.

"I'll talk to Alice about getting your things," she said. "And we can go over the paperwork with the social worker tomorrow. Okay?"

Nash mouthed the word *okay*. He smiled and patted her hand.

"I love you," Del said.

I love you, too, he mouthed.

She called Lindsay from the car on her way home, willing her voice not to shake. "I know it's a lot to take on, believe me," she said. "And I know the way he looks makes you uncomfortable. I get it. But he's my only family. I don't want strangers taking care of him."

"I know, babe."

Del swallowed the tears that threatened. "They don't even look at him, Linz. He's not a person to them. Imagine if it was Reed? You'd do the same thing. I'm bringing him home."

"Okay," Lindsay said, after a few seconds. "Let's bring him home."

"Really?"

"Of course. How can I say no to you? You're having my baby." She gave a little laugh, and Del's chest grew warm. "But he's not your only family, Del. We're a family, too, okay?"

"Thank you," Del said, tears in her eyes.

A month later, she watched her brother's face light up as she placed his nephew in his arms. The baby stirred, opening his eyes, gazing up into his uncle's face. They locked eyes, and Nash smiled. Del snapped a photo with her phone.

That's not something you see every day.

TWENTY-SEVEN

Piloting Memories

S. Salazar

I don't know her, but I follow the old woman coaxing me forward. I tour this museum in comfort despite its unfamiliarity. The woman wears a mossy-green top, her silver curls tumbling to her hips. She turns to see if I'm still here. I am. Our eyes meet, her crimson lips mirroring my smile. We spiral dim hallways. Firearms and photographs are stationed behind glass panes that reflect someone's worn features back at me. The woman stops abruptly and gives my hand a familiar squeeze. My gaze follows hers to a Mk III target tug plane suspended from the ceiling by thick cords.

Suddenly, my plane, too, was suspended in air, the target in sight. The cockpit hummed, goggles tight against my face. I aimed at the yellow target tug trembling ahead. *Pop, pop.* Scarlet paint splattered the fabric drogue trailing the plane.

"Got 'er!" I cried into the radio.

I didn't remember leaving my cockpit. I did, however, remember her leaving her cockpit, a helmet perched in the crook of her elbow. Her eyes darted toward me, blonde locks knotted tight at her neck. Her hips swung with a confidence unknown to me. As she approached, the guys hollered and high-fived me. Her smirk flashed red as the drogue.

"I'm pretty hard to get," she goaded, extending a hand to meet mine.

I squeeze her hand. I *do* know her. I push a strand of gray behind her ear; right here, right now, she isn't just the woman from my memories. She nuzzles into my arms.

"You're back," she whispers, tears flooding her eyes.

We linger, clinging to a time much easier to remember.

"Got 'er."

TWENTY-EIGHT

Red Giant Looming

Laura Ansara

The horizon, once defined by mountains dotted with green and purple life, now lay bleak and brown. Kiera lifted her pack and hiked down a rocky gully where a waterfall used to adorn a cavernous spot, spraying cool drops on sweaty visitors. Of course, the stream had dried up years ago.

A man stood in the distance, his silhouette familiar and non-threatening. Still, Kiera clutched her weapon out of habit. A thieving survivalist was the last thing she wished to encounter today. His head turned as he heard her descend the trail.

"James, is that you?"

The man squinted to recognize her face. "Kiera!"

She jumped into his arms with a shriek of disbelief as their tears mixed.

"I can't believe you're here. It's been over twenty years," she said, slowly releasing him.

"I knew the waterfall would be gone, but this was our spot. You've been on my mind, of course," he told her.

"Yes," she looked down. "You too. Perhaps reliving the past is all we can do to cope with a lack of future."

He nodded. "This place symbolizes the best parts of our relationship, out of all the happiness … and regret. I guess I'm trying to escape inside the memories."

"We all are," she replied. "Yet it only makes us feel worse somehow, doesn't it?"

Tears flowed and they embraced again.

Kiera had intended to clear her mind with a good hike, but now she stood holding hands with her first true love. Her mind was anything but clear.

In normal times, they would have filled in the blanks of each other's lives. There was little point now. They walked back up the trail, hand in hand, about a hundred meters from the precipice that overlooked the vast views of the canyon. A line of people had formed. Kiera didn't dare go near what had become the famous step-off point for those who wanted to end their suffering.

The horizon transformed into the darkest oranges and pinks Kiera had ever seen. While the swirls of color created an undeniable beauty, the foreshadowing of the scene tainted its glory. The once whitish yellow sun was now a life-sucking inferno of orange, hovering over everything precious. Nuclear fusion wasn't supposed to happen for another five billion years, long after humanity had completed its course on Earth. But power mongers and their ruthless technology race led to the most failed intervention with nature ever imagined. Man's attempt to control the weather inadvertently sped up the end of the solar system's life force. The sun was prematurely evolving into a red giant, an expanding star that would soon engulf the Earth. Nothing could undo what had been done.

In a couple years, oceans would heat to the point of killing all sea life. Man-made cooling waters would sustain enough sea life to feed small populations of people until the end. All plant life would soon wither, leaving animals, and eventually humans, without food.

After Kiera and James said all they could, they walked back to her car. It was heartbreak all over again, for different reasons this time. She drove toward the exit and watched James in the rearview mirror. He was returning to the trailhead. Her heart leaped.

"The step-off point," she whispered. She raced her car through the lot, driving off the pavement to catch up to James.

He stopped to watch her get out of the car and pull him to the ground.

"Not this way! No!" she cried, pounding softly on his chest as they lay in the dirt. "There's at least another year or two left. See it to the end!"

"What's the difference? Now or next year? It's too hard to live through."

She glanced toward the step-off point. The people were gone.

"But it's not ending today," she replied.

The orange haze melded into grays of dusk. At least night time hadn't changed yet. Her husband would worry about her. She took James' hand as they both stood up. She led him inside her car and they drove away.

TWENTY-NINE

The Perfect Birthday Cake

S.V. Brosius

The ticking of the clock greeted Sara as she entered the kitchen with two bags of groceries. As she rolled up her sleeves to begin preparing the batter, the vision of the perfect birthday cake floated into her mind. The vanilla layers would be stacked with a generous amount of chocolate ganache throughout the middle. The chocolate buttercream frosting would encase the entire dessert, showcasing a few carefully constructed red roses with green stems on top. She watched the stand mixer whirl the ingredients together as the memory of a bright cherub face with two pigtails watching her with eager anticipation brought a smile to her face.

Once the carefully filled pans were in the oven, Sara began working on the buttercream frosting. The sweet chocolate aroma combined with the gentle puffs of powdered sugar clouds took her back in time as the defiant young teen with anger in her eyes stormed out of the house, smelling of chocolate cherry perfume and donning a low-cut dress that was bought without her approval. The worry, the frustration, and the fear of that night so long ago still worked a knot in Sara's stomach.

After the cakes were cooled and carefully assembled, Sara took her time smearing the frosting over the delicate surface. As she smoothed out every ripple with concentrated effort, the need to hide every part of the golden goodness from view spurred her on with a silent battle cry. The distraught voice of a young woman broke Sara's focus as her movements came to a halt. Tears gathered in her eyes. "It's your fault Dad left."

Hours later, the final steps of decorating the cake were complete. Sara sat at the dining table and waited. The ticking clock seemed to mock her as she sat, sipping chamomile tea and scrolling through her Facebook news feed. She was a bundle of nerves, wondering if all her efforts would be appreciated or blatantly ignored. Her fingers itched to send a text but knew it would be in vain. A loud yawn rose from her throat as she thought about merely giving up and going to bed. Then, the sound of the doorbell pushed all thoughts of restless sleep away as a renewed excitement and hope filled the sweet-smelling air. Sara didn't have to look through the window to know who was on the other side of the door. A relieved grin tugged at her lips as she opened the door and said, "Welcome home, Rachel. Happy Birthday!"

Rachel beamed in response and immediately flew into her mother's embrace. Now, everything was perfect.

THIRTY

The Devil's Daughter

H.D. Scarberry

I wiped my hand against the front of my dress and watched impatiently as Levi adjusted himself in his saddle. Deep blue eyes stared down at me, steady and calm despite my anger.

"You're so much like your damn Daddy," I said scornfully. "Stubborn as a mule!" Wiping my forehead with the back of my hand, I turned away from him and looked out over the fence into the fields.

"I've been called worse, Momma," he said, failing to hide the smirk creeping across his face.

"Yeah. That's exactly what I'm afraid of, Levi." I shoved my fist onto my hips and stared up at my son. "That little girl ain't nothing but trouble, and you know as well as I do that having her stay here is going to cause one hell of a commotion."

He stepped down from Smoke's saddle and took a deep breath before coming to stand in front of me. I watched as he fumbled the reins in his calloused hands, avoiding eye contact with me. I narrowed my eyes. It wasn't in Levi's nature to be unsure, of *anything*.

"I know that," he said softly. "But she ain't got nobody." He brought his gaze to meet mine, his breath short. "He's hurtin' her, Momma, and if she shows up with one more bruise, I'll put him in his grave."

I felt the breath slowly escape my lungs as I stared up at him. "Hurtin' her … how?" I asked as I searched his face, fighting the wave of nausea and rage in my stomach. Levi's face was motionless except for his clenched jaw.

"I think … I think I'd rather not say. Not to my own momma." He took a step closer to me as his eyes danced wildly. "I mean it, Momma. One more harsh word to her, and he's good as gone."

The sun was high above us, causing the sweat to bead on both of our faces. Dust rustled and then quickly fell as Smoke raised a leg, batting away a pesky fly. I turned once more and stared out into the fields and sighed before giving him my answer.

"If the girl hasn't got anyone else then who am I to turn her away and call myself a woman of God? But I swear, boy, if you make me regret this—"

"Oh, no ma'am, but … uh, you may want to get your ole switch ready."

"I don't think I'll be spankin' my twenty-year-old son, Levi!"

He grinned, the dip in his mouth making his lip protrude at an odd angle. "Nah, but your fifteen-year-old daughter's boyfriend is comin' up the drive, there, and she'll be running for it in three … two … one …"

I spun around on my heels just in time to see Katie high-tailing it across the backyard toward the driveway. "Oh, hell!" I muttered under my breath as I picked up the fabric of my skirt and started running after her. "Katie! *Kathryn Annette*, you stop right there!"

She whirled around, her long brown hair flowing around her as she ran backward, her boots kicking up the dust. "I'm sorry, Momma! I'll be back before ten o'clock, swear it!" She screamed as she turned back toward Seth's car and jumped inside in a flash of cowgirl boots and long legs. I stopped running and stared as they raced down the driveway, a cloud of parched earth flying behind the car. Turning back to Levi, I let out an exasperated sigh.

"Y'all are going to be the death of me, swear *that*!" I yelled, turning and stomping toward the house. "Go get her, then. I'll have a place for her at supper. I swear, you damn hoodlums. Wouldn't give ten cents for the bunch of you!"

Levi's laughter faded as I grew closer to the house. The screen door slammed behind me, and I fought the urge to smile. If they inherited one thing from me, it was the undeniable desire to fight for what they wanted, with all of their hearts. It usually made me proud—at least, in the few times when we wanted the same things.

THIRTY-ONE

Unrude Awakening

Donna Rhodes

I t is 7:20 a.m. as she stares incredulously at the human being descending the stairs, his leaden feet fiercely colliding with each step. Could he truly have come from her womb, this silent human who slithers about the house, fuels up from the GE refrigerator, and drops word bombs that send his siblings crying from the room?

Is it true that at one point in his life, she taught him to talk and walk, feed himself, use the toilet, say please and thank you? How is it that he now speaks foreign words and slouches around autonomously? Reminders of designated chores, curfews, and homework are met with vile responses like "Don't be so cringe! Why aren't you dope like Martin's mom?" among some of the more repeatable phrases.

Cringe? Dope? Yes! You just made me cringe, and yes, I feel like a dope trying to have a conversation with you!

It is 7:25 a.m. and he rummages through the pantry, grumbling inaudible tones under his breath. Her eyes bore into him, trying to imagine the feeling of his swaddled body against her neck, followed by his sticky peanut-butter-and-grape-jelly hand in hers, and those wet, sloppy, toddler kisses he slathered on her face. Did he really used to cry when she would leave the room?

She follows him as he lugs his body through the kitchen. Her view becomes purple boxer shorts barely hiding his bum, his head swallowed by the refrigerator. As hard as she tries, she cannot trace the transformation of her sweet little boy into this . . . this rude stranger. When did the dreaded evolution occur, or more appropriately, the digression?

It is 7:30 a.m. and her eyes follow him as he ascends the staircase, two steps at a time.

It is 7:40 a.m., five minutes after the agreed-upon time, when the front door slams shut and he is sucked into a gray Toyota that speeds away, the offspring of the *dope* mom behind the wheel. "Bye! Have a nice day. Love you too!" floats through the empty air followed by a sigh and eye-

roll.

The betrayal makes her feel alone and cold and heart sick.

It is 3:15 p.m. when she runs through the parking lot and into the emergency room entrance. She waits impatiently until a nurse escorts her through the double doors. "Third curtain on the right."

It is 3:15 p.m. and behind the third curtain on the right a sixteen-year-old boy is asking for his mom.

THIRTY-TWO

You Sneak In

Ania Ray

You always sneak in like it isn't your house. Like a paranoid burglar careful not to reveal her next step, you slip off the shoes you have worn for a decade. You tell me they're comfortable - reliable - so why spend hard-earned money for blistering leather? But we both know the truth: you'd rather pay for the foundation of my life than for the foundation of your calloused feet.

My thin bedroom walls echo the clink of spoon against glass against table top. Like you, it can't help but rest its bottom, wrinkled hand pressed up to firm back. I try to focus my eyes to the words floating on the dim-lit screen of my laptop, sentences flowing like the water you will watch filling the bucket tomorrow morning, because it's not enough to clean other people's houses. You want your own to glisten, too.

Books and stray pages cover me in a cocoon of paper and I rearrange my body to straighten the knots forming around my spine. I begin to crack my knuckles, but stop to keep the sound from interrupting your hushed it's-finally-me time. Have you ever noticed how the kitchen converts to a library when you sit there? The spritz of lemon travels from your tea beneath my door to tickle my nostrils and I think of home. But do you? I know you see Lysol more than you see me. I close my eyes and listen, praying that you won't open the door tonight. I wouldn't be able to digest the distaste in your eyes as you'd scan the mess around me.

As you make your way to the bathroom, I hold my breath. Your steps creak, a stark contrast to Morning Mom. Then, you move briskly, a waitress preparing her dining room, pouring tea for the thermos I'll carry to my 9:40 class. I'm no longer a child, but you say I'm still your baby. How is it possible your eyes sparkle like you slept for hours, and the bags under my own are so drawn? You must understand my weariness, but is it the same tired you are feeling tonight? With everyone asleep, the burdens of the buckets you carry and vacuums you drive are now the weights around your swollen ankles. The water runs and I exhale. The bristles of the toothbrush reach deep dental crevices like your duster did a few hours ago. The bankers and lawyers shouldn't complain tomorrow - er, today.

When you shut the water off, I lean over to switch off my light. The bathroom door opens and I lay my head down, my laptop winking shut, too. I told myself I would work hard at school so I wouldn't have to work like you one day.

But I seem to have made my bed a library table and tea is what I need right now. I'll wait till the morning, though; you add just the right amount of lemon.

––––––––

The clinking of glass and silverware stirs me awake. Papers and books are in a neat pile on the floor next to me and a blanket hugs me tight. When I open the door, you are in the kitchen, sweeping. You lean the broom against the wall to embrace me. The tea is already made.

Justice | Vengeance | Revenge

Part Four

She Versus The Universe

By Sasha Snow

THIRTY-THREE

London

W.A. Ford

Double deckers roar
Streets roll on
Numb hands clutched
A recipe
Devour all that exists

Positive sighting
Lit and alone
Eager hands creak
Sleek circles
Shark in home waters

Jewels adorn
Vulnerable necks
Nervous hands flutter
Compliments and curtsies
Trust earned in cycles

Elegant strokes

Budding artist
Graceful hands dance
No splatter
A success worth celebrating

Secret and lovely
A tiny thrill
Prim hands immersed
Wounds widen
Advantage over bond

The flow clots
On grass and stone
Trembling hands caress
Unfortunate soul rushed
Into the spirit

Strange eyes watch
No fear, no challenge
Guilty hands still
The other smiles
We should be together

Fluttering lashes cast shadows on cold skin
An unusual detail to notice on a stranger.
Dreams and denial war on the frostbitten face

It is not my war, but I refuse to look away.
Trembling lips release stuttering puffs of air.
I train my ear and lean closer

Madmen see truths beyond the light of day.

London

I strain to hear insight, warnings, meaning.
A string of names and a number on repeat.

I retreat and refocus on his humanity,
These are not souls I know and cannot offer allegiance.
He limps on, betrayed and defeated.

THIRTY-FOUR

A New Home

Shrutidhora P. Mohor

I love the tiny waves and the sound of soft splashes that they make as they belly-land on the rocky shore here. Their edges glisten momentarily before they get absorbed into the dry crevices of the boulders or simply get sucked in by the sandy soil. For many years, I watched this with sparkles of amusement in my eyes. Ever since I moved in here with him, my attachment for the water body, a major river flowing for miles from up north and about to meet the sea close to our home, has grown. I lived my days and nights by listening to its music, putting out my ears for a discordant note, a sudden missed beat, a false rhythm maybe, when on windy mornings the wind lashed on its surface, or on dark still evenings the prelude to a violent storm sounded like a sombre bass drumbeat on its surface.

He and I both shared this growing love for the river water. He was serious about his boat trips and fishing adventures, making it a point to sail away twice or thrice a week. I was an untiring watcher of the changing colour palette on the top layer of the river water and often tried to keep a count of how many shades of the same colour reflected there during sunrises and sunsets. A lone pelican or a couple of storks flew in to look out for their next prey, their eyes sharp and swift with a hunter's instinct, the riverine worms and flies either cautious and lucky, or casual and unlucky, devoured within seconds. At times during days of turbulent weather the river appeared enlarged, its already wide expanse at the turn ahead near the mouth of the sea was threateningly marked by rising water. Gazing at the frightening spectacle of one or two boatmen hurriedly steering their vessels away to safety and hearing the whiplashes of waves create a disharmonic orchestra on the water, I covered my ears and half-shut my eyes even though I continued to peep through and watch the scary scene. There is a strange attraction in the fear of water as well, I told him on such occasions when he suggested that I come away from the window and pull down the shutters.

Such was my attachment for the river water that he often said, as I sat on the front steps of our home and watched the sky play out its colours on the water, affectionately touching my chin, "How about a villa right in the middle of the river? Where you will be surrounded by this canvas."

My eyes brimming with gratitude, love and mischief, I said, "Why not one below there? Inside the river? A cottage under the water, hidden from prying eyes and envious neighbours!"

He nodded. He was always understanding, attentive to my wishes and dreams.

In order to lessen my fear of water on bad weather days he sometimes let me tag along, in order to teach me swimming. I gripped his wrist, stood at the banks in waist-deep water, and refused to go in any further. "Your enchant-ment with water will increase when you learn to play with it," he said time and again. I curved my shoulder up playfully and said once in response, "I will! When we have the villa deep down there, inside." I pointed towards the unseen bottom of the river. Thereafter, we sat down to enjoy a drink, a gin maybe, or on some days, plain lemonade. In between sips I observed how every time I drank from the straw channel, intense bubbles gathered immedi-ately below it. A few moved to the brim of the glass, most settled below. "There! They drowned!" I put my glass down and clapped in celebration of imaginary murder.

From time to time we threw small parties in our garden overlooking the river. Moist breeze settled on crispy fried bacon. Our guests admired the view as they dug their forks into strips of it. I smiled at him, the one eternal smile of happiness.

One quiet summer afternoon he brought home one of his colleagues. I rushed to show her around, the garden, the river, the sky hugging it, and invited her over to watch the sunset unfold on the river water. Since that day she frequently comes over, invited at first, uninvited after the first few times. Each time she has found me either at the riverside or doing the chores inside the house but with my eyes on the baby waves.

"You love the river water, don't you?" She asked once.

"I could be a mermaid! It must be so cool and comfortable down there. Myste-rious too!" I replied. My head pushed back lazily at the mere thought of the exciting life that goes on under water away from our sight.

For the first few weeks it is true that I felt a little uncomfortable here. I was scared too. The noise of the current of flowing water was deafening. Whenever I put my head out my eyes fell on the swirl of the water. A thousand forms of marine life whose names I have never known and some of which I have only seen on National Geographic, thronged this place. Initially, it seemed like a web. I was worried thinking that if I step out I am bound to get trapped in its fine net. I imagined tentacles of shoots and roots encircling my feet and stamped the invisible obstructions away, looking panicked. The large creatures pushed forth aggressively, the water immediately above their mouths floating up and sinking down in rings of different sizes. The smaller ones huddled together hoping to be safe, or hidden alone behind a leafy plant or underneath a horizontally lain branch with sprouts of poisonous flowers at nodal points. I shuddered, thinking of my possible plight at the hands of any of these living organisms, plants and animals, and withdrew my head inside and promptly shut my eyes. The gushing sound of water crashed against the bed and the walls while I imagined being in the safety and comfort of my bedroom, warm and dry.

But I became used to it over the weeks. I befriended my new neighbours although I still did not exactly know their names or the names of the species to which they belong. I have in fact grown to love the cool atmosphere here. Now, I possess the vision appropriate for a lover of aquatic life. The surroundings are not just pleasant but quite charming. Wild water-plants adorn the side walls. Changing shades of green and blue and mauve and yellow cling on to thick moisture-filled creepers which look like colourful ribbons used for decoration on our last anniversary party. I smile as I admire the beauty around. See, I knew it! I want to tell him, the mystery of the deep down under is unparalleled! Such interesting living creatures, each one struggling to survive, looking out for prey and predators alike, such a fascinating life cycle at work!

I miss talking to him. I am sure he too does.

One day, I make a plan.

A plan to meet him.

I visualise a tunnel, a long one, its outside damp and slithery, but warm and cosy inside, something like a tube rail which will begin from here where I am and end inside our bedroom where he is.

I shall crawl through it, wading my way through creepers and stray willows and the occasional water-cobra pit, a dozen eggs waiting to be hatched, the mother cobra primitively protective, and then after a long dark journey I shall alight in our bedroom, right next to our bedside table. I shall embrace him from behind, a sudden surprise hug, and the green shoots on my arms will pass on to him. He will take out the thorn girdle stuck somewhere in my hair and throw it aside and ask me, "So, is the villa down there likeable?"

"I love it!" I shall say and pick up the thorn strap from the floor, loosened from a thorn bush down under, and put it around his head. I shall then take a step back and utter in reverence, "You are my Lord, you look just like Him!"

One of the best things about being down there is the reverse view of the world. Till some time back I have seen the world from up there. I had to lower my gaze to look at the waves, the plants floating on the surface, the sky enacting itself on the top layers of the river water. Now my view has changed. I love the way I can see the waves from the bottom, a distant reverse view of the sunrise and the sunset filtered through many sheets of water, of the roots of plants which grow on the surface of the water, of how the gentle breeze combs through the few inches of water on top, or the strong wind which tosses fiercely the waves making them frothy and sizzling.

I watch all that from below. I also love watching him, of course, especially at dawn.

He does not use a watch to see the time for setting sail. He knows it from the colour of the sky. The moment at which the sky assumes a mix of ink blue and ink blue-smeared pink is the moment for him. It is the right time to flip the coarse, thick age-old rope out of the short pole, heave a push to the old boat, dislodge the oars from their complacent postures leaning against the ground, and jump into the boat himself while steadying the direction with the measured rowing of the oars. On some days he does not need both the oars. There is probably a low tide or the water near the shore is murky, and the boat wobbles along smoothly by itself and by either of the oars. It is on such days that he arranges the fishing equipment with one of his hands while he steers the oar with the other. On days of high tide however he is all eyes on the waves as his boat slips uncontrollably into the water, and threatens to go adrift anywhere. The loud sound of displaced water hitting against the rocky shore-line appears to be like that of a forever-thirsty man gulping water down his parched throat. He concentrates on getting the boat steady and by the time he has negotiated the unruly waters of the high tide the sky has changed its hue to a splintered pink and yellow. The horizon bears signs of a possibility of a breakthrough but for quite some time thereafter it remains only as a possibility of daybreak. A line of mellow yellow starts to lighten up the horizon only when he has reached the deep seas and from the shore he and his boat look like an unreal moving dot on the crest of waves.

One day as he tugs at the last knot of the anchor and pushes the boat with his other hand into the water and himself gets ready to jump into the boat I cannot restrain myself anymore. The eggs of his ankles look like golf balls. I want to run my fingers over them. I want to rub my lips against them. It's been long, I say to myself and I extend my arms up through the lid of the iron trunk. I grab his feet and call out to him.

"Honey!"

He struggles to get free and tries to kick my hands off. I tighten my grip, pull him down towards me, he loses balance and falls. His boat wobbles away.

"There! It's going away! Go after it, honey! You swim well, go after it!" I nudge him mildly and point towards the boat floating away, the water beneath its surface disturbed into uneasy movements. "You know what, honey, since that day, the day when you told me I must learn swimming and forcibly held my head under the water for long and as I was sinking I saw a glimpse of your colleague at our balcony screaming something at you, her face nervous and her eyes as large as our goldfish bowl, I have *actually* learned how to swim well enough. Perhaps I am as good at it now as you are. Isn't that great? Now, hurry! Go for the boat! And do tell me if you need my help. I can overtake it fast! Faster than you too." I long for his appreciation. I anticipate his words of praise for my newly adopted skill.

He stares at me. His lips look like burnt straw. It pains me to see him paling into the state of a terrified, lifeless being. I want to comfort him. I adore the look in his eyes, as astonished as a man exploring the first signs of life on an alien planet. I dote on his expressions, as scared as a baby encountering for the first time the ominous grumbles of an overcast sky. I continue to look at him with unbounded attachment. It is then that it occurs to me that I have never asked him over to my new home. I bite my lips in regret. I move closer to him and stretch out my hands in affection.

"Honey, this is so remiss of me..." I mumble apologetically. "Please step into my new home. It's right behind us there. My home has to be your home too, doesn't it, sweetheart? Welcome home, honey. We have finally got a villa deep down under. Come!"

THIRTY-FIVE

Black Water

Zira MacFarlane

The sunlight blazed. The forest hummed. Creatures thronged around the man until he walked into the clearing. He had helped the local godbotherer cut these trees, to burn the stumps and salt the roots. All the better to create a space to talk. No order for the man, no life for the god, just dead earth-an even field for all. His bare feet felt the moss of the forest floor give way to cinders and blades of wood. A charred shard of ironbark sliced his heel. Another wound. Penance. He had once shed blood and now bloody footprints followed him through life.

He stood in the clearing, bowed under the weight of what he had brought. Gifts, tools, and precautions. Little things to trade for safety, once owned by those lost to these woods. Maybe that alone would be enough to buy his wish. The godbotherer had told him how much gods loved to trade.

He placed a carved wooden footstool in the centre of the clearing. It had been made for him by a lover. The lover had had little skill for woodwork, but he was fond of it. Every time he ran his fingers over the flowers etched into it, he remembered the softness of that man's skin, the roughness of his lips, the smell of roses and coarse moonshine steeped into his clothes.

He took a seat on the stool-after all, even taking a seat offered by a god could be dangerous-and he waited. At the highest point of the sun, a child walked into the clearcut.

The man's heart sank; he knew the form the god had stolen. Quin had gone missing several moons before. No body had ever been found. But this wasn't the Quin who had blessed their village with cheer and mischief. This thing looked broken. Pale skin, fixed smile, eyes that wept black water. It bypassed the offerings and spoke.

"Ah, Anders, it's been so long." Alongside the dead voice was a trickling of ichor from its mouth.

"I come to you again, in a place of bargain. This is not your swamp, there are no waters here but what you bring. However, I come to ask for absolution. I have suffered for my sins. I wish them to be gone."

"And what do you offer in return?"

"Entertainment? A game of skill, of wits? I've brought several."

"An interesting idea, but what's the fun in wits? How about-"

The broken child paused. Anders felt the drip of rain patter on his head and shoulders, slickly creeping down his spine. It was strange, almost oily. He kept the entity in his eyes as best he could, not blinking, barely breathing.

"A test of courage? You do pride yourself on being a stoic. Just look at those feet of yours. Do you think that nothing can scare you anymore?" It chuckled, almost like a brook, black water pouring from its mouth. "Can you speak your sin? Feel its weight in my eyes, speak it in my tongue? Can you do it without one scream?"

Anders blanched. He felt his heartbeat quicken, his tongue thick and heavy in his mouth. His first effort to speak came out a hoarse squeak. And he felt something stir within him. He coughed, gagged, drops of black water sprayed from his lips. It was as though there was a storm swelling within him, being released with each effort at speech.

"I… I killed my lover." As he spoke, Anders sobbed and retched, tears flowing from his eyes, black water from his mouth in spurts and jets, mingling together on the ground. But he did not scream. "I killed Aeron. I heard the song in his heart. I saw the flowers in his hair. I knew that he could never be mine unless that song was quenched, and I killed him." The rain was falling faster now, his back was soaked.

"Oh, but that's not all the truth, is it?" The broken child leaned closer, suddenly inches from his face. "You were afraid. You gave the body to me." Its skin had paled, its teeth had shifted, sharp and straight like some strange fish. It stared into him, voided black eyes crawling across every wrinkle and blemish on his skin and soul. "You wanted to be sure no one found it, and you made Aeron mine, that man who loved freedom and joy. That man who loved you, you made him mine."

"Yes! Yes. I gave his flesh to you. I beg to be absolved. Please!"

The relentless flow came to an end. He could taste turpentine and tar, brackish water coating his tongue, sliding down his throat. He coughed, vomited, kneeling, hands on the footstool to steady himself. The rain had not yet stopped, but there was a new scent to it, floral, sickly, almost rotten.

The broken child was on the other side of the clearing, as if it had never moved. Face back to that of Siani and Tristan's Quin. It smiled sweetly, and blinked. "Of course! You were very brave."

Anders heard the sarcasm dripping from the words but started to breathe more easily. The gods did like their games.

Its head snapped towards him again. "Mind you, I can't absolve you. You never sinned against me."

Anders realized that it was no longer looking at him. It was not smiling at him. It was smiling at something above him. Shit. When had the trees closed in like this? Where was the light? The bloody ashen mud beneath him was churning, stinging the cuts in his feet. He could hear the songs of insects, strange birds, stranger frogs. And there was still the rotten scent of flowers in the air. He looked up.

"Hello... love..."

A familiar face, with the rents he had carved across it. Dead flowers, woven into a tangled mass of hair. A maw, split like an eel's, steadily dripping black water. A smile with all its warmth now gone.

Aeron looked down at Anders, watched his old eyes flicking back and forth, trapped in that drowned, wretched vessel that had once been his. Long tangled hair, rotten flowers ready to dissolve at a touch. Cold, wet skin. Cold, dead eyes. He could see Anders's fear in them. Wondered if the gaping wounds still hurt, wondered if the fire of breathless lungs still burnt in his chest. Wondered if Anders's soul could feel the memories of that body drifting far beneath the surface.

"How long will he live?" Aeron asked the god. "Will he ever pass over?"

The Black Water, form still overflowing from the body of Quin, perched on Aeron's old chest, poking at Anders's eyes. It dragged a finger down his cheek, splitting the weathered skin, showing waterlogged flesh and fat. Aeron felt his new body shiver, its gorge rise. He turned his head slightly and choked a cry back.

"Oh, I'll let him have a long life. He did win his little test of courage. I'll even help fulfill his deepest desire. He now owns you. Or your flesh at the least.

And what good would I be if he could not enjoy it for a very, very long time." It prodded at the dead face again. "I left him his eyes, all the better to see the fruits of his passion."

"And what would you do with him?"

It shrugged. Surprisingly human in its indifference. When Aeron couldn't see its face, the back of the child looked just so, just a child playing.

"The pile of flesh? It belongs to him, not me. No longer forgotten, now back with those who knew it." It clutched at Anders's jaw, forcing the head this way and that, peering over the wounds. There was a ghastly cracking sound as the skull swivelled on the neck. "Take it, leave it, no different to me. Do you want to forget him? Do you want to forget that flesh and the past it holds?"

Aeron smiled; he knew that the god wanted to offer kindness. "Never. Those wounds will always be a part of me, though my flesh no longer has them. That flesh will always have been mine, even though it is now his. Thank you for your compassion, but my past is mine, and I would never have it any other way."

"Ah, I suppose that I have carried these bones to those who loved them, and with that my work is done." The Black Water laughed, a chuckling brook, both aged and melancholy and fresh and joyful. "Farewell, Aeron. Visit me again. I do so love those who know me." The child lay back on the earth, waters swelling around it. The ashen mud crept over its face, ichorous water dragging it beneath the surface.

A brief voice, echoing from the sounds of life around. *"A gift for me, and a gift for you. I'll be taking this. Such a beautiful memory."*

The footstool that he had once gifted to Anders had begun to sprout, fresh green vines and leaves surrounding what was now both a sapling and a stump. Something old and something new, very much its leitmotif. As Aeron watched, the sapling grew to a bud, a bulb. It quivered, bursting open to show purple and gold, a single flower. He sighed, reaching out and plucking it. The love of a god. Something to cherish.

The Black Water had left puddles in its passage, one was flat and wide enough to gaze into. Study his new reflection. Short hair, now sandy blond. His creased mouth, which he'd so often made laugh before. The rough lips that he had heard speak such tender words. A handsome nose, broken in several places – Anders had often "defended Aeron's honor", whether he'd wanted him to or not. Burn scars, pockmarks from working hot metal. Several proud piercings, his brow, his lip, a bar across the shell of his ear. He stroked his face, coarse stubble pricking his coarser fingers, and twined the flower behind his ear. An old face, one that he had adored. It would take some effort to get accustomed to wearing it himself.

As he gathered up a set of vines, growing fresh at the forest edge, he couldn't help but laugh. That old godbotherer knew more of the bottles of her sanctuary than the arts of the godlike. After all, how could you purge life from a place? Creating space, creating order, that was an eternal climb up a gravel slope. As his new feet stung, he also questioned how one thought that blood shed out of volition washed away that which was shed from violence. Anders's penitence was so very like him, so very on his own terms.

Aeron tied the vines into a rough net. He put his hands under the armpits of his old body, saw Anders's eyes staring up at him.

"Worry not, old love. I'll find somewhere for you to rest. Somewhere with beauty, somewhere quiet. Maybe you'll find peace in my old bones." He smiled, he could feel the weight of his grief, but its burden was bearable. "I think I'll find you some place amongst roses."

Storyweaver, guide my steps and sing my path.
Wolves, run with me and my heart will burn with Joy.
And if I should be lost, Black Water, carry my bones to those who love me.

-- The Petitions of the Wanderer
Aeron's Prayer

THIRTY-SIX

Chopin in Candlelight

M.C. Rodrigues

Thunder rumbled in the middle of the night.

The woman, however, did not stop the music. Her hand's movements, broad and intense, at no point were shaken by the growl of the storm, or by the thick droplets of rain that crackled in hasted *stacattos* over the roof of the theater. They resounded in such a manner that if the man standing beside her did not focus his hearing, it would not be possible to listen to the details of the beautiful piece she performed.

Chopin's Nocturne, opus 9, number 1. How fitting.

"Keep playing, *ma chère,*" the man purred over her ear and laid silky kisses on her neck. The woman sighed.

The song weaved below her fingers, in precise tuplets and trills that brought a satisfied grin to the man. It was his favourite song. It craved perfection.

His lips strolled over her neckline until they settled on her heaving cleavage. The *pianissimo* cadences quickly grew in a fiery crescendo until she hammered ecstatic chords that echoed along with her moans as the man sneaked his hand under her dress.

"Are we alone?" she pleaded in a faltering whisper.

"Yes. Not even the Phantom of the Opera would dare disturb us in my theater."

A second thunder reverberated, and the lights flicked in menace.

"Careful, love, he might hear you and drop the chandelier over us," she teased. The man chuckled.

"Are you afraid of ghosts, *ma chère?*" He slid his fingers deeper up her inner thigh, ripping a blissful lament out of her.

"Never..." The woman's voice was barely audible. "Not while... not while you're with me."

Thunder blasted a third time. A primeval roar that shook the very foundations of the old building and killed the lights for good.

"Merde," the man whined as they were both engulfed in darkness. "Stay here, *ma chère,* I have some candles in the back."

"Candles?" She put the hem of her dress in place, covering her bare legs. "Is it safe with this much wood and cloth around us?"

"A fuse must have blown, but I'll have to wait until morning to change it. Don't worry." He placed one last kiss over her shoulder. "It's perfectly safe."

The man ambled across the place, his unwavering steps creaking over the wooden floor until he reached backstage. He did not need the light to orient himself. He was familiar with the distance between every door and knew where every pin was placed inside his theater.

It did not take long for him to reach the drawers of a closet, where several candles were stashed for eventualities. The man brought the thick beeswax stubs and placed them ritualistically around the piano. The rip of a match cut through the darkness as he distributed the fire through the stubs, one by one.

Flickering flames filled the penumbral stage in haunting shadows and hellish orange lights. The woman in the red satin dress, flushed and slightly disheveled by their former action, looked absolutely ravishing sat by the grand piano in candlelight. He thought the image was splendid.

"Now, *ma chère,* play it again."

The wailing notes of the Nocturne filled the theater again, its melody frayed by the constant murmur of the storm. The piece sounded like a recording from a gramophone, the man thought.

He let the woman tend to her technique-no lustful distractions this time-and reveled in the music. Eyes closed, head tilted back, and a smile on his face. The last chord sequence dropped in an agonizing *fortissimo* that dimmed like faltering flames occasionally blown by a breeze until it faded, dissipating in the air. He could almost grasp the ineffable remains of that last subtle note.

"Brava," he announced between slow resounding claps, before pulling the woman into a lavishing kiss.

They almost knocked down the piano stool in their desire, as the man pinned her against the floor and made his way through her skirts once again. The woman heaved and agonized below him, her voice filling the stage in a daunting crescendo until exploding in a high long note of golden ecstasy.

A flick of metal glinted in the man's right hand.

In swift and precise motion, he slid the silver razor in a line over the woman's neck. Her hands trembled and hurried for the wound, but he held them in place as the blood squished through the cut and bathed the man's face. A few seconds is all it took for the light to leave her eyes, eternizing the pleasure mixed with horror on her beautiful face. Such a sight made the man finally squirt himself inside of her.

The man gasped for air for a moment or two and got up, admiring his latest work. He was covered in red, deep and bright as the late woman's satin dress. A sadistic smile took his thin lips. Now they matched. He loosened his collar and sat back at the piano, for his pitch-black heart craved for music.

Chopin filled the murder room once again. The blood pool spilled and dripped over the stage, but the killer did not mind. He would fix that in the morning, along with the burned fuse. Now it was time for a celebration.

An image flashed in the dark.

The killer blinked to be sure, but the comer by the curtains was as empty as ever. He shook his head. The excitement pumping in his veins was making him see things. But then, near the scenery panel, there it was once again.

This time, the killer jolted up.

"Who's there? Show yourself!" he howled, but again, the mirage disappeared.

He did not sit. The hair in his arms prickled, and the nape of his head glazed ice cold. The killer was not superstitious. Why, then, was he feeling this way?

"Are you afraid of ghosts, *mon chèr?*"

The killer's eyes widened in astonishment.

It was the first woman. The one pianist he followed for months in his longing youth until he realized what he hungered for was more than the flesh between her legs. There she was, dashing long hair, astute eyebrows, and a silky gown, as if she had not aged a day. Her image, however, was translucent.

It did not prevent the first woman from leisurely strolling towards him. "I am not afraid of things from beyond. You cannot touch me."

The ghost smirked. "Are you certain?"

The killer dropped stiffly over the piano stool against his will. As much as he would fight it, he could not get up. His arms gruesomely raised in front of him and rested on the marble keys. His skin felt glacial, like he just took a dive into a frozen lake.

"How are you doing this?" he spat.

Answering his question, another figure appeared. The second woman, holding him down by his shoulders. A third set of hands held his right arm, a fourth held his leg, then the fifth, the sixth, and so forth. All of his women, trapping him.

The ghost's faltering expression twisted in a victorious smile as she approached, leaning until her face was only a disturbing inch away from him.

"Now, *mon chèr,* play."

As if controlled by a puppeteer, the killer's fingers resumed the absent melody and Chopin's nocturne echoed, again and again, until his digits ached.

The first woman circled around him, listening to the music. Her countenance was unreadable. After countless rounds, she strolled to one candle, sticking a translucent barefoot by the stub.

Her face twisted in a devious smile.

The candle tilted to the side, spilling its flame across the stage. It wasn't long before the fire spread. Wood creaked and charred, fabric crisped to cinders, and metal sizzled and blazed alight.

The man, however, kept playing.

He did not stop when the fire reached the piano and the cords were consumed, plunged one by one in dissonant shrieks. He did not stop when the flames glued the sole of his shoes to his feet, turning them into an amalgam of burned skin and leather. He did not stop when his fingers filled with crimson blisters, when the stench of carbonized fat was too nauseating to bear, not even when he convulsed after inhaling too much carbon monoxide.

The music stayed, long after the killer was gone.

An accidental fire was what the newspapers announced the day after. An incautious theater owner who placed candles on his stage and scorched himself and his mistress along with the building.

A tragedy soon to be forgotten.

The ruins of the old theater were later turned into a store complex that burned to the ground after a reckless employee decided to smoke next to highly flammable goods. Then, it became a supermarket that was incinerated after an electric malfunction, until people deemed the site cursed and gave up on it.

In every incident, rumours speak of a melody that was heard within the flames. Sinuous and lurking, like a haunting lament.

Chopin's nocturne, opus 9, number 1.

THIRTY-SEVEN

False Moon Rising

The Gathering

Tía Lorena picks up on the third ring. "Nora, what's the matter? Did you have another fight with Nathan?"

Nora climbs down the withered deck to the beach. She steers clear of the burnt offerings, a small pile of charred fish bones and melted candle wax.

"It's not going to work, Tía," Nora says miserably. "He still doesn't want to talk about it. Coming to the beach house was a mistake. I'm sorry for putting you and Tía Kata out."

In a warm tone, Tía Lorena says, "Are you apologizing because you need to or because you couldn't receive one?"

Nora wipes a tear from her cheek. "I don't know," she says honestly. "I thought coming here would make things better. I actually thought he would put in the effort and change, but he still talks to her. He's not even hiding it anymore. I don't think we're going to last the weekend."

"Be patient," Tía Lorena says. "Kata and I made sure the ritual was done exactly as Tatarabuela showed us."

Nora lets out a skeptical laugh. "Tía, at this point, I don't even think brujeria can save our marriage."

"Have faith, mijita," Tía Lorena says. "It's a new moon tonight, and a new moon means new beginnings."

Nora groans. "Have faith in what? On some dead fish and some scribblings Tartarabuela left us? Sure we prayed, but how is that going to fix anything, Tía?"

The line goes quiet for a moment.

"Mija," Tía Lorena says sternly. "Our prayers do not fall on deaf ears." Her words were heavy with meaning. "Did you leave your offering on the ofrenda like we told you?"

Nora reaches for the back of her neck, and wraps her forefinger around a lock of hair. Recently cut.

"Yes, Tía. She has her precious lock of hair."

"Then be patient, Mija. Your part is nearly done." Tía Lorena says.

The conversation ends and Nora slips her phone into her back pocket. A shiver crawls up her legs and over her spine, but she doesn't go inside.

Nora breathes in the briny air, letting it fill her lungs until it hurts, until her breaths match the tempo of water meeting earth. Something about being at the beach house peels away a layer of her anger and frustration and washes it away with the lull of the crashing waves. Her body eases and settles, and she swears she can hear a hum between her exhales and the roaring tide.

In the distance, a single globe of light rises over a cresting wave. With curious fascination and awe, Nora watches it ascend, breaking the horizon line and over the blanket of stars.

A new moon rises from the sea and Nora realizes it's heading to shore, toward the beach house.

Nora wavers, unsure as the globe of light teeters before falling and disappearing into a wave. She doesn't know why, but she has to be there when it comes ashore.

Nora's gut wrenches, fearful for that small light struggling. Nora rushes toward the water.

Her heart knocks against her ribs as another wave topples over and snuffs out an aura of jade green light under the water.

"Hey," Nora says, shouting. "Hey!"

Nora's bare legs crash into frigid water. She cries out.

The deck lights flicker behind her and Nathan's shadow appears on the deck.

Nathan calls for her, but Nora can't hear him, the hum and the thrashing of water drowns him out.

Wading through the water, Nora sees a woman emerge from the seafoam lying prostrate on the wet sand. The woman is young and naked, her body draped under a tangle of inky black hair. For a moment, Nora wonders whether she sees the pale bioluminescent glow from the new moon surround the woman before it fades.

Nora goes to her knees and rolls The Woman over. Nora hesitates before pushing strands of hair from The Woman's face. When she does, honey-brown eyes meet hers. Nora's breath hitches at the indecipherable familiarity that jolts between them the moment their eyes meet. "Hola," Nora says as if greeting a loved one.

The Woman's lips, blue and chattering, twitch as if to speak.

"What?" Nora says gently, bringing The Woman close.

Instead of words, Nora feels the imprint of a sharp smile and cold teeth press against her cheek.

—————

I met a lady in the meads,
Full beautiful—a faery's child,
Her hair was long, her foot was light,
And her eyes were wild.

—————

Nathan goes up and down the beach, his flashlight cuts up and down the black waves. Nora watches through the kitchen window until he disappears behind the seafoam-colored curtains. She pulls open a tin of Tía Kata's dried chamomile and drops it into the kettle. The soothing aroma that blooms in the kitchen reminds Nora of childhood summers. She remembers picking the delicate flowers and searching for the faint perfume of belladonna. But that was a long time ago.

The wind outside begins to howl. If her tías were here they would soothe away the storm with hot chocolate dusted with cinnamon.

The kettle whistles. Nora picks out her favorite childhood mug from the cabinet. She pours the tea into the Little Mermaid mug before breathing deeply.

The Woman is curled up on the couch wrapped in a tasseled seashell blanket. Her black hair has dried into curls, framing her honey-brown eyes.

Nora can feel The Woman's gaze follow her as she moves across the room.

"I'm Nora," she says. She waits for a response but it never comes. "This is my tías' house," Nora holds out the mug. "Nathan, he's the one who carried you in, he's my husband."

The Woman wraps her fingers over Nora's and smiles with just a hint of teeth.

"What's your name?" Nora says.

Instead of answering, The Woman gently takes the mug, and sips the steaming tea.

"Oh," Nora says before turning to a small end table by the couch. She picks out a pen amongst bundles of dried wolfsbane, an herb that hangs over every doorway in the house. Nora pushes them aside and pulls out a stack of conch-shaped sticky notes. She holds them out to The Woman.

The Woman shakes her head. She taps on the mug.

"That's okay," Nora says. "All good things in time." Her tia's words ring in her head and out of her mouth.

The back door swings open and Nathan trudges in. He shrugs off his coat as he enters the living room. "I didn't see anyone out there. Not a soul."

"Really?" Nora says, surprised.

"Yes, really," he says, his voice snapping.

"I didn't mean anything by it," Nora says.

The Woman shifts forward and the seashell blanket slides down exposing her brown freckled chest and shoulders.

Nathan doesn't bother hiding how his eyes follow the curve of her neck or how they linger over the slope of her breasts. He digs his hands into his jean pockets so deeply, the buckle of his jeans glint.

"Can I talk to you alone?" Nora says to Nathan. She bites her tongue before she turns to The Woman and forces a smile. "I'll be just a minute."

The Woman takes Nora's hand and squeezes it, Nora squeezes back before letting go.

Nora's smile softens, tongue bruised.

Nora and Nathan disappear into the kitchen.

"What was that?" Nora says.

Nathan rolls his eyes. "Are we going to do this now? You're the one who invited her into the house."

"Well, we should call my aunts," Nora says.

Nathan leans on the kitchen counter and crosses his arms over his chest. "No, it's late. Why would we?"

Nora's shoulders deflate. "Well," she says, her stomach twisting.

"You're aunts wouldn't mind," he says. "It's the right thing to do."

176

Nora's mouth runs dry and her heart rises with every beat into her throat.

"Trust me, " Nathan says. He waits for Nora's answer. "Isn't that why we're here?"

"Okay." Nora nods. "You're right. I'll make up the guest room."

Nora turns to leave, her eyes downcast.

"I love you, Nora," Nathan says.

She doesn't answer.

He grabs her, gripping her forearm tightly.

Nora holds her breath.

His phone rings and Nora recognizes the ringtone.

"Are you going to get that?" Nora says under her breath.

The phone rings again before Nathan let's her go. Nora can feel the blood return to her arm and fill the imprint of his hand.

Nathan silences his ring tone, but his mistress's name continues to glow on the screen.

"Don't answer it," Nora says, something hot rises into her chest. "It's late."

"It's work," he says and brings the phone to his ear.

"Don't answer it," Nora says again. She looks him in the eyes, quiet and still. Her cheeks flushed.

"Hello?" Nathan says, answering the phone. "Let me call you back."

Nora leaves the kitchen and takes the keys from the clam bowl by the front door. "I'm going to get us some food," she says and takes her raincoat from the driftwood rack.

"Nora, wait," Nathan says. "It's pouring, I'll go."

"It's fine," she says and walks out the door. She lets out a deep breath and leans back against the front door. She hears Nathan speaking to someone else. The porch lights flicker.

Nora pulls the hood over her head and walks down the creaking porch steps to the car, but stops in front of the living room window.

The Woman is there. Waiting. The Little Mermaid mug in her hands, her black hair draped over her shoulders and chest; the blanket splits open.

"I'll be right back," Nora says. She can barely hear her own voice over the rain.

When the lightning strikes, the bioluminescent glow surrounds The Woman again, but disappears when the thunder rolls in.

The Woman's lips curve into a smile with just a hint of white teeth.

A flash of light and crash of thunder.

Nora's heart pounds and she runs out into the rain and to the car. Water pounds over the car roof and she quickly cranks up the heat. She plugs her phone into the dash and calls her tía. Tía Lorena answers on the first ring.

"I'm sorry it's late," Nora says, she holds the steering wheel so tightly her knuckles turn white.

"What's wrong, Mija?" Tía Lorena says. Nora can hear Tia Kata speak in the background. "Hold on, I'm putting you on speaker."

"Everything," Nora says miserably. "This was a mistake. I'm sorry, I'm really sorry." Her voice cracks and she wipes her eyes with a damp sleeve.

"Nora, tell us everything," Tía Lorena says.

"Start from the beginning," Tía Kata says.

Nora breathes in deeply, their voices like chamomile and hot chocolate.

I saw pale kings and princes too,
Pale warriors, death-pale were they all;
They cried—'La Belle Dame sans Merci
Thee hath in thrall!'

A torrent of rain runs down Nora's windshield as the smell of fish penetrates her car's upholstery. She stares out the window at the beach house and tightens her grip around the steering wheel. She doesn't want to go inside. Sighing, Nora grabs the bag and runs through the rain.

"I'm back," Nora says, calling into the void.

In the kitchen, she tears open the plastic bag. Popping open the styrofoam containers, she calls out again. No one answers, so she walks into the living room. The television is on but no one is there. "Hello?"

Nora checks the deck. Nothing. Nothing except a small pouch behind the family ofrenda. Guessing its contents from the pile her aunts left under the deck, Nora pushes the pouch back into place with her shoe. Nora enters the house once more when the clock strikes midnight. It's late. Maybe they went to bed.

Deciding to do the same, Nora stores the food in the fridge before heading for her room. When she climbs up the stairs, a distinctive chime tickles her ears. Nora stops. At the top of the stairs Nathan's cell lights up. Nora reads the display. Six missed calls and numerous unread texts.

Then she hears it. That familiar sound. After six years of marriage, Nora recognizes her husband's grunts, his moans, and the intake of his breaths.

He wouldn't. Not on our vacation. Not in our bed.

Trembling, she grabs the bedroom doorknob.

Nathan yells just as she opens the door.

"Ah, ah, ah," he says, panting.

Nathan and The Woman are sprawled naked on the bed. The Woman is on her back, her body sweetly relaxed under his as he jerks and pumps into her. With a final grunt he slips out of her, his member soft and glistening.

Nora holds her breath as Nathan trails soft and open-mouthed kisses over The Woman's chest. When his lips are just above The Woman's heart he latches on. He sucks the sensitive flesh into his mouth like a starving babe.

Nora looks up and The Woman is staring at her. Right at her. The Woman grins and wraps her legs around Nathan.

Something changes.

Nathan is now struggling against her thighs. His eyes widen as they meet Nora's but not in remorse. In fear.

The Woman's lips twitch and Nora catches a brief glimpse of teeth. Sharp. So very sharp.

Nathan groans. Another. And another. He groans into The Woman's flesh until the sound becomes a haunting scream, a one worded plea.

Nora shakes her head at the word. Her name. Nathan screams. The sound is muffled but Nora understands. Help.

Helpless, Nora watches as his mouth becomes fused to The Woman's skin. Saliva, tinted pink, drips out of his mouth and trails down her breasts.

The Woman undulates and her skin ripples. She sighs and a thin fleshy rod uncurls from her dark hair. It stands erect. At the end of this appendage, just above her brow, dangles a ball with a luminescence similar to a new moon. A false moon infinitely more beautiful in its purity.

Nathan panics. He scratches at The Woman's thickening skin, his nails flicking off as The Woman grins. And like the new moon hovering above The Woman's head, her skin begins to glow. This glow flows into Nathan. He struggles with all his might but The Woman flexes her thighs forcing his wet hips into hers. Tears fall down Nathan's face.

In seconds, his skin is death pale. In minutes, it's translucent.

Nora lets out a breath at the sight. Whether it be in her blood or the brujeria, she understands, she knows what must happen.

The change starts with Nathan's eyes. He doesn't need them. Not anymore. The Woman doesn't need them either for she has her own. So his eyes shrink until there is nothing there but a frightening emptiness. If Nathan could cry he would, but you need tear ducts for that and he has none. His stomach, intestines, bladder, lungs…He doesn't need those either.

The Woman grins a smile much too large for her face and extends her webbed hand. Nora lifts her hand in response. There is a brief flash of recognition before Nora blinks. Breathing heavily, Nora touches the short strand of hair behind her ear.

Such a small sacrifice.

She would do it again, she realizes.

She would have given more.

Slowly, Nora shuts the door.

In the kitchen, Nora grabs her keys and her phone from the clam bowl. She dials her tía's number. On the first ring, she is outside of the beach house. On the second, she is pulling open the car door. On the third ring, Tía Lorena answers.

"You were right," Nora says with a smile that shows just a hint of teeth. "About the new moon."

THIRTY-EIGHT

Fantaisie Française

Elaine May Smith

Françoise Labrune has been a chambermaid at The Pontchartrain Hotel in New Orleans for half of her thirty years, so she has a good idea what a man like you hopes for when he checks in for the night. She starts her shift extra-early, ignoring your "Do Not Disturb" sign, feeling a surge of excitement tingling through her supple body as she slips in, silently securing the lock. She knows just what to do before taking your breakfast order.

She tiptoes over to find you asleep in bed. You're half-awakened by her white linen apron chafing softly against her silky black skirt and her stiletto heels clicking delicately on the wooden floorboards. You wonder if you're still dreaming as she works her way around you, crouching briefly to gently rustle some papers into the trash. As she reaches to dust under your bed, just inches from your face, you catch the stupendous sight of her taut bosom squeezed into the lacy cups of a plunging brassiere, straining at the pearly buttons of her barely-opaque blouse.

You secretly watch her feather duster fluttering over every surface, and her lithe form stretching for the top of the wardrobe, causing her skirt to hoist just sufficiently for you to detect where her fishnet stocking meets her mouth-watering thigh. Your eyes follow the slit of her skirt up to the curvaceous beckoning of her buttocks, where the muscles expand and contract in rhythm with her handiwork. She pauses to sweep the ringlets of hair back from her glowing temples and strokes the beads of perspiration from the nape of her slender neck.

The golden bangles on her slim wrists are tinkling in the air and twinkling in the hazy morning sunlight as she bends over to polish the dresser mirror with a strong sense of purpose. You're torn between stealing a glance at her perfect reflected features and spying on her tantalising hips swaying within your reach. Turning to rest momentarily, she raises one foot onto the bedside table to adjust her garter-belt, allowing you to glimpse her satin French knickers, loose at the frilly edges and clinging tightly at the creamy epicentre, where you're curious to explore, long and deep.

You smell her irresistible scent infusing your potent body. You imagine the sensation of her dexterous hands going to work with you under the covers. You're aching to press into those succulent breasts, to taste the delicious warmth of her pouting lips, and to grind yourself into her hot moist skin.

As she hears your deeply masculine desires becoming vocal and urgent, she clicks her way towards you, lifting her soft long lashes to meet your eyes directly with her own intense gaze, licking her lips in acknowledgement of the thirsty work she has performed, and in anticipation of the tasks yet to be demanded of her.

"Voulez-vous, Monsieur?" she asks coyly.

Your desperate demand, *"Drain me dry!"* is met with willing submission, as she kneels and sinks her fangs in your neck.

THIRTY-NINE

Fly Bait

Zira MacFarlane

*C*lang.

The hammer again. Audrey staggered from their bedroom into the forge. The wasted figure stood, sunken eyes blazing with fear, before the red-hot anvil. His arms, so strong and sure before he left to fight on foreign shores, now shook under the hammer's weight. She scrambled over to him. He hadn't begun to scream, not yet.

Sparks were worming over his skin. The leather apron had slipped. Underneath he was naked. He shuddered as his mouth worked without sound, a thin dribble of blood where he'd bit his lip. He was hearing *them* again.

"Robin." Half choked on coal smoke, burnt hair, sweat, scorching skin, Audrey spoke gently. "Robin, you're safe. I'm here."

His head whipped round, his voice an urgent hiss.

"Audrey! Get behind me! You're in the thick."

The flies. They came when the tinnitus was bad and then came hell, Gallipoli - the trenches, screaming horses, abandoned corpses, the mounds of dead, the mud, and the flies, the endless *fucking flies*. On the hottest days, flies blotted out the sun. And though she might not see or hear them, they had followed him home.

"Robin, my love."

His hands trembled as he swung the hammer. If she startled him on an upswing, he might let go and crack his skull.

"Lay the hammer down and come to me."

"The flies. I must drive away the flies. They bring the dead." The hammer fell from his hands, raising dust. He slumped to the side. His wasted frame shook with fever.

She carried him bodily to their time-weathered riders' bench. While he'd been away, she had kept the forge, growing strong. In turn the war had consumed him, till he was but a husk. She sat there all the night, cradling him like the babe they'd never had. His body twisted against her, quietly whimpering, mumbling fragments of the war that clung to him, that clawed at his mind and stalked his dreams. The coals burned to ash as the smoldering rage in her gut flamed anew. Tomorrow, tomorrow she would try again.

The bench provided by The Ministry of Pensions in the North was angular and narrow. Anything to discourage the poor bastards who'd survived Europe's bloody game of empires. Audrey tried to soften her face and steel herself inside as she waited between a hard-eyed widow and a soldier who sang low as he scratched at the stump of his left arm.

"Robin Winters."

A slack-faced, portly man, missing the laugh lines common to his age, called from behind a barren desk. He barely glanced up at her approach.

"Clearly, you are not Robin Winters."

She swallowed, tried to smile politely.

"Robin is dreadful ill. I'm the wife. Pleased to make your acquaintance."

"What brings you then?"

"I need to plead his case again, sir. With the malaria and the tinnitus and the shellshock, my husband's an awful wreck." She faltered under his dispassionate stare. One last gamble. Robin would hate her, but what else could she do? "He can't work. If he keeps on, he'll hurt himself. A military pension-"

"File says he's a blacksmith. Good trade. Fox hunting begins next week."

"Sir, it's dangerous. He sees things. He sees the dead come back for him."

"How fitting. His file indicates he was a coward." November frost in tweed. Not a twitch of compassion. "Lucky to be alive. Spinelessness is best dealt with on the field. Summary justice."

Her stomach burned. He cut her off before she could protest.

"Find a priest. Absolution might ease his soul. Don't come back." A vicious smirk danced around the corners of his mouth. "I've half a mind to tell the Peelers about him. They hate cowards, especially lazy Irish riffraff trying to weasel out of an honest day's work."

She tamped down her fury. Imagined snapping the bastard over her knee like a badly wrought paling. Left. She'd do Robin no good from gaol.

———

On the path to the forge, she smelled her husband's fear. Gunpowder. Blood. A low buzzing. Flies hovered at the door. Her nape prickled, her eyes frozen wide. Every sound seemed too loud.

"Robin?"

Maybe he truly *was* hounded by the dead. She could smell the corpses, crawling back for him. Swallowed. Felt her throat stick. Stepped into the forge.

There. On the bench. Sprawled like he was waiting for his horse to be shod. Service pistol still hanging from his hand. Head tipped back like he was napping. Sandy hair, clotted red, white bone. Wall behind him slick and black, glinting orange with flickering flame.

She fell back on her haunches. Called out his name. Tears spattered a half-worked horseshoe in the dirt. The dead had claimed him after all.

She sat on the rider's bench all through the night in the light of the dying coals, holding him close as her anger roared.

———

At dawn, Audrey rose. Washed the body, laid him out on the kitchen table, read the poems. Keened. She poured the salt and earth onto his chest, placed tobacco for the journey in his hand. She kept his soul as best she could. But her sadness was poisoned by fury, leaving no heart to celebrate the life that had been stolen.

A knock. The slack-faced man from the ministry stood in the doorway, a grey horse spattered with mud limping round the yard behind him.

"Terribly sorry, I was passing your forge and my horse cracked a shoe. Luckiest place for it, I suppose. How much for a new one?" His eyes narrowed; lips pursed as he studied her further. Stared at her, draped in forge leathers and Robin's cast-off clothes. A far cry from the glad rags she'd dragged from deep in her closet just yesterday. "Say, you're that Irishman's wife, correct?"

Audrey paused, gritting her teeth before she managed to speak.

"He's away."

"Drowning his sorrows, is he? Bring him here, I'll wait. If he can't do his job, he'll face the penalties of those who feign illness. You'll thank me for it in the end, mark my words."

She stared into his face, gorge rising.

"I can help. Just follow me, bring your horse."

She hitched the mare at the shoeing post, trimmed the hoof and pried off the broken shoe. More cast iron than wrought. Melted down scraps likely. Shoddy work. The man settled on the rider's bench. Right where she'd found Robin.

"Hard work and God, that's what he needs. Not charity."

Audrey found a horseshoe in the forge. The last one Robin made. She laid it on the anvil. Took up his hammer. Swung high. Smiled. In earnest this time. She'd grown so very strong in the years since she had seen her husband off to war.

"For Robin."

Crack of bone. Spray of blood.

"For me."

She swung again. Radiant in her anger and her joy.

When she was done, she tied his foot to one stirrup and sent his horse scrambling down the empty road. She scrubbed down the forge and the bench once more. Swatted away the flies as she worked. Damn, but they could breed fast.

It was a damp day, hot for September. There was a low droning all around her. She returned to Robin's shrouded body, to start his lonely wake. To celebrate a life. To mourn its loss. To cherish every memory of his love and his pain.

FORTY

Sprinkles

Ednor Therriault

S he turned off the bedside lamp in her Utah motel room. The cool, clean sheets felt good after a long day on the freeway, and she fell asleep in less than a minute.

Just after midnight the closet door swung open silently. He stepped out into the room and stood motionless for several moments, listening to the steady rhythm of her breathing. In the moonlight that filtered through the gauzy curtains, he could see her chest rise and fall under the blankets. He felt himself relax.

Checking the door to make sure it was locked, he walked over to the side of the bed. He carefully picked up a pillow and folded it around the .22 automatic in his right hand. He always used the .22 because it rarely exited the skull once it entered. No muss, no fuss.

She startled him by taking a quick, snuffling breath, then she rolled over to her other side. But still she slept.

"Sarah," he said.

"Hmm," she said, still sleeping. Then she jerked awake and saw him. Scooting back against the headboard with a gasp, she covered her bare breasts with the sheet. He smiled, the dim light revealing the contours of his face. Yes, he thought. She recognized him. He raised the pillow-wrapped gun.

"Why…" she said.

He pulled the trigger and there was a muffled pop. The slug entered her head just above her right eyebrow, leaving a neat little black hole. She hadn't even put a hand up to ward off the bullet, like most of them do. She fell over on her side, and a stream of blood slowly leaked across her forehead onto the clean white sheet.

He threw the pillow on the floor and put the gun in his coat pocket. From his other pocket he withdrew a small white paper bag. Inside the bag was a chocolate donut. He pulled out the donut with a gloved hand and took a bite.

Walking slowly around the bed, he looked at the woman while he ate the donut. Crumbs and colorful sprinkles fell onto the carpet and the bedspread. That was okay. That was the whole idea.

Instead of popping the last bite into his mouth, he dropped it onto the carpet in front of the bathroom on his way to the door. He brushed the crumbs from his hands, buttoned up his long coat and looked around the room. Nothing amiss, outside of the nude, dead woman in the bed. He smirked and walked through the door, pausing momentarily to make sure it clicked shut behind him.

FORTY-ONE

The Cough

Andy Schmidt

The sound of it jolts me awake. The loathsome break in the night suffocates my ears, my mind. I cannot help but listen to the nauseating mixture of mucus and blood tickle his lungs and escape into the muggy air. I hear his pain in every breath, each a terrible gasp for air, a fish out of water desperately gulping for a single drop. Revolting pity for this man drives my incessant insomnolence. I suppose I should consider myself lucky though. I can still breathe.

I check my pocket watch against the faint moonlight. Zero four hundred hours and still no more than a few winks of rest. The stinging sores on my neck are hard enough to ignore as ravenous insects gnaw my raw skin and feast on my blood night after night. But after a few weeks, the shrill buzzing and constant swatting became a normality. Harder still was learning to fall asleep with the uneasy feeling between dire rest and sudden wakefulness; never knowing what calm nights will be disturbed by a scream from your fellow soldier as a bayonet impales his sleeping stomach. These dirty holes in the ground where men sneak about eviscerating each other are something I never imagined I would experience. God truly has forsaken all on the island.

I've always been a heavy sleeper. Well, I used to be. My wife would tease me that I'd never wake to her elbow jabbing in my side as I hogged three quarters of the bed from her. She would find me fast-asleep at my desk with my head sunken in a pillow of leather-bound pages. All night I'd dream there, fantasizing that someday I would support my family by writing such enticing words as the ones my head rested upon. I'd even sleep through the cries of my two-year old, yearning for consolation after a nightmare. I still keep a photograph of the three of us embedded in the case of my watch. It's the one thing I own that isn't stained with dirt or blood anymore. My commanding officer walks by and notices my bloodshot focus on the photo. He kneels, resting a calloused hand on my arm. His eyes—rigid sapphires—catch the light in their many facets and connect with my own.

"You'll see 'em again soon, corporal. If we outlast those bastards just a little longer, we can all go home to our families and get outta this shithole. Now kick the lads up. We've got a lot of ground to cover today."

"Yes sir," I croak.

God, my throat is parched. I can only imagine how *he* feels.

I go to each soldier down the line and wake them. They groggily rise from the soil and collect themselves. He's the last one in the line, isolated from the others. We have to keep him distanced or we'll all catch it. That cough is a military casualty. Once it takes control you lose your aim, then your breath, then your sanity. The stertorous man's head is leaned away from me, obscuring his state of lucidity; his arms quiver and wearily clutch to his chest. I give him a gentle prod with the butt of my rifle, avoiding a direct touch.

"Sarge says we have to move on."

His head turns laboriously toward me. Sharp, steely eyes cut into me though drooping eyelids attempt to conceal them. The terrible rasping noise hardly suited the honorable man, much more deserving of lucky breath such as mine. A word attempts to escape his bloody, dry lips but the cough usurps his air. Poor bastard.

Another day of it. The anxiety, the shock, the rush, the kill. No matter how stealthily we crawl through the foliage we are never veiled, never safe. His cough always gives us away. We lost four men today, two the day before. How long has it been since they discarded us here? Six, seven weeks? I can barely keep track anymore. The major general predicted four days of deployment on the island. Just four days and the enemy would inevitably surrender. What a load of shit. I bet he barely gave a thought before impetuously sealing our fate with the ink of his pen. The major general clearly never muddied his boots with *this* enemy. He's never heard their horrific cry as they charge us, wild night beasts bearing bayonets or even sharpened sticks once their bullets deplete. Never seen the heaps of entrails and severed limbs scattered about after their wounded use precious last seconds to explode themselves when we get close enough to confirm casualty. No, they will never surrender.

Another night of it. The dirt, the bugs, the uneasiness, the cough. We spent the entire day trudging to a new position and this hole feels like the last. What does a man become without a restful moment? I lay my head on my rucksack and take out my watch again. The wan crescent hovers above me, shrouded in wispy layers of smoke. I can barely make out my family's smiles against its light, let alone recognize my own in the photograph. That smile is like the moon that illuminates it, a somber remembrance of brighter nights buried beneath smoke.

His cough pierces the night again. For God's sake, can I not have one minute of peace? Eventually the bout dies down, replaced by quiet, yet irksome wheezing. As much as that cursed man torments me, I cannot help but admire him. Through his pain he endures the bugs, the tension in the air, all of it. A real stoic. I still can't believe that a month ago he snuck into the enemy's bunker, unaccompanied, and massacred that entire squad. He's always been a quiet one. Well, he used to be. He secured us another week's worth of rations, ammunition, precious drinking water and a safe position that we didn't even have to dig for. Didn't gloat or anything. He's a damn hero. Much more of a hero than me, and he knows it.

Our first day on the island we attacked the main port village. Apricot hues glimmered atop the sea foam, reflecting incendiary artillery strikes as a great tidal wave of men crashed against the beaches. We charged through scorched and blackened streets decorated with mangled bodies and debris. Our swift momentum sliced through the enemy holdouts, hot knives through butter. The maneuver was brilliant, a tactical masterpiece until the enemy vanished. Standard lines and gunner positions were abandoned, but the village was far from empty. The bastards were out of uniform. Common clothes disguised them, malicious foes camouflaged amidst innocent civilians. Everything turned to disaster. Every dwelling became a threat. No one knew who to shoot.

Fire and chaos and a blurry scramble from one cover to the next. Searing gusts tossed floating embers around the air, periodically singeing the skin of my squadmate and I. We were separated from our unit, lost among flames, but somehow still together. The air cracked and a bullet ripped through my buddy's face. I dropped down and grabbed him by the armpits and pulled his body behind the only nearby cover, a thick bamboo fence. Another high caliber round struck our refuge and I peaked around to spot the sniper. A figure crouched by the side of a thatch-roofed hut—not yet ablaze and just down the road—aiming his rifle my direction. The edge of the fence splintered, wood chips blasted away and a loud crack slapped my ears a second later. Had the bullet been a few inches lower, I would have faced a similar fate to my friend, who I now looked down upon.

What was left of his jaw loosely dangled to one side by few remaining sinewy threads. His agonized scream gurgled through bubbles of lurid red fluid gushing from the immense cavity beneath his nose. My half-faced friend gaped up at me wide eyed, grabbing at my arms ferociously. The warm rush of blood cascaded down my hands and pooled beneath my knees. His dilated pupils rolled back into his head and he convulsed on the ground. I couldn't stop it. I tried to erase the grisly scene from my mind but my treacherous eyelids refused to shut. His seizure ended and the trembling in my bloody hands slowly quelled. His body lay there, unmoving save for the occasional muscle twitch and lethargic flow of blood still pooling beneath me. Two pairs of haunted eyes affixed to each other unblinkingly, one stale and lifeless, the other suspended between horror and wrath.

I broke cover and vengefully dashed towards the hut, leaving behind my companion's bloody cadaver. The side of the building was clear. The shooter must have moved to a new position, leaving only the smell of fresh gunpowder and burnt flesh to fill my nostrils. I heard the back door of the hut slam closed. I crept to the back and found a weathered door which was easy enough to kick down. Inside, a young child clung to her mother's charbroiled corpse. Hardly any traits of the woman were still recognizable except for a few ribbons of dark brown hair, weaved into an intricate style. Our fire bombs consumed her. Light from the doorway behind me shone on the woman and child, splitting into starry streaks as my tears welled.

A blurry shadow moved on the edge of my vision and I was tackled. We tumbled and my back slammed hard against the floor. Frenetic hands grappled around my neck and shoulders; a knee pinned down my groin. I wriggled under the weight and managed to slip my arms under the hold. All of those painstaking hours of training in hand-to-hand combat were finally being put to good use. I shoved his knee to the side and bridged my back, flipping my attacker as I whirled around and reversed our position. The man stared up at me, eyes bulging with vindictive rage. He appeared to be a common villager, dressed modestly, but there was something more to his strength and ferocity. This fucking bastard was one of them. The grisly image returned to me. A face with a crimson pit where a mouth should have been, strands of dangling fresh on the sides. We wouldn't even be here if they would just surrender. This village never would've burned. My beloved would stop worrying about her husband dying on some meaningless island. The poor burnt woman and her child, laying just inches away, never would've suffered if they would just *stop*.

I tightened my grip around his throat and bashed his head into the wood floor. His skull let out a gruesome crunch. He sputtered and spat at me as I strangled his breath away. He desperately kicked and thrashed about as I stared into his struggling eyes. Within their depth, abyssal hatred slowly turned to hopeless embrace. His neck strained against my fingers for one final glance at the woman, then to the child, and back to me. The stiffness in his muscles waned. His eyes stilled. It was done. I released him and sat there, only now noticing the intensity of my own panting. The child crawled over to the man and brought a delicate hand up to the stubble on his cheek.

"Papa?" she cried.

My stomach lurched, knotting into itself. What have I done? How could I mistake this child's father for my enemy? The world around me churned and the stench of smoke dissipated. The absence of gunfire and the child's wailing swathed my ears. I died there, sitting on my bloody knees, entombed in an empty void and became an insensate husk. All was darkness.

Then a gentle ocean's tide seeped back into the sandy shore, feeling returning to me as a firm hand settled on my shoulder. It was *him*. His silver eyes pierced my desolate state with a look of disgust; or was it sympathy? My body succumbed to exhaustion, my mind to shame. I don't remember leaving the hut or finding the next hole to sleep in. I only remember falling asleep and returning to my void.

He never told a soul about that day. He really was a quiet one. The cough stabs at me from across the trench, jarring me from my half-conscious recollection. Awareness of my uncomfortability returns. Bug bites itch and gritty clay grinds the flesh under my fingernails. I fidget onto my side and see the other men in a deep sleep despite the interruption. How is it I can sleep through my wife's jabs, my little girl's cries, the bugs and dirt and yet this cough torments me? How can I sleep with the lingering memory of killing an innocent man with my bare hands? Another fit of coughing. It's getting worse. Each desiccated gasp is contrasted by an eruption of harsh, wet phlegm. If only we had some medicine, even a spare flask of water to ease his throat and alleviate my own restlessness. We drank what little drops we had left two days ago.

"Wake em up, nightowl," my sergeant barks at me. "Time to move."

The humid air does little to cool us despite the absence of the sun, just cresting over the horizon. Blankets of soft pink light penetrate the morning smoke and mist and gently rest on the tropical flora before us. The further we trek inland, the thicker the vegetation grows, increasingly slowing the coughing man. The dense jungle drowns his lungs, each breath sinking him. The rest of us stagger ahead, barely keeping in step. The oppressive sun peaks overhead and harsh bursts of red light flush through my exhausted eyelids. I stagger, fatigued and delirious as the sweltering heat wicks away my precious moisture. Methodical movement and a pressing fear of being shot at any moment fills the day until the sun finally sets, its fiery memory still hanging in the air. Sarge looks over our ragged troop and orders a halt near a dim cave. We advanced only half the distance of yesterday, despite no enemy engagement.

Night creeps around us and we assemble camp by the deep hues of twilight. My enervated muscles fail to keep my pack from plopping down to the mud. I rummage through it and weakly grasp the splintered handle of my shovel. I can't do this. I just want one night of rest. My body topples to the mud as well, and I watch the other men dig beneath a darkening skyline. The wispy apparitions ripple in the wind with entrenching tools in hand, digging graves. The mirage disperses as another raucous fit of mucus hacking begins. I feel a taut and uneasy string tied between each of the men and catch glances of contempt at the sick man. The fog in my mind billows. How are we still here fighting this pointless war? What gain is worth this amount of human suffering? We're never getting out of here. I'll never get out. I'll never sleep again. Please... just one night of sleep.

Brisk whizzing passes my ears and cuts through my fog.

"Take cover!" my sergeant yells.

Every man bursts into movement. The air fills with thundering pops. Muddy clumps spray up from the ground as invisible needles envelop us.

"Make for the cave and return fi-" the sergeant's shout is severed as a bullet shreds through his throat.

He falls. Dozens of bloody splatters dance off his body as bullets overwhelm the corpse. The sudden realization of my responsibility as corporal banishes all cloudiness for the time being.

"Make for the cave and return fire!" I shout out.

A lump forms in my throat at the reiteration. My men return shots toward an enemy cloaked in darkness, the only light produced by muzzle flashes and the final blue shades of dusk on the horizon. We sprint to the cave. Deadly silhouettes, frag grenades in hand, begin to flank us. Screeches behind, gaining on me. *Oh fuck, oh fuck.* Some of the shrieking shadows reach their marks, rupturing flesh of friends and foes alike. The concussive blasts deafen my ears with excruciating ringing. Slivers of bone and metal shards lodge into my leg, tearing holes through my uniform and tissue. The rainstorm of hot blood showers my backside and thick globs ooze down my neck and arms as I run for dear life. I trip on the rocky entrance of the cave and a soldier pulls me into their impromptu line. It looks like I was the last one alive to make it. My hearing gradually returns to me and through the muffled noises I make out stifled coughing within the short pauses of gun fire. Shit. He's still out there.

"Only lay barbed wire when we are all behind the line!" I shout. I grab my two closest soldiers. "You two, get him out of there!"

A brief moment, then both soldiers hit the soft loam, riddled with bloody holes. Two lives wasted. Fuck, we won't survive this. Low ammunition slows the enemy's fire, the threat replaced by a mass of wild screams surging toward our line. A man approaches unscathed, almost shot down by our own had it not been for his recognizable cough. He hobbles past, panting and spewing blood onto the cave floor. Someone lights a lantern nearby and the spark reflects in those intense, silver eyes staring back at me. My spine chills. He knows what I've done. I shouldn't be the one in charge. I'm a worthless murderer. The barbed wire is laid at the barricade. Friendly machine gun fire pings off stone walls. Sounds of explosions respond, the barrage of bullets dropping waves of suicidal fanatics detonating a few feet shy of their quarry.

The final bullets are shot and the ringing in my ears subsides again. Stillness. Gun smoke circles in the air, twirling around shafts of golden light from our lamps. I hear shouts of the enemy language in the distance. Hurried sounds of bodies rustling through bushes rapidly fade away from us. Is this a trick or did something else catch their attention? The stillness extends another minute, then hundreds of indiscernible taps, like fingers drumming on a table come from afar.

"He's going to get us all killed!" someone shouts.

"How are we supposed to run with him dragging us down?"

"You're dead fucking weight old man."

The condemned man lies encircled by a dozen exasperated men, coughing blood into his sleeve. Some of the men punctuate their insults with kicks to his sides and head. Even more blood spews from his mouth onto boots of the very men who wouldn't be alive without his service. I order the men to stop but the confrontation persists. They are blinded by rage, grief, tiredness, and despair, completely lost at their wits' end, ignoring all presence of danger. I know that blindness. That unbridled inferno within them once burned within me too. I want to join their screaming. I want to finally put an end to that disgusting wheeze. What's one more pitiful corpse on the battlefield? His head tilts up just enough to reveal those steely eyes. They stab right through me, piercing flesh and bone and secrets. He's seen my greatest shame. All this time he kept it and showed more honor than any man.

I fire a single round into the ground. The yelling subsides. Every man looks at me, their faces painted with livid expressions. The stillness returns, the only remaining sound are lungs, grating bellows stoking a feeble fire.

"We can't risk leaving the cave. They could be plotting another ambush this second. We will wait for light and hold our ground. Alternate sentries to watch the line through the night. Now, reload your weapons, clear the rest of this cave, and get some goddamn rest." The last, exhaustive effort in my voice dies off, my adrenaline tapped dry for this final command.

Disdainful glares and silent acknowledgements shoot back at me. The moment to finally end the cough passes away. The men disperse and turn their glares toward the wretch, muttering curses under their breath. I move him to a secluded area of the cave for everyone's sake. Soon after, the men fall asleep. Exhaustion is rampant. A smart soldier knows to sleep while you safely can, even if you're standing straight up. I can't help but feel I am the most debilitated of them all. I haven't slept more than a few minutes since that cough began. That was days ago, certainly weeks now.

I pull out my watch. The glass is shattered and the hands are motionless, destroyed. Shrapnel must have ripped through. The disregarded bloody sores in my leg stained the photograph inside, the smiles lost beneath red. My mind drifts incoherently as I try to process it all. All I want is to rest. Just one fucking night of sleep or I will die. Then it comes back to me. I've died before. That day revisits me in full, a lucid dream of starry streaks over a burnt corpse. Hateful eyes curse me for burning his wife alive and orphaning their child. I look down at the charred woman with her meager tresses of woven hair. Not dark brown, but strawberry blonde, the color of my wife's hair. Her cheekbones, the shape of her nose, they're subtly there, burned away yet barely noticeable. The child crawls up to me, silent and resolute, and cups my face with her tender hand. My own daughter's face looks back at me but for the first time I am the one crying in the night.

His cough snaps me out of it. Fuck, I was almost asleep, even if it was the nightmare lulling me back into my void. I just want one night of rest. Just one night. *Just one god damn night.* Sounds of the sickly man echo off the cave walls, relentless noise of a man that should just die. All of the men want it done. It would be better for everyone. He *deserves* to die.

I stumble silently, my feet limping inches away from sleeping soldiers reliving terrors in their dreams. I glance at the cave entrance and notice the sentries asleep at their post but I don't care. Only one thing holds my attention. He's awake, yet he wavers with closed eyes, clasping his knees in stupor, his lungs retching putrid air; a thin fragment of what he used to be. I move close to him and quietly lower to my knees. *Just one night.*

I tighten my grip around his throat and gently press his head into the stone floor. My hands recall it all, this sensation of feverish tensity. He shakes alert, sputtering and spitting out bloody mucus. It sprays onto my face as I strangle his breath away. I feel his bodily slime drip past my eyelids, trickling down my lips, off my chin. He continues to lie there, limply accepting his fate as I stare into his gray eyes. Within their depth, repugnance slowly turns to soft condolence. He does not look away or blink, until at long last, his ragged breath hushes. His eyes still, and my secret dies, never having left his lips. It was done. I release him and collapse to the ground. Stillness. Not a single sound.

The Cough

My eyes are forever imprinted with yet another cursed gaze staring back. For one night I close them and ease into my void to rest.

The sound of it jolts me awake. The loathsome break in the night suffocates and imprisons me. I cannot help but gasp for air and shudder as blood and mucus choke my windpipe. I just want to breathe.

FORTY-TWO

The Oak

Rick Hansard

"What do you mean you can't? Hell, Ben, if you can't cut down one tree, I have other crews on the county's approved list that'll do it."

"You ain't listenin', Turner. My crew is there. We were dropping it this mornin' 'cause it'll take most of the day to get it chopped and loaded. I said they can't start because of the old man."

"What old man?"

"There's some old feller that's standin' in front of it… said he owns the tree and ain't nobody gonna cut it down."

"Your whole crew can't move one little old man?"

Ben responded in anger.

"No, Turner, they can't. You work for the county. Nobody can sue your ass! I own my business. My guys put their hands on some old man and he breaks a hip, he'll sue me out o' my underwear."

Turner rolled up the papers that were spread across his tailgate. He got in and drove to the site. He was furious. Rain had put him a week behind on clearing this stretch of the new road. Now the ground was finally dry enough to start dozing but one tree stood in the way.

When he arrived, Ben's crew was standing to the side. At the base of the huge oak stood an old man in overalls and a flannel shirt. The guy appeared to be around eighty. He was leaning on a cane. Turner's second man, Tommy, walked up to the truck window. Tommy had a great way of getting to the point.

"Old man's name is Graves. When the county took this land, it included this stretch at the back corner of the old man's farm. He fought it but lost in court. Legally, we can have the sheriff move the old man. If you do that you should do it now. One of the neighbors has already called local TV. You don't want this on the six o'clock news."

Turner shook his head, "So all of this is because…"

Tommy interrupted, "There's more. I talked to this lady who has been his neighbor for fifty years. Here's the rest of the story. About forty years ago the old man lived on this farm with his wife. One day, she ran off with the old man's best friend. They left in the middle of the night and never came back. The old man lost his mind. Never remarried, almost never leaves his farm. If you look close there's a heart carved in the bark with the name 'Mary' in it. Neighbors say the old guy comes out here a lot and just sits by the tree. So, this ain't just about the tree to that old man."

Turner looked at two bulldozers sitting in the field, then at Ben's crew standing by their bucket truck. He got out of the pickup, slamming the door behind him.

"I don't need the sheriff. The county owns it now, he's trespassing. Ben, you come with me."

The two walked up to the old man. His face was haggard, but he had piercing blue eyes. Turner wasted no time on introductions.

"Mr. Graves, the county owns this land and this tree. Ben and his crew are gonna cut this tree down. You can walk out of the way, or we will carry you out of the way… you decide."

The old man's voice was soft as a whisper.

"But this is my Mary's tree." Tears filled his eyes. The old man sighed, looking down as he walked away. He leaned on his cane a safe distance from the tree, turning to watch as the chainsaw came to life. Moments later, Ben called to his crew as he cut aggressively through the massive trunk.

"Watch out, this thing is hollow. It can twist and could fall any damn where!"

At that moment, cracking sounds caused Ben to drop his saw and run as the huge oak twisted then fell to the ground. Ben walked back to the tree.

"Turner, come here. Tell everybody else to stay back."

"Why?"

Ben didn't answer. Turner walked toward him but stopped when he saw the two skeletons crumpled together in the gnarled stump.

Rebirth | Life | Joy

Part Five

Happy Plant

By Alisa Hartley

FORTY-THREE

Third School

Ednor Therriault

Coming from the old school, I've been scrambling to keep up with the new skool. Adapt or die, right? Technology, communications, cultural and professional dynamics—it's all changed. By embracing change, though, this dinosaur has survived well beyond the Jurassic period. Along the way, I've discovered the delightful fact that there's a *third* school: the school of creative pragmatism.

It's an attitude. For us creatives, it gives us an advantage over our competition, especially when we are competing only with ourselves. Going outside traditional methods or expectations to do what it takes to get the job done is the dictionary definition of pragmatism. The school of *creative* pragmatism kicks in when ordinary pragmatism doesn't get you there.

Example: I used to play in a band in Missoula, Montana, a town that fairly vibrates with the creative energy of artists, writers, actors, dancers—free spirits of every stripe. Our favorite place to play, the Union Club, was a gleefully notorious bar known for generous pours, a killer jukebox, a spacious dance floor, and best of all, a broad cross-section of Missoula. Bikers, ranchers and truckers shot pool and tequila with hippies, college kids, greasers and punks. Our band's music was the great equalizer. We took old country songs and ran them through a rock 'n roll blender. What we poured off the stage were familiar tunes reassembled to kick ass and keep the dance floor packed. After some initial resistance from both country and rock camps, people got the idea and we built a solid following.

Now, this was back in the dark ages before cell phones, texts, Twitter—any digital communication we could use to promote the band. All we had was word of mouth. How were we going to rise above the mundane? What would separate us from the other bands? Missoula's always been lousy with talented musicians, so bolstering our band with a couple of hired guns seemed the obvious answer. We knew better. We had to entertain and enthrall, not just impress with our musical virtuosity (something I've never claimed to possess anyway). So we changed the question: How were we going to keep people entertained in a new way? I decided to apply the principle I've used many times since my college days. If you have an idea but you're not sure it's allowed or appropriate, do it anyway, until it fails or some authority puts the kibosh on it. Simple. Want to set up a microwave on the bass amp and hand out hot burritos to the crowd all night to celebrate being voted Missoula's Best Band? Do it. The bar manager may get a whiff of refritos and unplug your oven, but guess what everyone will be talking about tomorrow? We hatched enough crazy ideas to build a reputation. We gave away a White Trash Honeymoon, complete with a night in a dive motel and dinner at Double Front Chicken. We gave free haircuts onstage. We were unpredictable (make no mistake, some ideas crashed and burned), but that became a part of our draw. Other bands? They didn't dress the part. They didn't involve the audience. They played the same old tired radio songs and tried to sound exactly like the record. They missed a fabulous opportunity for unbidden creativity.

Working without a net isn't for everybody. We were pretty much blackballed in the press for a year after manipulating the local media one summer by staging a phony feud with a sister band that culminated in a live "fistfight" on air at a college radio station.

We had a good run, and that band spawned dozens of other musical projects over the years, but I think we'd all agree that it was never as thrilling as those nights at the Union Club when a packed house was cheering on some stunt or performance that was so far outside the box, it *became* the box. It was our sandbox. We could do whatever we wanted, until we were told that we couldn't. (Usually that involved members of the legal, insurance, or law enforcement communities.)

You can call it a guerrilla approach to creativity. An idea is sometimes successful when it seems, on the surface, to be exactly the wrong thing. Old school minds might tell you that a certain thing won't work because it's never been done that way, but that's because their view from the tar pits prevents them from seeing innovation. Be brave. Be fearless. Be illogical. Trust your gut, not a spreadsheet. Use that sentence fragment. Ignore that chart of acceptable Pantone color combos. Drop that pirouette into your pop 'n lock routine. Kill your darlings.

Learn firsthand why something's never been done before. In my experience, what you frequently discover is that the only obstacle was fear of failure. Or the occasional arrest for a misdemeanor.

Class dismissed.

FORTY-FOUR

Blue Raspberry

Leanne Su

I t's a hot, oppressive summer day, the type where the air is so wet your clothes never dry and all the old folks fan themselves with a newspaper, shake their heads, and say "Oh, it's a scorcher." You're sitting by the neighborhood pool, feet dangling in the water, the tops of your pasty thighs burning in the sun and your ass uncomfortable on the scratchy pool deck, but your towel is so far away and you're very comfortable where you are.

A shadow blocks out the sun and you tilt your sunglasses up.

"Hey," you say.

"Hey," she says back, sitting down next to you.

You know her from calc, and you're pretty sure you took some art elective together junior year. She's on either the softball or volleyball or cross-country team, or some combination of the three, and she has that kind of effortless cool you don't even bother hoping to strive for.

There's a bead of sweat on her temple, and you watch through your tinted sunglasses as it chases its way down her face, onto her clavicle, and under the curve of her sports bra. You snap your eyes away as she turns to look at you.

"Out for a run?" you ask, heart pounding in your ears more than you'd like to admit, but you chalk it up to the mind-numbing heat. Maybe you're getting heat stroke. She nods and toes off her running shoes, mumbling a quiet sorry as she peels off sweat-stained socks and stuffs them in her sneakers. She scoots forward and dips her toes in, leaning back on her forearms.

"Yeah, I definitely wish I wasn't," she says ruefully. "It's a fucking scorcher."

You want to poke fun at her for sounding like one of the old folks who fans themselves with a newspaper, but you don't think you're that close. Instead you just nod in somber agreement.

"Yeah," you say.

A silence stretches between you, gooey and syrupy and not quite awkward but not comfortable, either.

"I heard you got into one of those fancy technical schools in California," she eventually says. "Congrats."

"Ah," you say, mildly caught off-guard. You're so used to keeping to yourself and your four friends, you always forget that other people perceive you. "Yeah, thanks. Gonna be cool to get out of this bumfuck town."

She snorts, but her face looks kind of sad or maybe disappointed, and you wrack your brain to try and remember if she's staying in-state or something.

"You're headed to one of the Ivies, right?" you ask, really hoping you're right.

She nods and you let out a little sigh of relief. She doesn't seem to notice.

"Yeah, gonna play softball for them," she says, kind of distracted. It doesn't seem like she's terribly excited.

"It...doesn't seem you're terribly excited," you say slowly. Normally you'd be way too anxious about crossing a line, but the sun is making you loopy and you just noticed that she has a bellybutton piercing, holy shit, and you're not sure that you have more than two brain cells to rub together right now.

She lifts one of her broad, tanned shoulders.

"Yeah, I got offered a full scholarship to play in-state," she says. Oh damn. "But yeah, I wanted to move too, so. You know."

"Oh, neat," you say, and then internally slap yourself in the face. Who the fuck says *neat*. "Nice."

"Ricky's staying in-state," she offers up. You're not sure what to do with this information. You're pretty sure Ricky is her on-again-off-again boyfriend who's also on something between two and six sports teams, but you have no clue if they're on or off right now.

"Kind of a bummer, you know. We were talking about trying to make it work this summer."

Okay, so they were on, and now they're off.

"That sucks," you say, trying to be sympathetic but not sure how. She shrugs again.

"It's alright," she says, breezily. Maybe a little forced. It is weird, you think absently, that she would choose to sit here with you and spill her heart out like this.

She pushes herself upright after another few minutes of languid silence. There are little bumps on her forearms where they were pressing into the ragged pool deck.

"You headed out?" you ask, trying to not sound disappointed. You probably fail.

She shakes her head, ponytail swishing behind her. It smells like apples, and you immediately feel like a creep for noticing.

"Nah, I wanted to grab a freezy pop from the grocers. You want anything?"

"Oh sure, a popsicle would be real nice," your mouth says before your brain can catch up. She nods as she pulls her socks back on, making a face, maybe at the way the damp fabric drags across her toes.

"Wait. I don't have my wallet on me," you say as your brain finally catches up.

She waves dismissively at you.

"It's like a dollar, don't worry about it," she says, lunging forward to stretch out her thighs. You pointedly don't look at her ass.

"Besides," she says, cracking her neck. "Don't wanna leave you thirsty."

Your brain short-circuits. She grins, lopsided and confident, before taking off.

That was flirting. Right? That had to have been flirting. You wait for her to turn around the corner and then scramble to your feet, stumbling your way towards the reclining chair where you left all your stuff. You fumble your way to your phone and frantically scroll to the group chat.

hot trash summer
u guys
help
u kno jasmine

narcy narc
is she the girl who went to prom with ricky?

hot trash summer
y
es
do we know if she's like
not full hetero

like mb not full homo but like
u kno what i mean

à la elêvætör
o
m
g
bitch
B I T C H

hot trash summer
alastair u r not helpful

narcy narc
!!!
biiiiiiiiiiiiiitch
get it

hot trash summer
MARCUS U R NOT HELPFUL EITHER

crunch wrap supreme
I mean she's on the softball team, right?
That has to count for something?

hot trash summer
thank u, belle, for being the only useful human

crunch wrap supreme
Also, BIIIIIIIITCH

narcy narc
lol

hot trash summer
goddammit
where's hikaru
hikaru is my only friend

You hear a beeping sound and drop your phone in a panic as you whirl around to find the source of the noise, the shatterproof case once again saving it from an untimely death. It's just a little cardinal, stopping on the roof of the pool house to cock its head and cheep at you. Still, you place your phone back on the lounge chair and grab your towel, spreading it back out on the side of the pool and returning to your previous position.

You feign casualness as you hear rubber soles slapping across the pavement from behind the fence. She drops down besides you and hands you a popsicle, the plastic crinkling when your fingers brush up against each other. You mumble a thanks and pretend your heart isn't about to hammer its way out of your chest, pushing yourself upright and unpeeling the wrapper.

She kicks off her footwear once again and scoots next to you, feet dangling in the water alongside yours. Her toes are painted bright blue, chipped and fading but still vibrant through the ripples of the pool water. You take a tiny bite of your popsicle, wincing a bit at the sharp cold against your teeth.

"Hey," she says. You turn to look at her. There's a blue raspberry freezy pop dangling from her hands, and she has a look in her eyes that kind of scares you and kind of thrills you at the same time.

"Hey," you manage to respond, somewhere between a croak and a squeak. She reaches out to loosely grab your right hand. A drop of melted ice sugar has dripped down the popsicle and onto your wrist. You watch through the haze of a fever dream as she brings it up to her mouth and licks it off.

"Um," you say, lightheaded. She grins at you and gently returns your hand to your side.

"You wanna catch a movie sometime this week?" she asks, casual as all hell. You blink rapid-fire. What the hell is going on.

"Sure?" you ask, this time definitely a squeak.

"Sweet," she says, and makes to stand up.

"Wait," you manage to get out before she leaves. She looks at you quizzically and for the first time you see a flicker in the veneer of confidence she has up, the tiniest crack in the facade.

"I, uh—I'm not. I don't want to be, like, your experiment, or whatever—"

The words spill out of your mouth, feeling like marbles against your tongue, because honestly you would be *fine* being her experiment, but you also know that your friends would be very upset with you if you didn't at least try to stand your ground.

"Oh, don't worry about that," she says, shoulders loosening a little, and for the first time you consider the possibility that maybe she's as nervous about this as you are. "I'm not experimenting. That's what the locker room is for."

You try to not think about *that* visual and immediately fail.

"Okay, um," you say, trying to figure out how to word your next question. "Uh, why—why me? I guess?"

She laughs and looks a little sheepish.

"You know how we were partners for that one project in calc? It was kind of close to the end of the school year, some time in spring."

You nod, having some faint recollection of the day she was talking about.

"I'm really bad at math, and you were just like, really nice and also super competent, and I dunno. That just kind of did it for me."

"Wow, you really are a big gay nerd," you say before you can stop yourself, and are immediately mortified. "Oh my god, sorry."

She laughs so hard that she curls over this time, and you can't help but join in, even though your face is burning hot and you're still unbelievably embarrassed.

"Yeah, guess so," she finally manages to wheeze out after the giggles have subsided. She smiles at you and you smile dopily back, holding her gaze in the hot summer heat.

"Okay, well," she says, starting to walk backwards while still looking at you. "See you Friday? We can meet here and I can drive?"

You nod furiously, feeling kind of dumb because you're pretty sure you look like a bobblehead, but she trips over a pool noodle and barely manages to catch herself so you feel a little better.

"Yeah, sounds good," you say, and she grins at you and gives a little wave one last time before tossing her empty freezy pop wrapper in a bin and taking off on her run again.

You stare down at your wrist. There's a faint blue stain from where her lips touched your skin. The popsicle is still melting in your hand, all but forgotten, beads of ruby red sugar splashing down onto your thighs.

"Holy shit," you whisper to yourself. You awkwardly get to your feet, careful to not smear more of the popsicle juice than you already have. You scarf down what's left and toss the wooden stick in the trash, rinsing your sticky hands in the shower by the pool and hurrying back to the lounge chair. There's a series of messages in your group chat that you promptly ignore in favor of scrolling straight to the bottom.

hot trash summer
i have a date this friday / ??????
holys hti??????

à la elêvætör
BIIIIIIIIIIIIIIIIIIIIIIIIIIIIIIIIIIITCH

crunch wrap supreme
Omg
So proud of you
They grow up so fast…

à la elêvætör
girl get it
like fr tho get it

hot trash summer
fjsdklfjad
what is happening even

narcy narc
HELL yeah girl get it
u better give us deets
also where the fuck is hikaru
@Hikaru "Fuck you I'm a delight" Oyama
hikaru come celebrate

hot trash summer
aaaaaaaaa
!!!!!

You put down your phone, unable to stop smiling. The heat melts away around you, leaving you feeling light and airy and buoyant. You slip into the water and watch as the stain on your wrist washes away, wisps of raspberry blue in its wake.

/ /

Hikaru "Fuck you I'm a delight" Oyama
100+ new messages wtf
What'd I miss
Wait
O shi

narcy narc
lol

Hikaru "Fuck you I'm a delight" Oyama

Blue Raspberry

O sh
O SHIT
YEAHHHH GET IT
Damn Jasmine????? Did not expect that one
Lol
Hell yeah girl get it
Hot trash summer strikes again <3

FORTY-FIVE

English Ivy

Sophia Therriault

I stretch to the sun, angling my broad leaves toward it, drinking in the late afternoon rays. The cat comes to stretch out on my sunny windowsill, extending her legs in front of her as far as they can go before tucking them neatly underneath her. The sun is warm, and she likes it. Sometimes, the cat will rub her face against my leaves, brushing her whiskers with my stems and petioles. Her cat hairs get stuck all over my leaves and soil.

Sometimes the Waterer cleans some of the hairs away, plucking them off one by one and shaking her head.

"Dumb cat," she says.

She doesn't know our feline-flora relationship.

On some days, the Waterer comes along and pokes her finger into my soil, squishing some of the dark earth between her finger and thumb and saying things about how wet it is. Sometimes she leaves and comes back with water, drenching my dry soil and watching the water drain all the way to the bottom of my terra cotta pot. But sometimes she does nothing, plucking away cat hairs and shaking her head.

A few days ago, the Waterer brought another plant to sit beside me in the window. It stands in-between me and the blue-green succulent to my right. This new plant is taller and broader with skinny, waxy leaves. She is lovely in her glazed blue pot, the color of the sky. In her soil is a tiny brown bird, glazed like her pot, and facing away from the window. I often lean out toward the glass, pressing my leaves against it to show the little bird how to look at the sun, but it doesn't move.

English Ivy

Someday, when my leaves spill over my pot and down the wall out of the sunlight's reach, I will have a bird of my own in my soil, drinking my water and watching over the rim of my pot. Someday, I will have a glazed blue pot, the color of the sky.

FORTY-SIX

La Table

Sasha Snow

I am awake. I am alert. I am aware. Please don't leave me here.

My name is Matsalsbord. I'm from a far-off, distant land called Sweden. My four legs are held together by screws and bolts. My varnish is worn at the corners and that one spot where Jessie spilled a spray bottle full of vinegar. It was more of a 75/25 solution, rather than the recommended 50/50, so it left a scar.

I didn't mind, though. She was my little girl. I watched her grow up, from crawling beneath me to towering above me.

And Mom, she was so attentive. Oiling my varnish, cleaning up from meals and craft projects. Wiping up every speck of grease, glitter, or goo.

I was once more than just an object. I held keys, grocery bags, family dinners, festive holiday decorations (my favorite being the Thanksgiving cornucopias), runners, candles, or Tom, the family cat. His fluffy, delicate paws pranced over my paint, tickling the grain of my tabletop. He was often scolded off of me, but he was my friend, too, purring while lying across my lumber.

I commanded the dining room. It was the center of the house and I was its king. Everything happened around me. School projects to dinner to family meetings, I was the center of the world. My universe. My life.

Jessie made forts out of my skeleton, piled high with pillows and blankets. Dad helped our little girl with her algebra homework on my back. Groans of laughter at dad-jokes warmed me, birthday parties' cake crumbs with sticky ice cream drips tasted fed me. Family dinners gave me purpose.

But now, tossed to the curb, like a broken lamp or rusted skillet, I'm left to be weathered by the sun. Only the memories of my previous life remain. I wait for the inevitable heavy item pick up. Trash day is coming for me, faster and faster. I'll soon be covered in banana peels, coffee grounds, and other forgotten furniture.

Will I go into a compactor? Will I be unscrewed, torn apart piece-by-piece? Maybe I'll end up on a barge to trash island, one last hurrah for me. The wind on my grain. The smell of rotting food surrounding me, but at least I'll see one last sight, have one last adventure, create one more memory of the ocean. I'll push myself overboard, float to the bottom of the sea, forever left with my thoughts. I just want to remember Jessie.

Brake lights illuminate. My time has come. I'll say goodbye to dinner parties and sandwich crumbs and jigsaw puzzles. And laughter and love and happiness.

But wait, this is a family. With bungee cords and twine. They caress my frame, test me for wobbles. But I am still sturdy, just worn. They want me. They like me. Maybe they'll even grow to love me when I sit in the center of their dining room.

FORTY-SEVEN

Shoes

Maggie Friedenberg

These shoes don't fit.

Sure, they fit just fine when I tried them on in the store. A little stiff, but all new shoes have that in common. They felt comfortable enough when I walked the length of the shoe aisle. I didn't know they would rub against the tender skin of my foot, raising fluid filled blisters that hurt with every step. I didn't know they would burn angry, red welts into the backs of my ankles.

At the end of the day my legs ache. Throughout the night, the muscles seize, waking me up. I know from class that electrolytes will help with muscle cramps so I get up and walk to the fridge to grab a sports drink, the pain increasing with every step. It tastes terrible but after a few chugs, the cramps subside. Back to bed, and even though I'm exhausted, sleep evades me. My heart pounds. I can feel the beads of sweat forming on the back of my neck, under my hair.

It wasn't supposed to be this hard. I graduated, top of my class. I aced every test, every clinical, every simulation. The professors were confident in my abilities. I scored the interview and got the job all my classmates were clamoring for. I bought crisp blue scrubs and an ID holder that says *I make a difference!* And these white shoes.

The other five people who started at the same time as me? They seem to be getting the hang of it. They smile and joke and get their shit done. Their shoes fit just fine.

I need to break in the shoes. I drain the blisters with a lancet and put antibiotic cream and bandaids on them and at the end of the next day there are new blisters under the old ones because the shoes don't fit.

Six acutely ill people in need of constant care. Medications to be administered, test results to check, phone calls to doctors and family members. Document, document, document everything. This one needs their drugs crushed in applesauce and spoon-fed to them. That one needs them mixed with water and flushed through their feeding tube. Remember to flush with saline before and after you give the medication. A clot has formed in this one's central line; we need to administer TPA. Don't give it too fast. They could die. Don't wait too long. They could die. I'm on my feet twelve hours without lunch, or even a pee break, but nobody cares if I die. I kind of want to die.

It's my daughter's first preschool field trip and I am missing it. Apple picking and a hayride at a nearby farm. But I leave the house before she awakens and I get home after her bedtime. On my days off I am so exhausted and sore I snap at her when she asks me for a snack. Her lower lip trembles as tears form in the corners of her big, green eyes, framed by long, dark lashes. *Mommy is so sorry.* She is everything I ever dreamed of and I'm missing out on her because I thought this was the way to make our life better. Better isn't supposed to feel like this.

Along the route to work in the morning, there are a lot of trees. I think about what it would be like if I drove my car straight into one of them. Would I die right away, or would there be pain? I park my car and go inside and start my rounds and after an hour I'm so sick that I run for the staff bathroom and heave up my guts. I can't do this anymore. I'm going home.

I don't go back.

And the day I hand in my resignation and my ID badge I'm wearing my comfiest flip flops and I'm smiling for the first time in months. The shoes didn't fit. They never fit.

Author & Artist Bio's

Laura Ansara has always been drawn to dystopian science fiction. A dark ending with a pathway to hope is always preferable to the happy, tidy one. She writes from a corner bedroom in Ohio during serendipitous moments of peace in an otherwise active household.

S.V. Brosius is an author of paranormal romance and poetry who also loves to cook and bake! She lives in the Midwestern U.S. with her husband and two children.
The beauty she finds in the written word inspires her every day.

Rebecca Carlyle is based in Seattle, and her favorite accessory is an oversized mug of coffee. Her love for storytelling has always been a passion for her, but has grown stronger throughout her college years and since graduating. In 2020, she published her first novel, *Finding Alice,* and plans on a follow-up novel soon.

Robin Chapman is a part-time writer and birth photographer, where she aims to show women their strength and beauty through her writing and images. She's a full-time mom of four, imperfect Jesus-follower, and normalizer of failure living in Alaska with her ridiculously good-looking husband, Andrew. She serves up solidarity and grace with a side of humor.

Shannan Chapman is a writer, a mother, grandmother and wife who lives in Tucson, AZ. She loves to travel the world, meet interesting people and write about them. She is currently (still) working on her first novel.

Fred Charles is a writer, artist, and musician from Philadelphia. He is co-owner of Loud Coffee Press Literary Magazine.

Darren Faughn always finds peace placing pen to paper. He wrote his short story before the contest even came to fruition, but it took him weeks to finalize what he wanted to submit. He hopes to one day publish his own book of short stories and anecdotes. Placing in the top ten added more fire to the flame to birth a career of his own in the writing world.

Rick Hansard loves writing short stories and poetry. He and his wife enjoy encouraging young people to use their imagination to write, paint, sing, and share life through telling stories. Rick has a large collection of mixed genre works he hopes to publish soon.

Mike Kloeck is a short story writer, editor and chef who lives on the Oregon Coast. When he is not writing or cooking seafood fresh from the Pacific, he can be found walking on the beach, enjoying the surf, wind, rain and occasional sunshine.

W. A. Ford is an indie author based in Philadelphia, PA with a lifelong love of reading and writing. She descends from a long line of storytellers and relishes in hearing and sharing family folklore. You can find her creeping around her hundred-year-old house with her feline familiar or on Instagram at @willow-ford213 and @thefarbackroom.

Maggie Friedenberg is an independent author of contemporary fiction and romance. Her lifelong love of books and writing began when she was only three years old, and her debut novel, HOLDING PATTERN, will be published on June 3, 2022. Maggie lives in Philadelphia, PA with her husband, three children, and cat.

The Gathering is a trio of Hispanic women from Southern California who love fantasy, folklore, and mythology. They met at Cal State Northridge in a writing workshop and their names are **Joanna E. Benitez**, **Leslie Gonzalez**, and **C. L. Verdin**. Together they write speculative fiction that is drawn from their cultural backgrounds.

Alisa Hartley is an intuitive artist, writer and creative based in Calgary, Alberta, Canada. She is passionate about exploring different artistic mediums including but not limited to: photography, poetry and watercolour painting. She enjoys collaborating with other artists and strives to build a sense of community in the art world.

Joe Hopkins is a writer out of New Mexico. Joe truly loves the southwest and all of the rich cultures that call the region home. He hopes that through his writing, he can help people feel closer to a part of America that is often forgotten.

By day, **Ariel Kay** is a data analyst, and by night she is a writer, avid gamer, and devoted reader of summaries for horror films she's too afraid to watch.

She has recently discovered a love for flash fiction and is working on her first novel. Originally from the United States, she moved to London eight years ago where she still lives with her husband, two rabbits, and an anthropomorphized robot vacuum named Elliot.

Jacqueline Layne lives in Central Florida with her husband and her two daughters. She is fervently writing and rewriting her first novel, *The Aitalus*- a task made more difficult by the happy squeals of small children playing in the yard of the elementary school behind her house, where she writes. She promises her writing isn't always sad. Like, pinky promises.

Thomas Leventhal lives with his family and their two dogs in Southern California. His writing has been greatly influenced by the many odd and strange folks he has met over the years. Thomas has been an avid film photographer for over 40 years and has recently taken up painting.

Zira MacFarlane is a non-binary queer biologist dwelling in Toronto with a small menagerie of cats, geckos, snakes, and humans. They are an amateur writer, and love using horror and fantasy to explore ecological themes and stories of queer love and pain. Their days are split between seeking out the quiet spots of nature hidden in all cities, telling stories with their friends and family, and trying to discover the latest mischief their cats have caused.

Stephen Mills was born outside of Seattle, Washington, and joined the U.S. Navy in 1996, where he was stationed in Florida. He currently resides in Arizona. Stephen has enjoyed books throughout his life, with interests ranging from non-fiction and biographies to historical fiction/adventure and dark fantasy.

Matt Micheli is a horror and dark fiction writer out of New Braunfels, TX. You can find his work in various magazines and anthologies. His novella "THE WHITE" is slated for release in December of 2022 by D&T Publishing.

Shrutidhora P Mohor is an author from India writing in English. She has several single titles published by Ukiyoto Publishing since 2019 as well as contributions to many anthologies. She has an eye for the quirky, witty, odd aspects of life, and a special place for unfulfilled, unstructured romances. With a Doctorate in political theory, she has been teaching Political Science at the undergraduate and postgraduate levels for over fifteen years.

Ted Morrissey's novels have won the International Book Award, the American Fiction Award, the Manhattan Book Award, and, most recently, the Maincrest Media Award for *The Artist Spoke*. His novel excerpts, short stories, poems, critical articles, reviews, and translations have appeared in some 100 publications.

A lecturer in Lindenwood University's MFA in Writing program, he and his wife live near Springfield, Illinois, with two rescue dogs and about a thousand books.

Ellis Morten is a queer writer and cat lover based in Brooklyn, NY. They are excited to take the plunge into horror writing and hope to be scaring readers for years to come. Currently, they are working on several projects and trying to fund their unending desire for more tattoos.

Jordan Nishkian is an Armenian-Portuguese writer based in California. Her prose and poetry explore themes of duality and have been featured in national and international publications. She is the Editor-in-Chief of Mythos literary magazine and published her first novella, *Kindred*, in 2021.

Clara Olivo (she/her/Ella) is an Afro-Salvi poet living in diaspora. Born and raised in South Central L.A to Salvadorean refugees, Clara weaves history and lived-experience creating diasporic poetry that amplifies ancestral power and pride. Her words capture the traumas and triumphs of living in diaspora and how displacement, colonization, and survival have shaped her life. Since finding her voice, she has performed in open mics and ceremonies from Seattle to Washington D.C and has been featured in publications such as The South Seattle Emerald, Valiant Scribe and Quiet Lightning's Literary Mixtape. Clara lives in a quiet home on unceded Duwamish land with her partner, dog and an ever growing number of houseplants.

A former schoolteacher, **Catherine Peacock** lives on the banks of the Delaware River in Milford, Pennsylvania. Her short story "Annesh of the Taaraddi" appears in the anthology *An Odd Sized Casket*, published by Owl Canyon Press. Her story "The Shibboleth of the Divide" appears in the anthology *From the Corner of My Eyes*, also released by Owl Canyon Press.

Ania Ray is co-founder and head coach of Quill & Cup, a fiercely supportive writing community of women who commit to making sustainable progress on their work through accountability & coaching in mindset and craft. Ania is the author of *The Cromwell Rules* and *Breaking the Rules* and is currently writing the third and final installment of the women's contemporary fiction series. She currently resides in Costa Rica with Cody, her husband and co-founder of Quill & Cup, and their cat, Bahama Blu.

Donna Rhodes is a retired high school English teacher and author of *Creating Futures: The Life Of Richard Aguilera Ruiz*. She resides in Olathe, Kansas, with her husband and four-legged friend, Harper. Reading, writing, piano, cooking, and collecting recipes she never intends to make keep her busy and out of trouble.

M.C. Rodrigues (she/her) is a cardiologist by day and a writer by night. She gravitates between various genres, but has an affinity for stories about queer characters. A lover of black coffee, chocolate and cozy wool jumpers, Rodrigues lives in São Paulo, Brazil with her husband and two dogs.

Erica Sage is an author and English teacher who lives in Washington State with her family. She is the author of the young adult novel JACKED UP, published by Sky Pony Press, as well as adult short fiction published in the anthology XVIII (Eighteen), published by Underland Press, and Underland Arcana magazine. You can find her in the trees, or on Instagram and Twitter: @erica_sage .

Born in Seattle and raised in rural Idaho, **S. Salazar** has always felt at home in the mountains. After graduating from the University of Idaho, she began writing more seriously. Her work has been featured in *Harpur Palate*, and her current works in progress explore what Latinx heritage means in families where it isn't openly discussed.

H.D. Scarberry is an author and artist who hails from a small town just south of the Tennessee border. Her current published works include two novels and one short story collection, as well as a poetry collection which was published under a pen name. Her art is available on her Etsy site.

Hello, I'm **Andy Schmidt**. I like to think about stuff, and sometimes make art out of it. I also thoroughly enjoy apple pie.

Born in Reno, Nevada, USA, **Elaine May Smith** was raised in Scotland during the Oil Boom. She is a Member of the Federation of Writers (Scotland) and Poetic Genius Society. Having traveled extensively, she now writes a variety of genres from her home in Dundee.

Sasha Snow is a writer, photographer, and filmmaker. She has a degree in TV/Film Production from the University of Texas at Austin and now lives in sunny Los Angeles, California. In her spare time, she enjoys creating short films and taking pet portraits for her production company, Albino Hedgehog Productions.

Megan Speece is a thriller author, horror buff, and dog person. She lives in the beautiful Pacific Northwest with her husband and two dogs, and can be found spending her weekends at the beach, exploring everything Washington has to offer, or settling in with a good horror movie. Megan is currently working on her second in series novel as well as a few independent projects.

Leanne Su is a second-generation Chinese American woman from Seattle, WA.

She is currently studying as a Ph.D. candidate in aerospace engineering at the University of Michigan, researching high-power electric propulsion. When she's not breaking or fixing thrusters, she's usually embroidering, writing, or taking cursed pictures of her cat Pudge.

Coming from the Dallas area in Texas, **Billie Spaulding** spends his time worshipping his mini-dachshund, smoking cloves and making homemade Mexican food.

Operating from his home base in Missoula, Montana, **Ednor Therriault** uses music and writing as his well-worn paths to human connection. He's published seven books of nonfiction, and is currently working on number eight, due out spring of 2023. As Bob Wire, he's played his "maximum honky-tonk" everywhere from nursing homes to festivals for 25 years.

Sophia Therriault lives in Missoula, Montana with a cat who thinks he's a dog and a dog who thinks she's a cat. She is currently studying psychology and creative writing at The University of Montana. Sophia's album, *Bruises*, was released in 2017 by her two-person band, Red Dress. She is the proud waterer of ten houseplants, including her very own English ivy.

Annie James Thomas is a New England-based writer, former TEDx speaker, and music lover. She is a co-founder and editor for Loud Coffee Press literary magazine. This is her fiction pen name.

Mae Wagner is an author of various works, including a memoir, *Girls, Assassins and Other Bad Ideas*, August of 2022. Mae currently lives in a small lake Erie cottage in Pennsylvania with her husband, their dog, cat, and an unwavering search for adventure, beauty, and light.

Lightning Source UK Ltd.
Milton Keynes UK
UKHW051045260922
409449UK00006B/87